SON OF ORDER

Dragons Wake

K.D. MENZIES

Dedicated to my father, Donald Menzies, who passed while I wrote this book.

Contents

JaCol Publishing Inc.
Copyright 2018 © by JaCol Publishing Inc.
Illustrations Copyright © 2018 by JaCol Publishing Inc.
SECOND PRINTING
December 2020
All rights reserved
JaCol Publishing Inc.
195 Murica Aisle
Irvine, CA 92614
818-510-2898
Editor-in-Chief: Randall Andrews
Managing Editor: Jessica Collins
www.jacolpublishing.com

ISBN: 978-1-946675-23-1

Cover art by Christina Myrvold

1

Chapter 1

Olympians, wizards, and mortals marveled when I, the son of order, married chaos in a Milpitas, California church, but when she died, no one marveled about my mourning. They should have.

Over six months had passed since my wonderful Vedi's death, and my grief sat between the first two stages—denial and anger. Anger crested the horizon like a would-be rising sun, but the earth in my head stood still for a reason I dreaded discovering, keeping that angry sun from reaching higher.

Nothing made sense except the knowledge that something wasn't right with me. I knew I needed to move on but only the tiniest of steps seemed clear. I endeavored to take the ones I could.

Laying paving stones one night for my mother's church comforted me. It isolated me from people in general but more specifically from my memories of Vedi. I intentionally chose a cloudy night because on clear ones she spoke to me.

As for the task, it allowed me to apply my inborn dragon penchant for order. I could lay out the stones each the same distance apart, the same inset into the ground and in a straight line. I enforced order, and chaos said nothing about it. I needed to hear my own thoughts and them alone.

My thoughts spoke to me for a few short minutes before I heard the voice of a mortal.

"Thank God, I found you."

This one I could almost forgive for the interruption, my best friend, John. His foolishness, however, received no such mercy. My eyes glowed purple as they did when I needed to see in the dark, but also when I was angry. "It's almost pitch dark, you fool. You could stumble over something."

He held a broken broom handle in one hand and blood soaked the knees of his jeans. He grabbed my shoulder and clung to it. "I have stumbled, thank you, several times."

"But why?"

He waived the broom handle behind him. "I found a vampire."

"There's no such thing. We've talked about this…"

A man's angry scream from the darkness stopped me from finishing. John moved behind me. I saw the source of the sound. A man in a business suit ran at us, crossing the church's lawn. He moved at a speed no more normal than me, though speed on foot was not my thing.

If the purple glow in my eyes gave him pause, I couldn't tell. He ran into me with no hint of wanting to stop. The impact reminded me of hitting the ground after a hundred foot fall. I sprouted my wings in time to dampen the force of the collision before it could be transferred to John's mortal bones. The wings slowed us enough that I had time to grab John's belt and toss him away before he could get pinned beneath us.

The man drew back his head, inch-long fangs attempted to bite my neck. My hands hardened as I pushed his face away. I felt the tips of my fingers become claws buried in his cheek. His eyes widened as the force applied pushed him off me and into a roll.

John jumped on the man and drove the broken broom handle into his chest. The man grabbed his shoulder, pulled him down and rolled on top. John impressed me by having enough presence of mind to push the handle further into his chest. If the man's heart evaded the first effort, the second one did the trick.

The man's hand grasped John's neck. I wasn't about to let him crush his windpipe, so I leaped at the man, knocking him off. His back hit the ground and the broom handle pinned him like a butterfly in a collection.

He pointed at me. "Aiden Ferris, we are watching you."

I'm not sure what I thought besides a running argument between John and me about the existence of vampires, because what I said next was silly. "See John. He's not a vampire. A stake to the heart and he's still alive."

John pointed at the man. "Look again."

Where the man had been, a skeleton lay.

"Okay. I'll admit that's very vampire-like, but I'm still not convinced."

John wagged his finger. "Look again."

A pile of dust leached into the ground. Only the broken broom handle and John's blood and sweat remained as evidence of the struggle.

I moved John to a tree he could lean against and gripped his shoulders with my clawed hands. "Okay, John Eisenbach, what have you been up to?"

Plastic shards fell from his cell phone as he pulled it out. It zapped his thumb as he tried unsuccessfully to turn it on. He dropped it. "My research, I found this community of vampires through my research."

"Which research? For your degree or to find sellers for my artifacts?"

"Both."

I knew there was something less than honest in his answer. It's something I can do. I grimaced. He revised his answer. "Okay, both and also another bit of research I've been doing to help you."

"How does getting things, like whatever that was to chase you, helping me?"

"You've been in a deep funk for far longer than psychologists say you should be. I thought I'd find you some evil worth your attention. You know, to give you something to do."

I reverted to full human form, losing my claws and wings. "I

3

don't need anything else to do besides figure out where my life goes without Vedi."

"I'm sorry then, but don't you need to do something about these vampires?"

I walked back to my pile of paving stones. "Whatever these are, I need to do something about them but only because of what that one said to me."

"That they know who you are?"

"Yes, that's the reason. John, I don't have to fight evil. I have to stay out of trouble."

"Then you're back?"

I dropped a paving stone I had started to lift from the pile. "I'll need to see your research in the morning."

Chapter 2

I knew John would be disappointed if he knew what I planned to do with his research, so I didn't tell him. After he left for classes, I drove into the east hills to meet Oliver, my handler.

Oliver's an Olympian who, besides keeping me out of trouble, is the Olympians' fixer. Stray magical artifacts, stray Olympians, stray titans, or any other magical creatures, they're all his business. He puts them back where they belong and cleans up any mess they may have caused. I wanted him to do that with these things John found. Then I could get on with mourning.

The vacant lot was too vacant when I arrived. Oliver's green 1964 Deville was nowhere to be seen. I had arranged the meeting via text message the night before, in between laying paving stones. I double checked Oliver's text back. It read, "go to the vacant lot in the hills—9 a.m."

No plumes of dust rose from the approach winding beneath the lot. I turned and waved my arms. "Oliver, I'm here."

I typed those same words into a text, but it wouldn't send. My phone's battery died. It hadn't seen a charger in a couple of days, thanks to my being out at nights.

Oliver could have arrived by some magical means, so I gave him one last chance to be there. "Oliver," I yelled.

His voice didn't respond, but something reacted. I sensed its gaze at my back. I spun to a giant tabby house cat, three feet at the shoulders. It hissed, and a chill ran down my spine. It stood in the open, far from any potential cover, but still it vanished.

My hands hardened, my claws formed, my wings sprouted; I wanted to intimidate. I turned in all directions.

Again, behind me, I spun to another giant cat. This one had the color patterns of a blue-point Siamese. Its hiss compelled me to bare my teeth.

If Oliver intended to test me, I failed. My claws and wings revealed my nature for whomever to see, and the cats, however large, didn't justify it. At least I could say I held back from roaring. That second hiss tempted me. Instead, I only bared my teeth, still normal human in transformation.

The second cat vanished like the first and a man's voice came from a boulder up the hill. "Now calm yourself, boy."

Calm eluded me. "I'm here to meet someone and you're not him."

The tabby appeared, as if out of thin air, and hissed again. The man peered over the boulder's edge. "Back off, boys. I've got it from here."

The cat vanished. The man, dressed like a rancher, made his way down from the boulder—walking and sliding as he approached.

I took the time to gather myself back to full human.

He dusted off his hand and extended it. "Ezekiel Roe's the name, but call me Zeke, and you're obviously Aiden Ferris."

"Obviously, yes. I'm not usually that obvious. Those things freaked me out for some reason."

"No, reading your file, I wouldn't suppose you've seen the Children of Galinthius before. If it's any consolation, those two haven't ever seen a dragon before. I guess that makes you even."

I only knew the Children of Galinthius from what Oliver told me. They're the Olympian's enforcers. If the day ever came that my presence on Earth could no longer be tolerated, the Children of

Galinthius would show up and teleport me away. I hoped to never meet them.

"Why are you here? Where is Oliver?"

Zeke brushed the dust from his gun holster. "Oliver had an emergent situation involving trees that shouldn't be planted outside of Hera's grove, so he asked me to substitute for him."

"Why did the cats come along? Am I in trouble?"

"They're my partners, and no you're not. I'm the Children's of Galinthius human liaison. Those two report to me, but I report to ones above them."

I could tell his answer, though honest, had unmentioned qualifiers, qualifiers I might know if I could translate hisses. "And you know it's my nature to continue satisfying all the conditions of my being here."

"Like I said, son, you're not in trouble. Now, you wanted help with something. What is it?"

I got printouts of John's research from my car and showed them. He flipped through the pages and handed them back. "These are the Empusa. Are they bothering you?"

"One of them attacked me last night, called me by name and said they were watching me."

"Well, that's not good son, not good at all."

"So, you'll handle it?"

"I'll talk to my superiors and someone will handle it."

His answer was honest but the word 'someone' bothered me. "Someone who will keep them out of my life?"

"If you weren't your father's son, I'd say 'sure' and feel good about it, but for you I must tell you I can make no promises, but odds are good."

"Odds aren't good enough when I have mortals to protect, and now that my wife is dead, I can't heal them. Someone needs to keep these Empusa out of my life."

Zeke moved his hat to his chest. "I'm so sorry about your bride, but trust me, son, the power she brought you would have upset things more than these Empusa ever could."

I choked backed tears. Zeke grabbed my shoulder. "I know what it's like to be pulled away from the love of your life. Because of that, I'll do whatever I can."

I wiped my eyes. "Whatever you can is all I can ask of you. Thank you."

He gave the side of my shoulder a pat. "You go be with this mortal friend of yours and wait for me to contact you. I'll let you know when we've got the Empusa to promise that you and your friends are off limits."

"Twenty-four hours?"

"That or sooner."

In that moment, Zeke's sincerity rivaled anyone I'd ever met. I left him in the hills and tracked down John at the university. I became his shadow, confident I could protect him while waiting on Zeke, but I didn't realize who else needed my protection.

Chapter 3

John shook his head when I told him about Zeke and getting the Empusa to leave us alone. He didn't say anything about it. He started to a couple times between his classes, but he would open his mouth, raise a finger, close his mouth, and shake his head. I could tell he hated my solution but couldn't think of a reason I should hate it. He treated me to silence until dinner.

Our order taken, he laid out his silverware in deliberation. "You got any paving stones left to lay?"

I smiled. "You speak. You finally speak."

He wadded his napkin in his fist. "Well, do you? Any paving stones not yet laid in perfect order? If not, then what next for you?"

I tapped his fist. "Calm down. I'm moving on from stones."

He released his napkin. "Please don't joke about it. You seriously need to work through this."

"You of all people know I'm lousy at jokes, and that's not what I'm doing. I'm going to do something bold tonight, and I want you to help me."

He sat up. "Bold? Well, that sounds like my old friend. What do you have in mind?"

I activated the weather app on my phone and slid it over. "It's supposed to be a clear night tonight. I want you to drive me up near the observatory."

He slouched. "You sure there aren't any more paving stones to lay at the church?"

He knew what a clear night sky meant. I'd been hearing Vedi's voice talk to me from clear night skies since her death. He worried I was going crazy. I did too. "I need to confront this. I need to figure out why it's happening. There's only one way to do that, and since we need to stay together until Zeke contacts me, we may as well try it tonight."

He picked up my phone and handed it to me with a smile. "Being there for you will be better than not. Let's do it."

I asked John to wait by the car while I walked far enough away so I could speak without him hearing. I didn't want him answering questions not directed to him and possibly dispel my hallucination. Even a hallucination of Vedi would be precious to me.

That night's sky displayed the Milky Way. John's laptop illuminated his car's cabin, so I guessed he missed the sight. What a shame.

My ears attuned to the dead air as I waited for her voice. It came, though at first, I couldn't make out words. Like whispers on a swing, her voice caused my heart to leap and then to fall. It came and went and came and went until in its coming I made out words. My name, she said my name. Other words followed but trailed off. *"Aiden, my bro..."*

Her tone pleaded. I wondered. "Vedi, what are you saying to me?"

Her voice steadied. *"Aiden, my brother needs you to save him in Yosemite."*

"Hunter? What could he need to be saved from?"

My jerk of a brother-in-law, Hunter Asta, managed to be the dumbest and toughest warlock on Earth. I couldn't imagine him needing my help or deserving it. I waited for Vedi to answer but she didn't. This had always been a one-way communication. I hoped with such a request it might become two-way, but no.

I hated Hunter, but I loved Vedi and she loved her brother, stupidity and meanness and all.

I flopped down in the car next to John. "We've got one more place to drive tonight."

"Where?"

"To find an old friend of yours in Yosemite."

He started the car and revved the engine. "Road trip? I like road trips. Who's my old friend?"

"The guy who kidnapped you and tied you to a chair in the middle of the desert."

"Hunter? Yes, he is an old friend."

I shook my head. "I don't know why."

He chuckled. "We had a long time to talk. Just him and me and miles of empty desert for over two days."

"Well, the voice told me he's in danger and we're going to test it out."

With a phone call to my mother-in-law we confirmed Hunter's whereabouts. His coven rented a set of cabins in the area, and John managed to locate them using his laptop. It took two hours to get there.

Pulling up, we saw bodies littering the ground. Blood stood out more than any other feature. John began to throw up. I grabbed his shoulders. "Get down, stay down, and lock the doors after I leave the car."

The locks clicked after I shut the door and I darted into the camp.

Intermittent screams came from the woods, but I saw what I came for in the middle of the camp's clearing. Men in business suits had Hunter tied to a tree with metal cables and they were dousing him with gasoline.

I ran into the fray. "Hey, what do you think you're doing?"

One moved at me in a blur, and I knocked him to the side. He slashed my shirt three ways in that split second of proximity. The others, four of them, bared their fangs. I recognized their fangs. They were Empusa.

"Hunter, how'd you pick a fight with these things?"

He wriggled against the cables. "I can't let vampires invade my turf."

I brought out my claws and wings, no question these things merited that much transformation. I hoped to end the fight with intimidation rather than kill any of them. I wanted as little complication for Zeke as possible.

"Get out of here!" I yelled.

The Empusa didn't run, instead, they spread out along the edge of the clearing. I put Hunter's tree out of its misery and yanked the cable. His diggings weakened the tree enough that when I pulled the cable it caused it to creek and lean.

"Hey, watch it, man," he leaned and his feet left the ground.

I pulled a two-foot-long splinter from the tree and waved it around. That's when they decided to leave.

As I helped Hunter free himself, he said something worrisome. "I could have handled them on my own, but my folks won't fare so well."

"They know about your parents?"

"Of course, they do. I bragged to them about them."

4

Chapter 4

I stepped toward the parking lot. "So, they know where your parents are, and I'm guessing you also told them who they are?"

Hunter writhed out of the cables and followed. "I didn't tell them where they live, but I sure told them who they were messing with."

I pointed at the broken tree. "Apparently being the great-grandson of the wizard Dak didn't impress them?"

"Well duh, Aiden, he's dead, and guess whose father made that happen?"

Yeah, our families have some major history, but I wasn't distracted from Hunter's failed synapses. "As usual, Hunter, you're stupid. Now your parents are in danger, and you put them in it just so you could try to intimidate these things with your relation to a man who's been dead for almost a century."

"Hey, man. Members of my coven are dead all over. Take it easy on me."

I wagged my head. He took no responsibility.

I knocked on the car. "John, it's us. Let us in so we can get out of here."

Hunter struggle to sit before lying down across the back seat.

The beginnings of bruises crossed his arms from the metal cables. I imagined similar marks hid under his clothes.

"Are you okay?" asked John.

Hunter arched his back and grimaced. "Nothing a good night's rest can't fix."

For Hunter, that meant internal injuries bad enough to need an emergency room if it weren't for his great grandfather's magic running through him. I tapped the steering wheel to get John back on task. "Drive us out of here."

"Where are we going?" asked John.

"As far as we can get before midnight. We'll get Hunter a hotel room, and you're going to stay with him."

"What about you?"

"I need to get to the Asta's."

Gasoline fumes from Hunter and the remnants of regurgitated curry from John forced us to ride with the windows down. Hunter slept or passed out, I'm not sure which. John and I couldn't talk over the wind, but I could tell from his smile, his hopes of me fighting the Empusa were probably too high.

We stopped at a motel outside of Stockton. With no time to talk, I took a cab to Milpitas and the sidewalk in front of my in-laws' house.

I had called Zeke on the way and asked him to meet me there. I started to call my mother-in-law to see if she might be awake at two in the morning, but the front door swung open and I heard her voice. "I dare you to step onto my property."

She blamed me for Vedi's death. Sometimes I wished she was right so I'd know who to punish. "Ms. Asta, I need to talk to you."

"I wish you'd step onto my property, so I can show you what I think of you, you putrid disgusting lizard."

Up until then, 'son of death' was her favorite term for me. Apparently, I merited further use of her creativity. As for the threat, she knew a dragon of order couldn't step on private property without an invitation, so she taunted me more than she threatened.

I pulled at my shirt. "Ms. Asta, I just got back from saving

Hunter from several Empusa. He told them about you, so I fear they may be coming for you."

She slammed the door. Her words muffled through. "And why should you care?"

The porch light came on and the door re-opened. Mr. Asta appeared in his bathrobe on the step. "You know, dear, he can't lie. I think we need to invite him in."

She huffed. "Oh, do what you want."

Invited, I entered. Mr. Asta gestured to a chair. "Is Hunter okay?"

Ms. Asta answered for me. "Of course, Hunter's okay. We couldn't kill him if we wanted to, and I can't say I haven't tried."

I raised a finger. "As Hunter goes, he got hurt pretty badly. Enough that he let me put him up in a motel to rest."

Mr. Asta grasped his wife's wrist. "Well, then we're glad you were there to help him. How did you know he needed help?"

I didn't want to tell them Vedi talked to me through the sky so I pondered for words. Ms. Asta studied me with an unsettling smile, as if she knew something. I rushed out an answer that caused a sharp pain in my abdomen. "A member of the coven told me."

It wasn't a lie. Vedi was a member of the coven, but the mere resemblance to deception was enough to cause me pain. I feared sweating and further discomfort, but headlight beams on the window changed the subject.

"That would be Zeke," I said.

"Zeke? Who's that?" asked Ms. Asta.

"He works with the Children of Galinthius. They're going to protect you."

She stood. "What? The one's Oliver had to hide my family from for a generation? You brought them here?"

Mr. Asta took her hand with both of his. "Aiden, are you sure about this?"

"Zeke's got my best interests at heart. I'm confident of that, and part of my best interests is keeping your family in it. You're all of Vedi I have left in this world."

Ms. Asta averted her eyes. I suspected she knew something

about Vedi's voice from the sky, but I needed to meet Zeke before he reached the step.

He shook my hand. "Son, when does your handler get to sleep?"

I laughed. "As soon as I do."

"So, this is where the descendants of Dak live?"

I grabbed his shoulder. "It wouldn't be wise to let your cats in."

He lowered his voice. "I know, son. My bosses would just as soon see this family dead if it weren't for Oliver claiming jurisdiction."

"So, no cats?"

He nodded but grimaced. "In that same vein, I've got mixed news on the truce front. It turns out the Children of Galinthius owe a lot to the Empusa's late matriarch."

The pain in my gut moved lower. "They're not going to help me?"

"I didn't say that. What they won't do is anything to harm the Empusa. They still think it's in the Empusa's interest to leave you and yours alone."

"So ...?"

"They've gotten the Empusa to agree to leave you and yours alone as long as you and yours leave them alone. That means you agree to a truce."

I gulped. "I'll do that, but I hope you realize what that means in my case."

"Your file says something terrible will happen to you if you break your word. I'm curious if you know what that is?"

"I only know it's something like death, perhaps worse. None of my teachers knew of a lawful dragon who broke its word. Does my file say?"

"Nope, just that it's no small thing for you to agree to a truce."

"If it's what it takes, I'll do what I must. Now, let's go see two of the people this truce will protect."

I made introductions quick, patted Zeke on the back and left. I had the truce I wanted, as long I could keep my end of it, and two potential loose ends were in a motel near Stockton.

Chapter 5

Hunter and John's motel room faced the rising sun, which I arrived with. Hunter sat on a bed in boxers only. Brown stripes of bruises ringed his body. According to John, they had been black a few hours earlier.

I told them about the truce and its conditions, how the Children of Galinthius refuse to harm the Empusa but see it in their best interest to leave us alone.

Hunter objected. "They tried to kill me. I don't back down from a fight."

"Hunter, this isn't just some rival coven or street gang. These are the Empusa."

"Empusa? What kind of stupid name is that for a bunch of vampires?"

John started to open his mouth, but my stare convinced him otherwise. Four hours sleep in the last forty-eight hours took its toll on me. I sat on the other bed "The Empusa aren't vampires, but what they are, have connections with the Children of Galinthius. That makes them big league."

Hunter pounded his chest. "I'm the great-grandson of the

wizard Dak. I'm big-league." His sentence punctuated by a pain that drew his hand to his back.

"Hunter, if you go after them, I'm not going to want to save you."

Hunter turned away.

I took John outside to talk in private.

John shook his head. "Aiden, what?"

"Hunter hates me, but he likes you. I need you to talk to him so he understands. We need this truce to work."

"Maybe I need this truce to work. Maybe Hunter needs this truce to work. But you don't need it to work."

"Yes, I do."

"Aiden, you're running away and hiding from things, the Empusa, or whatever they're called, and your grief."

I wondered how many times I'd have to explain this to him. "I'm doing my best to face it, but I can't face it while you and everyone else that matters to me are in danger. I need time."

His eyebrows frowned. "After six months you're still in denial. You hear her voice."

I nodded. "And she was right. Hunter was in danger. She even told us where he was."

He held up a hand. "Okay, okay, you have a point there, but it doesn't change that you're still not moving on with your life."

"John, we can talk about this later, but please, for now, talk to Hunter."

"I will, but what's right for Hunter and me isn't right for you. People regularly disappear around the Empusa hang-outs. You've read my research. They're doing bad things and the Children of Galinthius aren't going to stop them. How can you, the son of order, agree to this?"

"I'm agreeing to a lot of things lately. It's because I need time to collect myself, so I don't do anything monstrous."

His eyes burned into mine. "How monstrous is being a coward?"

John's seriousness defied his nature. I took a step back. "What? Where did this come from?"

He cocked his head. "Son of order? The Olympians worry your

father would go insane if he realized he had a son out of wedlock, but I'm not sure that's possible. Your father wouldn't recognize you. Not as any son of his. Not the way you're acting. Son of order? You don't care about any order beyond your nose. You're a coward."

He wanted to get to me and had. "You can call me a coward if you want to, but I care about order. It's a tyrant that I can't be, and that's hard for me. Vedi helped me do that like nobody else could. Now she's gone. I fear that without her, the world may be a better place without me."

John's face softened. "And that's why she sent you to save her family from the Empusa? Because the world is better without you?"

The thought of Vedi struck me. A lump entered my throat, threatening to make speech impossible. I struggled to get out words. "I'm not leaving you. Just please talk to Hunter."

He returned to the room, and I sought out a depression off the highway. There I did something I'd never done before without a fight at hand. I sprouted my wings and launched myself into the air. My wings carried me high and fast in the hope of not being seen.

Oliver told me that as tempting as it may be, I must not fly for pleasure or convenience, but he didn't say anything about dealing with pain.

Scattered clouds passed below me. The wind in my face soothed me. I could almost think of Vedi without that lump in my throat, almost. The flight reminded me of something she said in the Himalayas, the day I realized she loved me as much as I did her.

"I want to see you flying in all your glory."

Wondering if perhaps she could, tears broke loose, dripping in a stream sprinkling my sides. I spread my tears over several square miles of California's Central Valley.

The long cry cleared my head enough for me to think.

I should take a long relaxing cruise. I could take John with me. Maybe it would help me. I flew back to the motel, taking care to descend with little notice.

I expected John to smile his contagious smile when I told him about the cruise idea, but instead he and Hunter were gone. I asked the desk when they checked out. The woman manager asked me who I was and when I gave her my name, she handed me a folded note in John's handwriting. "Hunter made a quick recovery. I am the brains. He is the brawn. Let's kill lots of vampires. Gone vampire hunting."

The manager read my facial expression. "Something wrong?"

"Yeah. My best friend's a fool."

6

Chapter 6

I needed to get to Hunter and John before they gave the Empusa the idea the truce was off. The printout of John's research showed nine hangouts around the bay area where, as John reminded me, people kept disappearing. They became items two through ten on my check-list of things to do that day, right after item number one, calling Zeke.

Zeke didn't sound friendly anymore and told me he couldn't talk about 'the never-ending problems of dragon-boy' over the phone. Instead, we set up a late afternoon meeting at an overlook of the Golden Gate Bridge on the Marin side. By that time, I visited six empty hangouts. Three remained on my list, and not much remained of my sanity.

I sat on my car's hood watching fog. Somewhere behind it, a majestic bridge spanned the bay, but like the location of my friend and my brother-in-law, all was shrouded. Zeke drove up and exited his car without my gaze leaving the fog.

"You sure are one needy dragon. Oliver must consider chasing down trees with the potential to change the balance of power in the universe a damned vacation."

Truths, falsehoods, embellishments, and inaccuracies littered what he said, but I thought I caught the meaning. "I am so sorry Zeke. Oliver and I are already in your debt, but I need to ask you yet another favor."

He kicked my car's tire. "Damnit, kid, you play the bereaving young widower too well. I'll do whatever I can to help, but I'm running out of gas here."

Instead of facing him, I tracked the progress of a pretty woman climbing the slope from the bay. "If your cats can find John and Hunter and you can let me know where they are, I can talk them down."

Zeke walked back to his car. "Son, the Children of Galinthius have a lot more to do than keep you and your in-laws out of trouble. Especially considering they'd just as soon put that witch family on a lonely rock in space."

The woman kept climbing closer. I feared time escaped me as we spoke. Soon she'd be close enough to hear us. I turned and called to Zeke. "That may be the case. That may be their attitude, but that's not the deal they have with Oliver's bosses. For my part, I'm doing what I can to keep the peace. They need to be able to say they did the same."

Zeke paused by his door. "Son, I was about to forget whose son you are. Appealing to their promises like that? That could hit home. I'll pass on your request; remind them of those promises, and who you are. I'll do that, but I can't make any promises."

"They have to do something."

He took off his hat. "That they do and that they will. Just be warned. They may come back with a plan of their own that you won't like in the least bit."

"Like what?"

He grimaced, climbed behind the wheel, and started the engine. "Listen for your phone."

He drove off as the woman reached fifteen feet below me.

"Hello," she said.

I wondered if she might have an earpiece, but she seemed to be looking at me, so I responded. "Yes?"

22

She talked to me. "Climbing rocks, cliffs and steep slopes are not what I'm good at. Can you come closer, so I can talk to you?"

I hadn't heard a request like that since my childhood. Who asks an adult they don't know to come closer so they can talk to them? I wanted to get to the last three hangouts as soon as possible but on the off chance she needed help, I climbed down.

When I faced her again, she smiled. "I am sensitive to the use of magic and its emanations from those who possess it."

Her greenish-blonde hair danced in the breeze, enthralling me until I thought of Vedi. My enthrallment lasted a brief second. The woman's words intrigued me because they were true. "Okay, so why do you want to talk to me?"

She cocked her head. "I've never seen so much magic emanating from someone before as I have you."

That was a lie, which both further intrigued me and alarmed me. "What are you really doing here?"

She pointed her chin at me. "I'm not here to lie to you. I overheard that you're looking for two associates of yours, powerful in magic, right?"

"What makes you think that?"

"Because you are powerful in magic."

She lied again. She didn't want to tell me the reason she thought they'd be powerful in magic. The fact that she lied to me twice told me she didn't know I knew when she did it. I had her at a disadvantage. I pressed it. "So, are you offering to help me find them?"

"I may have found them already."

This time she told the truth. I struggled to keep myself from grabbing her and shaking her. "Where?"

"About an hour ago, I saw an unusually powerful witch-boy wandering near the main branch of the public library in San Francisco."

I touched her shoulder. "Was he with a brown-haired white guy with a pleasant smile, not powerful in magic?"

She nodded. I started back up the slope. "Thank you."

Her last statement had one blemish to the truth. Something about the word 'near' made it the thing that didn't belong.

I had a riddle to solve and its solution, like a maze from fairy-tales, had the treasure I sought, a chance at peace. Could it be that Hunter was seen far from the library rather than near it? No. That would have made more of the statement false. So, if he wasn't seen near the library, and he wasn't far from it, what relationship did that leave? It had to be that he was seen in the library.

Why did this woman who had seen someone with more magic emanating from them than me, want me to think Hunter and John were near the library and not in it? Maybe I'd find out by going there.

Chapter 7

Being a dragon of order comes with limitations, like not being able to stay in a public library past closing without permission. Unlike normal people for whom not quite making it out the threshold in time is embarrassing, for me it's devastating. I'd rather be disemboweled.

So, when I arrived at the Main Branch of the San Francisco Public Library with only seventeen minutes until closing, I sought out someone in charge.

I approached a woman in a business suit who stood near the front desk. "Hello, I need to find two young men in here and I fear I'm running out of time before closing,"

"Something wrong?"

I must have been wearing my worry. She had a smirk, but I realized from her sincerity it was a resting expression.

"They're up to something foolish and I need to talk them out of it. It's extremely important that I do."

"What makes you think they're here?"

"A good tip."

She tilted her head. "Where do you do your social work? I haven't seen you around here."

"I'm not a—"

"But a friend in the cause, I can tell that."

I wasn't sure if she could tell I was a friend in the cause but she seemed to think so. She touched the back of my hand. "I'm Maria, a psychology grad student."

"I'm Aiden, a guy with one foolish friend and one foolish in-law. I need to find them."

She laughed. "I help social workers with the homeless as a practicum. In a few minutes, I sweep the library to make sure the homeless leave and find shelter. I'll bring you along. If those young men are here, we'll find them."

"The library will let us stay past closing?"

Her real smile came out. "However long it takes. Not more than a half hour. We can start now."

She was Latino, but something about her small frame and resting smirk reminded me of Vedi. I stared as I followed her. That lasted a few seconds before we came across a short heavy man with a swollen face and a more charming lack of intellect than Hunter's.

He grinned at my staring, as if he understood why, and I stopped. Maria spoke to him like one would a child. "Court, this is Aiden. He's going to help us tonight."

His grin changed to a grimace. "Oh good. Aiden, you and I need to protect Maria."

Maria patted him on the back. "That's sweet of you, Court, but I don't need protected. We're in a safe place."

He wagged his head. "Scary people are here. You need protected."

His words were true, at least from his perspective, so I interjected. "Are there two of them. One tall and thin with a butch haircut and the other average looking with a nice smile?"

"No. The tall one scared some of the scary people away from him, but he's not as scary as them."

I put my hand on his shoulder to make sure I had his attention. "Do you know where the tall one is?"

"I can show you."

Maria and I followed Court to a room on a floor near the glass ceiling. When we entered, we found John and Hunter sitting at a table. John jumped up. "Aiden, you've come to join us?"

I stepped into his space. "What have the two of you done?"

Hunter turned toward a window. "The hunter has become the hunted."

The line seemed out of place from him.

"Since when does Hunter quote literature?"

John smiled his way. "I think he's quoting Star Trek, actually, but he's right. We came here to find them, but they seem to have been expecting us. They're all over the lower floors and outside, just waiting for us to try and leave."

Maria approached. "I'm not okay with any gang war."

I grabbed her shoulder. "It's worse than that, Maria."

She lowered her shoulders. "What the hell are you guys talking about?"

I gestured to Court. "Protect her by making sure she doesn't leave this room until I sort this out. John and Hunter, you two stay here too."

Court nodded. Hunter stood. "I'm going with you."

I held out my hand toward him. "Hunter, no. There's a truce that just needed some time to work its way through to all of them. This is likely just a misunderstanding. I need to talk to them alone."

Hunter gave me a rare break and sat back down. I didn't detect fear like I did deception, but I saw it in him for the first time.

I sat John with a stare and left the room, closing the door behind me. "Lock it."

A rail from which all levels of the library could be seen became my perch. Things moved in places I couldn't see. I yelled, "Who here speaks for the Empusa?"

A lone security guard walked to where he could see me from the ground floor. "The library's closed now, everyone. It's time to leave the building."

A figure in a dark suit streaked from someplace out of view, colliding with the guard. A large belt flew from the guard and across the floor in the opposite direction. Disarmed, the guard needed my help.

I dropped down a level and then another and another on my way to him. Out the corner of my eye, I saw the guard attempt some sort of move on the Empusa, but the advantages of quickness and strength belonged completely to his attacker.

The ground floor greeted me with the guard's blank stare. His head facing an unnatural direction. The Empusa snapped his neck because he tried to enforce order in a public library. The creature could not have known who I was.

My claws appeared, my wings sprouted, and my eyes glowed, but one thing I shouldn't have done, I roared. My roar is a sonic weapon, sounding somewhere between the blast of a large brass horn and the roar of a tornado. It can be heard for miles.

The windows blew out and the ground tremored beneath me. A shock-wave threw the Empusa against a book shelf, and the book shelf fell from the force. Car alarms called out through the early night. What had to be dozens of business-suited figures scurried out of the building. Some crawling on all fours. Some fleeing out upper floor windows. In the blur of their movement, they could be mistaken for cockroaches scurrying from a burning shed.

I turned to the guard and touched his neck. My intent was to honor his noble sacrifice, but instead I saw his head slowly turn, his eyes shut and reopen, no longer blank. The broken skylight opened up the night sky obscured by a thick fog. No aspect of Vedi was present and yet I healed him.

The guard turned his head. "What just happened?"

Not wanting to cause myself any more problems, I answered with carefully chosen words. "Whatever you do, don't thank me. Thank God."

Chapter 8

I dug the guard's attacker out from under the books. He lay motion-less while I cleared every book. He jerked his head about and scur-ried out the front door, moving too fast for me to grab him. I managed to see enough of his face to recognize it if I saw him again. His nose was large and crooked, probably broken some time ago.

The mess I made of the library stung like an infected sore. I placed a book back on its shelf and noticed a tear in its sleeve vanish. Books around my ankles began to rise off the floor.

My wings were still out and the guard was behind me. That and what I suspected was about to happen caused me to turn. "Go and get the police."

He gave an awkward salute and limped away. The second the doors closed behind him, the books rose in a wave and landed in order on the shelves. At least he didn't see that.

The ability to heal was supposed to have come and went with Vedi and the ability to restore the inanimate, though related, was new.

Tortured by the broken windows, I flew to each one, and after placing one piece of broken glass in the general vicinity of the frames, glass fragments returned and fused into whole windows. Restoring the massive skylight completed the cleanup, I thought, until I noticed Court and Maria.

As I landed near them, Court laughed, but Maria scowled. "What are you?"

Needing to give an honest answer, respectful of her intent, I chose to give a limited answer. "I'm a magical being, but please don't ask for more details."

She walked around me as if a tailor inspecting a suit. "Does it embarrass you, what you are?"

Court chuckled. "Dragon-man."

That was too close to accurate. I tried to distract his thinking. "I'm Aiden."

He smiled. "I'm sorry, Aiden. I didn't mean to hurt your feelings."

He sincerely saw himself as sorry, which wasn't my aim, but at least he'd be unlikely to talk about me being a 'dragon-man' again.

John and Hunter approached and I put them to work. I asked them to make sure Court and Maria made it home okay while I took care of things at the library.

Once alone, I called Zeke. His first words were, "you're at the San Francisco Public Library main branch?"

This begged the question. "Yes. How'd you guess?"

He grumbled. "I think I heard you. That was you making that god-awful sound, right?"

"Yes, but you'll be happy to know I cleaned up after myself."

"Son, let's hang up our phones."

"What? Why?"

"I'm walking in the front door."

One of the doors swung open and Zeke's silhouette contrasted against flashing lights from the street. He pondered the scene. "Police radios and 911 calls spoke of broken glass everywhere. I don't see any."

I shrugged. "For some reason, I don't know, I suddenly have the ability to put things back together."

He took off his hat and held it over his heart as if he entered a mausoleum. "Saints be praised, or at least I wish that was right for this. You're becoming a growing problem, son. While you're gaining new abilities to alarm my bosses, do you think you've got one to erase that guard's memory?"

"I did my best to manage that one for you. I told him not to thank me but to thank God instead."

He waved his hat. "Great work there. He told a reporter, God used the devil to heal him."

Sarcasm's tricky to catch for me, but I caught that. "I'm sorry, Zeke, but when that guard's neck snapped just for trying to enforce order in a library, I lost it."

Zeke turned away and replaced his hat. "You recall, son, talking about agreements between my bosses and the Olympians about you?"

My hand shook. "Yes. This wasn't an appropriate time and place for my roar. I know that. It's the grief and my recent lack of sleep. It's hampering my ability to keep my cool."

He showed his profile. "That roar has no appropriate time and place as far as my bosses are concerned."

A chill crawled down my back. I swallowed and asked the dreaded question. "Does this mean I'm finished here?"

He took a long breath. "Not quite, son. You could have blown it tonight, but you didn't. The building's fixed and there's only one man telling stories about you. One man can be nothing more than the victim of a traumatic experience. We can keep it there, but when that number grows much past one, the potential for problems grows exponentially."

"And the noise?"

He took another deep breath. "There's no evidence to support an explanation their naturalist minds like, and a lack of evidence for a supernatural one. Count your lucky stars, son."

"Okay, I got lucky and have no intention of pushing it. Now, what about the Empusa? Did word of the truce not reach these particular ones?"

"So, your friends didn't cause this fight?"

"No, I found them in time."

He smiled. "Good work, son, and without our help. So, you've got them reigned in now?"

"I think so or at least I'm a lot closer than I was before."

He shook his head. "God damn, son. You can't even embellish, can you?"

I laughed. "You've read my file."

He didn't laugh or smile. "Well, okay, here's the unembellished truth from me. My bosses are acting suspicious, like their hiding something from me, and they haven't ever done that to me before. They respect my strategic mind, you should know."

"I didn't know, but I can tell you're not lying. Do you have any ideas as to why they're hiding things from you?"

He tipped his hat. "I'm still looking for a pattern. Until then, I'm not sure, but I know this much. Son, you need to get some rest, for both of our sakes."

Chapter 9

Lightning flashed as I drove to Maria's apartment. In the split illuminations, Empusa scurried about the edges of highway embankments. No doubt, they kept track of me.

I was right, it turned out. Amongst the Empusa, news of the truce still worked its way through their ranks. Zeke's cat friends would inform him once they were confident all the Empusa knew, at least all the ones that needed to. Until then, he thought it wise for John, Hunter, and me to keep a low profile.

News already saturated the south end of the bay where we lived —north of there, in and around San Francisco, not so much. Unfortunately, Maria lived near San Francisco, and the three of us thought we owed her protection while we waited.

We tried our best to be polite guests in her apartment, even Hunter. Two ambushes in two days sobered him. We tried to keep her calm, an unexpectedly easy task.

Her sofas' worn-down cushions valiantly held down the pungent residue of people who effervesced alcohol. We would not be the first of Maria's guests to sleep on them. There were only two, no problem for me. "I'll sleep on the floor. It's good for my back."

Rain cascaded outside, and John raised his eyebrows. He thought my statement curious. "You must be tired, Aiden."

I knew what he meant, that I slipped and spoke a partial truth. "I am tired, and I also see benefit for my back in sleeping on the floor. I'm not tired enough to pretend I do."

A knock on the door precluded a thunder crack. Maria started for it, but Hunter beat her there. He opened it a crack. "Hello?"

An arm pushed through and Hunter jumped back. A man in a pinstriped suit fell through the doorway, landing face down in Maria's entryway. She pushed him onto his back like someone used to handling unconscious bodies. I recognized his face.

The crooked nosed Empusa who attacked the library security guard lay before me. Maria felt his wrist and then his neck for a pulse. "I think he's dead."

Hunter knelt next to her. "But he just got here."

I tapped her shoulder. "Let me see what I can do."

I cradled the Empusa's head like I did the security guards. If a short enough time had passed since his heart stopped, I could heal him, at least in most cases. Not with Empusas apparently.

Instead of his eyes opening to a reprieve from death, they dissolved. The rest of him followed their example, leaving a pile of dust. The pile defied the wet air, withdrawing into the wind. Only a pendant the size of a quarter remained.

"What just happened?" asked Maria.

I picked up the pendant and closed the door. "I'm not sure."

A map rosette dominated one side of the pendant. The other showed four odd symbols. I gave it to John to see if the student of all things ancient could recognize them.

For his part, he copied them onto a napkin and rubbed his chin. "They translate into something, but I'll need access to the university library to figure it out."

Knowing his enthusiasm for such things, I thought it necessary to remind him of our situation. "That's going to have to wait until morning."

Zeke called before I could confirm John heard me. "My boys

helped spread the word and are confident the truce is in full effect. You and yours are now fully out of the woods."

I caught the stares of my companions. "That's great Zeke. Thanks."

"The boys want me to ask you about something before you get some sleep."

Cold came across my face. "And what would that be?"

"It's about the Empusa you fought in the library."

"It's not entirely accurate to say I fought him. I knocked him over."

"Was he alive the last time you saw him?"

I hated the way he worded that question. Taken literally, the honest answer, the only kind I can give, would be 'no,' but that would be to a question he probably wasn't intending to ask. I couldn't honestly answer it 'no' in that case. I had to clarify. "You mean, did I see him leave the library on his own?"

"Well, yes, of course."

"Yes. Why do your cats want to know this?"

"Because the Empusa haven't been able to account for him since the doings in the library."

John wasn't entirely wrong earlier. I was tired enough to slip in my devotion to the truth. I didn't lie to Zeke. I didn't even mislead him. I waited quietly on the phone for him to end the call, and he did. "By all means, son, get some rest. I think we're finally out of all this, but one never knows."

I grabbed the pendant. "Someone wants to frame us."

Hunter tapped my hand. "Fat lot of evidence they have after what you did to the body. Good work. You're starting to think like me."

"I was trying to heal him."

"Whatever, it worked for us."

Tired or not, I remained a dragon of order. I opened my hand. "I'm going to have to bring this to Zeke and explain what happened."

Hunter shook his head. "No, you just need to take wing, fly out over the ocean and drop this in."

"I can't do that. It's too close to a lie."

Hunter squinted. "Your lineage is so lame. Give it to me and I'll swim out after the storm passes."

I held it between two fingers. "I need to take this to Zeke."

Before I could moralize, Hunter snatched it and ran. I grabbed him, but he yanked away, denting the wall as he struggled. Not wanting to damage Maria's apartment any further I let go. He ran into the downpour, lightning flashed, and I ran out after him.

While nowhere near as fast as an Empusa, his great grandfather's magically perverted genes gifted him enough speed to lose me in the storm. Fortunately for me, he didn't inherit his great grandfather's brains. He wasn't going to get creative, so I knew with fair confidence where to find him, where the nearest road reached the shore.

Chapter 10

The storm gave cover to my wings, so I used them. I came across Hunter amid rocks and beach. He slowed to a jog as he neared the water, and I swooped.

Surprise gave him no chance to dodge or brace, and I sent him sliding across the sand. I planned to snatch the pendant as he lost grip of it, but he didn't. His grip remained sure.

I almost didn't recognize him as he rose to his feet, undeterred by the adversity I brought him. No brags, no taunts, no insults sent my way, just a determined drive into a violent sea, and words unlike an Asta. "My family, I need to protect my family."

I stood and called out. "Hunter?"

He walked backward into the waves. "I know what you think of me. Vedi thought the same. She never missed a chance to remind me how stupid I am."

"Hunter, please stop. I can fly faster than you can swim." He hadn't seemed to have heard me.

Water ran down his face. "But she loved me."

He reminded me of one thing we had in common. I struggled against a lump threatening to take my voice. "Let me deal with the pendant."

A forced smile crossed his face. "Maybe loving her stupid brother is what made it possible for her to love someone with a lineage like yours."

Grief, fatigue, and confusion nailed me to the spot as he ran into the foam. I wanted to give myself over to crying but feared I'd pass out. The inside of my mind matched the heavens. Clouds blotted out the faint lights of the firmament while rain poured, and the wind kept changing direction. I withdrew my wings.

Why did I expect him to give me the pendant, knowing it could put him and his family at risk? I found some clarity in the thought I could still tell Zeke about what happened. I just wouldn't have the pendant.

Hunter's course out to sea took him out of sight when I heard a woman's voice. "Aren't you going after the witch boy?"

The woman who sent me to the library stood behind me. The lump in my throat receded. "The magic you sensed in him will take care of him."

She cocked her head. "So, you're not concerned?"

Water on me evaporates rapidly, not because of an unusual body temperature, but due to order magic. My body tends toward being neat and dry. Vapor rose from me like an exhaust pipe and I didn't want to explain to her while yelling over the storm. "I should probably get out of the rain soon."

Her eyes wandered up and down. "Follow me. I know a place we can duck under some shelter."

I knew I couldn't trust her any further than John could throw her, but I wanted to know more about her. Perhaps I could discover the reason she tried to steer me near the library ambush rather than into it. I also wanted to know who it was she met emanating more magic than I did.

She led me to a cliff side, a solid cliff face with no overhang or shelter until we got within a few feet. It had an opening into a cave. I couldn't fathom how I missed it.

Inside, the light from a kerosene lamp made shadows dance hypnotically on the walls. She invited me to sit down on a rock. "Please, rest."

I accepted her offer. "Thank you for your hospitality."

"You must be soaked. Take off your clothes and let them dry."

I thought perhaps I should be flattered but I wanted a conversation. "I'm fine in that regard."

She turned her back. "Really?"

My mind struggled against my lack of sleep to find a way to get some answers without tipping her to my ability to know if she lied or not. "I have a question to ask you about what you told me earlier. When I found my friends, they were in the library. Do you remember exactly where it was you saw them?"

She pulled off her blouse, interrupting my fragile train of thought. I blushed. "Um, I can give you some privacy."

She smiled; at least I think she did. My eyes spent very little time on her face, though I heard her words. "You're the son of a mighty being, aren't you?"

I wasn't going to answer that question, no matter what she did to get it out of me.

She approached me like a leopard ready to pounce. "What do you suppose would be the offspring of the son of a god and a mortal?"

I held her at arm's length and got up. "Probably most unfortunate, would be my guess."

She scowled and returned to her blouse. I stepped back toward the storm. "I'm flattered that such a beautiful woman as yourself should find me attractive but—"

"You're gay?"

"No. My wife died recently."

"I'm so sorry. Too soon then. Perhaps another time."

That was all too sincere. I held my hand out of the cave before leaving. "I need to go now."

I bound up the cliff and moved out of sight of anyone standing by the cave entrance. I sprouted my wings and took off back to Maria's apartment.

On the way, I asked the howling wind for ways to explain to John and Maria why I let Hunter go. It didn't answer. I asked if I should say to Zeke about the fate of the missing Empusa. On that note, it seemed to sympathize. "Oh," it moaned. Of course, it didn't know what I asked, but my tired mind fared little better.

A spot on the floor called to me and John would have his choice of sofas.

Chapter 11

John took the news poorly. "You just let Hunter swim out to sea in this storm?"

I cared what John thought of my decision but my lack of sleep drowned out my concern. My back hit the floor and I closed my eyes.

"Aiden? How could you do that?"

"It's like he explained to me. It's his family. On top of that, John, I'm so tired. If I don't get some sleep soon, I might really do something stupid."

I'm not sure what John said after that. His words faded in my consciousness as I free-fell into sleep.

John and Maria left by the time I woke. My car keys dangled on a string about my wrist. I guessed Maria had a policy of tying guests' car keys to them. That's how she treated bums—like children. I knew that already, but I didn't know she saw me as one. This child, as she apparently perceived me to be, made sure to fix the dent in her wall before driving home.

Well rested, I wasted no time in setting up a meeting with Zeke. His unanswered question about the crooked-nosed Empusa sat on my stomach like swallowed hot coal. Zeke chose the Asta's front driveway. I guessed another difficult question awaited.

Zeke leaned on his car and tilted his hat back. "Hunter Asta, son, do you know what happened to him?"

I burned in two places inside. I answered to the hottest. "Zeke, the missing Empusa was alive and walking when he left the library, but someone brought his dead body to where John and I slept last night."

He squinted. "You don't say."

"Looks like someone wants to wreck the truce."

"First my bosses get evasive about things and then this happens. Something stinks about this whole assignment, son."

I stepped closer. "Any ideas, Zeke?"

He shook his head. "I still can't figure why my bosses would feel a need to hide something from me. I don't need that, you know."

I got the jab. I explained about Hunter. Zeke told me Mr. Asta had driven out to Half Moon Bay to pick him up. He told his mother he could barely move after swimming all night.

Remembering Zeke saying he had a valued strategic mind, I ran one last thing by him. I told him about the woman I saw in Marin and at the beach near Maria's apartment. The timings and nature of her appearances were too odd to be coincidence. She had to know something both of us wanted to know about all of this. He agreed and shared an awkward piece of advice. "Something tells me trying to jump your bones wasn't part of her marching orders. Son, she seems to have a real thing for you. You could exploit that."

I blushed and grinned. The grin made no sense to me and that fact made me blush more. "Yeah, and she seems to want to procreate. Your bosses and the Olympians would throw a fit if they thought I was taking a chance with that."

"You know what a condom is, son?"

That should have been a rhetorical question, but he meant it.

"Zeke, I'm a dragon, not a child."

We left that there. We agreed on the strategy, but the tactics would have to be mine.

When Zeke drove off, something occurred to me. I stood in my in-laws' driveway. For most that meant little, but for a dragon of order it meant I had an invitation. Without an invitation I couldn't have crossed their property line, but who invited me? Mr. Asta was away picking up Hunter. Ms. Asta, who hated me, had to be the source of my welcome, but why this time?

She watched me through her front window. I waved. She walked to her door and opened it. "You and I need to talk."

The oldest living direct descendant of my father's arch nemesis told me we needed to talk and meant it in all honesty. I gulped and went inside. She gestured me to a chair. "I want to thank you for trying to take care of Hunter."

I opened my mouth but caught myself. I didn't want to say her dead daughter told me to.

She noticed my hesitation and smiled. "I'm also pleased that you let him swim out to sea."

"He had the pendant, so I figured I could let him deal with it in his own way without me having to be dishonest."

She cocked her head and batted an eye. "No, Aiden, I couldn't care less about that blasted honesty of yours. Hunter is stupid and foolish. I'm happy that you let his foolishness run its course. It's the only way he'll learn."

The last sentence was less than sincere, especially around the word 'learn,' as if she wanted another result than learning. The cold implication stunned me. She grimaced, raised her eyebrows and after some time, grinned.

She leaned in and whispered. "I know, Aiden."

"You know that Vedi's death has left me broken?"

She took my face into her weak hands and shook my skin. "Spare me the blather. It's something more important than your feelings."

"What?"

"She talks to you."

"How do you know?"

"I see it in your eyes and hear it between your words."

I grabbed her hand. "Do you know how or why? I don't."

"When does she speak to you?"

"She only speaks to me on clear nights?"

She tilted her head. "In your dreams?"

"No, while I'm completely awake."

She winced. "When the moon rises?"

"She speaks to me while I'm completely awake and under a clear night sky."

Ms. Asta stood and pointed a finger. "Where does her voice come from?"

"The stars."

Her eyes widened. "No, it makes no sense."

I could tell she wanted it to make sense. She lied to herself. Denial is powerful, I know. I was there not long before. I knew better than to press her on it. As much as I wanted to know why Ms. Asta so preferred that Vedi might speak through my dreams or the moon, and not the stars, like my grief, the question needed time.

Chapter 12

I ate dinner at my unwitting adoptive mother Nikki's. She hadn't seen me in a couple of days and had good reason to worry. I read it in her, despite her inscrutable Japanese face and indirect words.

"The stones at the church are perfect, as usual," she said.

She placed a tone of pride on the last phrase. She's always been proud of my precision, but at times I wondered if she didn't think I took it to too great an extreme.

"You know me, Mom. There'd be something wrong with me if they weren't at least close to perfect."

"Close? But enough about that. Why haven't you contacted me in the last three days?"

I wiped my mouth. "Hunter got himself into some trouble in Yosemite and he needed John and me to help him. It was pretty intense. I got my first full night's sleep last night."

"You're such a good person, better than you have to be."

I filled my mouth with chicken and pondered the usual haunting question about Nikki and Patrick Ferris. When would Oliver see fit to tell them? Until then she'd continue to shower love on me instead of her real son. I loved my unwitting adoptive parents, a love fueled by gratitude and guilt.

She gave me the stare, the one I understood many mothers do; the one that grabs your attention even if you're trying not to look. "You don't need to help Hunter out of trouble. He is trouble. I don't know how you can tell where it ends and he begins."

"He's Vedi's brother."

"Thankfully, you didn't marry him. You married her. She's dead now. It's time you looked for another young woman."

I finished dinner and kissed her on the forehead.

As I walked away, she said, "My son should not be alone."

I agreed with her, that's why I drove into the hills that night to stand under a star lit sky. If Ms. Asta sensed her daughter spoke to me, perhaps I wasn't crazy.

The communications thus far traveled in one direction, so I came with no questions, just the hope of finding a clue. Why did my mother-in-law, an accomplished witch, have no trouble with the idea her dead daughter spoke to me, but did have trouble with her voice coming from the stars of a night sky?

I had to admit my motives were mixed. I hoped Vedi might hear me. My state of denial didn't need any of this, not her speaking and certainly not a two-way conversation. I didn't need it, but I wanted it and my odd exchange with her mother gave me an excuse to give it a chance.

It started out the same as before, nothing, then her voice, indiscernible, then scattered words, and finally a statement. *"Don't trust my mother."*

I thought those words convenient as they'd be the ones I'd choose. Too convenient. Perhaps in being suspicious I might be falling backward instead of moving forward in my grieving process.

She spoke again. *"She wants Hunter to die."*

Again, her words only confirmed my suspicions. Again, convenient for words supposed to be from Vedi and not my mind.

"Aiden?"

Yeah, I wanted to hear her call my name. Wait, though, why as a question? I pondered until she spoke more questions. *"Stars? I speak through the stars? Aiden, is that true?"*

Whatever the source of those words, the question was sincere.

They didn't know I heard their voice through the stars of a clear night sky. I knew that. Wouldn't all levels of my consciousness?

"Vedi?"

I waited for an answer. I waited as long as I could stand to. "Vedi, can you hear me?"

Nothing. The clear night sky embraced me with a void. I waited another hour and drove home to my bed.

Something pulled at me, making it hard to think. A daze set in and only morning woke me. Tears on my face were like a stranger's because I didn't remember crying, but a lump in my throat assured me they were mine.

The best rest I'd had in days still left my mind clouded. It worried me, but the clear areas worried me more. If Vedi's voice really was Vedi's voice, she didn't know exactly how she spoke to me. Something about it frightened me.

Also, the source being something other than myself, the truth of the other statements was likely more than speculation.

Ms. Asta wants her son to die.

I caught most of that myself when she dishonestly used the word 'learn' for another fate she truly wanted Hunter to experience from his recklessness.

I also found it curious how the crooked-nosed Empusa's dead body had been propped against Maria's door. How was it that it didn't disintegrate before it could be moved there? The one at the church could not have been moved more than a few inches before becoming dust in the wind. Who might have the magical abilities to arrange things as we found them at Maria's?

My attempt at healing may have canceled that magic, my order magic, and what magic is the opposite of mine? That of a direct descendant of the sorcerer Dak.

Fear flashed into my thoughts. John and I hadn't spoken since I told him I let Hunter throw himself into a stormy sea. He might be with Hunter. I needed to find him.

Searching the university library was a bit of déjà vu I didn't like, but to my relief, I found him at a terminal. I whispered, "John, we need to talk."

He turned away. "The writing on the pendant says pretty much nothing. It's just the guy's name, I'd guess."

I grabbed his shoulder. "That's not why I'm here. It's about someone wanting to get Hunter killed."

We found a study room so I could explain my theory. "I spoke with Ms. Asta recently and she told me she was happy I let Hunter swim out to sea. She said his foolishness needed to be allowed to run its course and that it would be the only way he'd learn."

"So, you agree with her, I take it?"

"That's not the point, John. It's that she was honest in every word but one, the word, 'learn'."

"From that you conclude she wants to kill her own son?"

"No, not that alone. It's a combination of things. That Empusa was killed and moved to our door without disintegrating. Only someone highly skilled in magic could have done that."

"Why would that have to be her?"

"That coven is full of hacks, Harold left Earth, and Hunter didn't try to set himself up."

"So, you're saying that leaves her."

"There's no one else we know of."

John resorted to an understatement. "That witch!"

He may have become too loud with them, so I moved closer and whispered. "When Hunter is told this, it should be you who tells him, but not right now."

He spoke in a hushed tone. "Why not now?"

"Because if it is his mother who tried to break the truce, we need to find that out for sure before Hunter confronts her."

He gave a slight smile. "I see you're back again."

"The rest has done me good."

When I explained my theory, I took care to leave out the clear night sky. I needed John on task. He needed to try and steer Hunter away from any potential schemes of his mother, without telling him why.

In the meantime, I needed to find a certain magically sensitive woman with bluish blonde hair and a desire to bare me a child.

13

Chapter 13

John's task required he anticipate the schemes of a powerful witch, and with only words in the ear of my thick-headed brother-in-law, thwart them. As much as he bettered most people in intellect, me included, I thought little of his chances.

I only gave him the task because I doubted I could do any better, and because the more active task of confirming who schemed to stop the truce before it started, had to be mine. The bluish-blonde-haired woman with the desire to bear my children had contacted me and me alone.

Some could sneer at my predicament, thinking sarcastically, what an awful burden, but their literal words would be truer than their meaning. A condition of my presence on Earth required me to secure the permission of the Olympians if I ever wanted to father an offspring, because it was imperative my father never know he had descendants. The more he had, the tougher it would become to keep it from him.

Vedi and I negotiated for such permission before she died. So, I found myself with no such permission and about to look for someone eager to make it happen, will of the Olympians be damned.

I visited a drug store to buy some condoms but decided not to. I favored caution as much as the next dragon, but some acts of caution favor over-confidence. This magically sensitive woman didn't seem the sort to be stopped from her goal by a piece of plastic. I could only count on the surest form of pregnancy prevention and I uniquely had the will to reliably use it. It would make the interactions more difficult to steer into the sorts of dialogues I wanted, but it could be the only path for the son of order.

Tactics decided, I entered her cave. I saw only her lamp but not for long. She stepped out of the shadows. "You're back? I thought I frightened you with my forward behavior."

I had to tell the truth with no deception and still trick her into revealing something other than her body. "You helped me two days ago. I'm hoping you can help me again."

She ran a finger down my arm, tracing the curves of my triceps. "In what way?"

She knew too well how to entice me. Vedi would have just told me to shave my head and get a nose-ring. I thought of her and took a needed breath. "Something involving a lot of magic happened that night a couple blocks from here."

Her eyes and hands evaluated my chest. "I was too distracted by your powerful emanations to see anything else."

She lied. She could see other things, but did she?

"You flatter me, but surely you saw this, an Empusa killed and his body preserved long enough to leave it on a doorstep."

Her eyes didn't lie when she looked impressed by my modest build. "No. I saw only you."

Her words lied, and she intended on keeping them that way, but a lie can reveal the truth if properly maneuvered. "A powerful witch's magic, you didn't sense that?"

She ran her fingers along my abs and smiled gleefully. "No."

She gave exactly the answer I could work with, a yes/no, but she also told the truth that time. It confused me. "Do you work for a witch?"

"Of course not."

Another truthful answer.

The tips of her fingers entered my pants. Now that was a Vedi move. It would stop there as a tease. I asked another question, although I'm not sure how I managed enough concentration to. "Did you have—"

She found my fly and pulled it down. That wasn't a Vedi move. I lost my train of thought and grasped the only remotely useful question I could think of at that moment. "Do you really like me?"

She laughed and nodded, her hand seeking and finding its objective. My mind ran to Vedi and directed my hand to grab her wrist and squeeze, forcing her hand to release me. I pushed her away and pulled up my fly.

She pouted. "What's wrong? I could tell you liked it."

"I'm not allowed."

"Not allowed? Who can command you?"

I sat on a rock. I found its cold useful in the moment. I didn't want to tell her enough to know of my lawful nature, lest she guess my ability to detect lies. I decided to turn the tables. "Since when does a woman pursue a man as aggressively as you do me?"

She sat on another rock. "Oh, I see. You prefer to be the aggressor."

"That's not the point of my question. What do you see in me that causes you to drop all the normal womanly ways in approaching a man and just go straight for me?"

She cocked her head. "I see the magic that emanates from people and I know that you must be the son of a god."

"And you'll throw yourself at any son of a god you happen to see?"

"No."

I noted her honesty. "So why me?"

"Because you are the most powerful and beautiful I've ever seen."

"How many have you seen?"

"You're kind are rare, but I've seen most, I think."

She believed she had.

"If you don't mind me asking, how old are you?"

She smiled. "I do mind you asking, but I have lived long enough to see many of you come and go."

I knew what she meant by 'go.' She meant die, but I became anxious for the more common meaning. "I have things to check on and should be going. I appreciate your conversation."

She stood and gestured to the exit. "Then you must be on your way, but please feel free to return whenever you wish."

I wondered what sort of creature seemed to know so aptly what I wanted to hear. I walked out of the cave and she spoke softly in my ear as I passed her. "Perhaps sometime you will allow yourself what you want."

If she knew, she might not be so eager.

Chapter 14

The first person I wanted to speak with called me as I drove back to the Milpitas, a coincidence of sorts, but not as convenient as it could have been. I had to ask Zeke to repeat himself, and he did. "I need you to come pay my bail, so I can get out of this county jail."

Oliver and the Children of Galinthius had deep contacts in high federal places. Misunderstandings occurred from time to time, but someone like Zeke should never have been more than a data reference away from being let go, no bail necessary.

"Why do you need bail?"

"They refuse to contact the feds."

"Why would they refuse?"

"Beats me, son. Politics I suppose."

Not only did I need to post bail, but he had to be released into my custody. Good thing for Zeke, they were more willing to call the Milpitas police to vouch for my character than they were the feds to establish Zeke's status. I waited until he and I were in the car before asking him the other questions his imprisonment begged. "What did you do?"

"Nothing."

My senses knew he thought as much, but of course, it didn't mean anything to me. "How could it be nothing?"

"Well, a police officer walked up to me and started asking me questions about my gun. He treated my permit like I got it out of a box of candied popcorn and asked me to surrender my sidearm."

"And you refused."

"No, I cooperated. I love the expressions on these little tin horns' faces when they call in the number on my permit."

"But he didn't call it in."

"Yep, and worse than that, he asked me what a private citizen needs a desert eagle for."

"How is that worse?"

"I told him a sissy .44 isn't quite up to the task of knocking down some of the things I need to shoot at."

"And that's worse how?"

"I failed to notice until then that he had a .44. He arrested me for giving him a hard time, and since they've refused to call in my permit, they've also charged me with illegal possession of a firearm."

Being in my custody meant I had lots of time to tell him what I found out from the sexually aggressive woman at the beach. She'd been alive long enough to see heroes in the classical sense, and she saw something involving significant magic the night the crooked-nosed Empusa was killed, but a powerful witch wasn't involved.

I figured since Zeke's bosses were protective of the Empusa, this information would get them interested in finding out about this woman. I waited for him to contact his boys, but I told one too many things.

"Why would anyone be asking if a witch was involved?" he asked.

I didn't want him to know I suspected my mother-in-law because his bosses needed no new reasons to want to blink the entire Asta family off to a rock in space. I chose my words with care to be honest and yet not reveal the suspicion. "In order to keep the Empusa's body from disintegrating before it could be dropped outside the door from us, someone would've needed significant magical ability, the sort a witch might have."

He tapped the dash. "Yeah, son, you don't lie, do you?"

I hate that question because it must be true, but it would also be the setup to trap me in a potentially fatal lie. "You've read my file."

"I've read your in-law's files too."

When we got back to our house, he asked me to give him some space in my backyard, so he could pass on what I found to his 'boys.'

This was my chance to call John and let him know we should no longer suspect Hunter's mother. I called him, but he started before I could say 'hi.'

"Aiden, you need to help me. Hunter's walking into a trap."

"What?"

I heard Hunter's voice in the background. "No, I'm not, and leave the screaming lizard out of this. He's not invited."

I rubbed my forehead. "What's going on, John?"

John started whispering. "Out of nowhere, his coven has decided to honor him at Eagle Rock tonight."

I couldn't contain my disdain. "Those poor eagles."

"Aiden, this isn't funny."

"Okay, sorry. What makes you think it's a trap?"

"Hunter's the only one who makes plans for the coven. That's suspicious, so I called Ms. Asta. She knows about it and refuses to go, also suspicious, but here's what really makes me believe it's a trap."

"What?"

"When I told her I was going, she begged me not to. She sounded way more desperate than she should be."

"Why would she care if you're there or not?"

"The Asta's like me, remember?"

"All of them?"

"Well, I'm not sure about Mr. Asta, but Hunter, and his mother really like me for some reason."

"And you think she's expecting bad things to happen at Eagle Rock tonight."

"Yes."

His confidence carried over the phone and I deferred to him. "Okay, here's what we'll do. You go with your phone on so I can hear."

"And you?"

"I obviously would not be an accepted guest, and nor would I want to be."

"So, you're going to sit at home and try to get there in time when things go down?"

I looked out my back window. "No. I'll be close by where I can match the sounds of your phone with what's happening."

John accepted my plan and hung up. He knew my word and so did I, but I feared I may have given it too soon. I needed to take Zeke with me, continuing to keep him unaware of Ms. Asta's potential malice.

He came back in. "You'll be happy to know, son, they're going to find out for us who and what that woman with the hots for you is, but they want you to stay away from her for now."

I stood. "Zeke, I hate to drag you around, but you've got to be in my custody and I have a suspicious coven meeting to observe tonight."

"So, son, it's 'take your child to work day,' is it?"

Chapter 15

Zeke had a good sense of humor about his circumstances. Until his court date, I kept him out of trouble instead of the other way around. I'm sure his bosses would have flown someone from half-way around the world to take temporary custody of him if they had anyone. Whatever Oliver dealt with must have been man-power intensive. Zeke changed his moniker for me for the time.

"Chief, why are we clinging to this dusty hillside?"

We had a rock between us and sliding.

"Because it gives us a good view of that big rock down there?"

"We expecting it to move?"

"The coven's going to meet there at sundown, and John's pretty sure someone's going to try to kill Hunter."

He pushed his hat against his head. "And why do we care?"

"Vedi cares and so does John."

He shook his head. "It's pretty bad when a dragon's being told what to do by a ghost and a mortal who wears his heart on his sleeve."

"Is that what John's file says?"

"He cares about too much."

I could tell his file must not say that but as far as Zeke was concerned, it did. He wanted to help me, and maybe Oliver, but he saw John and Hunter as liabilities.

Hikers in brown and black robes started approaching Eagle Rock, so I put a finger over my lips and we hunkered down.

I heard John's phone in my earpiece. Hiking up the trail, different coven members took turns asking to be introduced to Hunter's friend. John repeated a lie about him being a new member of the coven and Hunter acknowledged with verbal affirmations that weren't quite words, almost grunts.

As he came into sight, he spotted me and turned to Hunter. "Is it okay if I mingle with the others before the honoring?"

Hunter nodded, and John left him to join a group gathered around two individuals in green robes. "Hello, I'm John Eisenbach, I'm a new member."

The shorter of the two had his or her hood up. The taller of the two, a man in his early to mid-twenties, shook John's hand. "I'm Charly Chord, the coven's next leader."

Charly Chord had a confident smile. The lines on his face made it clear the smile lived there most of the time. John reached for his other hand and spoke with a feigned sense of awe. "What is this?"

He raised his hand enough and I could see what resembled a sword handle with a single bar-like guard, but instead of a blade protruding out the front, two metal ropes wound up his arm. I recognized it. Considering a low talent witch-boy held it, I might have thought it a replica, but a hot chill walking up and down my spine told me otherwise. This Charly Chord held Imhullu on his arm. The Imhullu, the wind weapon that felled Tiamat, one of the most powerful dragons ever to exist.

I turned to Zeke, "You see that?"

"Yeah. Chief, should I know what it is?"

"I guess not. Just that it could kill me, and it's amazing that squib could have found it before Oliver."

Zeke took off his hat and pressed a finger against his forehead. "Maybe Hunter isn't the target here."

I grabbed Zeke's shoulder. "Hold on. Don't call in your cats yet."

"But why, son?"

I didn't want his cats finding another reason to ship off the Asta's if it wasn't necessary, even if it meant risking my life a little.

I squeezed his shoulder. "He probably doesn't know what he's got. If he turns that thing on me, go ahead and call them, but until then, let me handle this."

"Alright, son, just remember I've got my job to do too, and it don't involve protecting Hunter Asta."

Charly let John touch Imhullu like one would a cast. His smile grew as he did. "That's a magical weather machine."

I patted Zeke on the back. "I'm right. He doesn't know what he's got. You can stop worrying."

I couldn't though. He probably knew enough to work up a strong wind gust, and two coven members were escorting Hunter to mount Eagle Rock. Charly walked toward him proclaiming something in Latin. It sounded like praise and whatever his words meant; he lied as he spoke them.

The two females who escorted Hunter placed a crown and a necklace on him and sat at his feet. Hunter waved and said, "Thank you."

Charly raised Imhullu toward Hunter. I sprouted my wings, readying to leap out and catch him. The plan seemed clear. The usurper of witches did not become better in my mind by wronging his own kind, but doubly worse. As soon as he displayed his wickedness, I would grab Hunter from the air, put him down, and find and gut Charly Chord for his entire coven to see.

Except the other green cloaked figure ran through the crowd and grabbed his arm, pulling it down, and removing Imhullu, taking Imhullu from him. The hood fell away revealing a long-haired woman. I recognized that hair style, bluish-blonde, just like my would-be seducer from the beach, only not her, a different face. They could be sisters.

John's phone caught the words between them. "What are you doing?" he asked her.

"He says not now."

Charly acquiesced like a dutiful child to a mother, but she gave him quite the un-maternal kiss as he did.

Zeke tapped my thigh. From his hunkered down position, he whispered. "What just happened?"

His concern regarding someone one in the coven, not an Asta, encouraged me, but something in the sky didn't. Clouds obscured many of the stars, the city lights shone against them, and silhouetted, two large winged creatures approached.

I answered, "I don't know, but it seems I didn't sprout these wings in vain."

He asked, "What?" as I launched toward them. They both turned as I did. In turning, they slowed and I caught one of them. I grabbed its leg.

A winged woman with the legs and talons of a bird shrieked and tried to pull free. She was a harpy. She tried to tear at my hand with her free talon and clawed hands, but she couldn't penetrate my skin. Flapping with panicked rapidity she pleaded with me. "Let me go."

I tightened my grip. "Not until I know you won't hurt Hunter Asta."

"Hurt him? I was sent to protect him."

She didn't lie, so I asked, "by who were you sent?"

She cocked her head back with pride, even while struggling to fly with me throwing off her balance. "We were sent by Thaumus, god of the seas."

I let her go, and after a short drop, she recovered and flew off toward the Pacific. I flew back to Zeke. "Thaumus?"

He pondered. "The titan? What about him?"

"What does he have to do with all of this?"

Zeke and I had a lot to talk about that evening. A danger passed, but what just came and stayed?

Chapter 16

Zeke and I had waited for the coven to leave Alum Rock Park. He shrugged. "That woman's hair has a bluish tint, right?"

"Yes, just like the woman on the beach. They look enough alike to be sisters, but they're not the same person."

He skittered along the hillside. "God damn."

I whispered after him. "Zeke, where are you going?"

"Watch me, son."

I did just that. He moved along the hillside like a mountain goat until he reached a point above the trail. There, he slid down an erosion cut down to the path, leaving a cloud of dust along the way. A few steps up the path he bumped into Charly's girlfriend. "Oops. Sorry, ma'am."

He tipped his hat and winked at me. After the last cloaked figure passed by, I jumped down. "What was that all for?"

"Son, I see why you want to keep that John fellow around."

"What are you talking about?"

He grinned. "We're going to need him."

"We? What are you talking about?"

"My boys are busy finding out who your blue-haired woman is.

That leaves it to me to keep track of Charly's blue-haired woman. Let's find out just how connected they are."

He took off his watch and showed it to me. In place of a time display, a digital map of east San Jose glowed. A light blinked over Alum Rock Park. I took the watch. "You planted a tracking device on her?"

"So now we'll know where she is at all times. If she goes off to meet someone, like say your beach lady, we'll know."

"And John? What does this have to do with him?"

"We can't have another event like your roar in the library, so you need your sleep, and that means to honor the conditions of my release, I need to stay where you are, probably also getting some shut-eye."

I had John come over to my house and pick up the watch, along with instructions on how to use it. John made yet another friend. Like with Hunter and Ms. Asta, I saw very little in common between Zeke and John, and yet Zeke suddenly cared about him. "Whatever you do, John, don't try to follow her yourself. We can't have you getting hurt."

With John gone, I pulled out the fold-away for Zeke and asked a question that had bothered me since my exchange with the harpy. "Why should a titan care about Hunter, and how did he know he was in danger?"

"I don't know, but I can arrange you a meeting with him. You can ask him then. In the meantime, you can get some sleep."

I made up the bed and shared the other question on my mind. "Okay, but why would he tell the harpy he's the god of the seas? That wouldn't be true since the war with the Olympians, right?"

"He said he's the god of the seas?"

"I'm not sure, but the harpy believed him to be."

Zeke laughed. "I guess it was only a matter of time with the Olympians all pulled out from Earth that some of the titans would become uppity."

"A potential job for your bosses?"

"Nah. Just an annoyance to the Olympians, as long as he doesn't interfere with mortals too much."

I looked forward to meeting Thaumus, thinking I could perhaps put him back in his place with a few well-chosen words, right after thanking him for his help protecting Hunter of course.

Four hours into sleep, John woke us to let us know Charly's girlfriend got in a car and headed for the east bay. I threw on clothes and snapped my phone into the holder on my dash. Zeke and I got on the highway ahead of her, used the slow lane until she passed us, and we followed.

At three in the morning, the road had few cars on it, making it challenging not to be obvious in tailing her. I dropped back on multiple occasions, relying on John to keep track of her whenever we lost sight.

North of Freemont, she pulled into the parking lot of a Christian school. I eased up to a curb and shut off the lights. A man in a suit and another bluish-blonde-haired woman stood outside a car, no doubt expecting her.

"Can you read lips, Zeke?"

"No, but that guy's an Empusa."

"How do you know he's not just some guy in a suit?"

"I read files, son, and I know that guy's an Empusa because I know who he is. That's Kern, one of their higher ranks."

Charly's girlfriend approached them and the other woman introduced her to Kern.

"What's that Empusa up to?" I asked.

"Are we sure it's not the women that are up to something?"

"Can you arrange a meeting between me and Kern?"

"What for, so you can thank him for saving Hunter's life too?"

"Everybody over there is lying to each other. And the last honest thing I heard one of them say was, 'he says not now.' Doesn't that imply there will be a time in the future?"

"Empusas, son, are almost as tight to their words as you are. Only difference is that they give theirs as a collective."

"They also have no problems lying, it seems. I still can't read their lips, but half of what those women are saying is lies and he's keeping pace with them."

Zeke closed his eyes. "Hold that thought, son."

"What? You're going to take a nap now?"

"No. My boys realized I'm awake so they're giving me a report."

I gave him a moment. Maybe I'd find out something instead of just continuing to mount more questions and suspicions. Zeke opened his eyes. "Telepathy is damned annoying, son."

I had my own experiences. "Yeah, tell me about it."

He blinked. "Okay, get this. Your beach lady is an Oceanid in Thaumus' employ."

"Working for Thaumus? That doesn't make sense. She tried to keep me from reaching the library in time."

"Those two over there are probably her sisters."

"Now, I'm really confused."

He took off his hat and held it upside down. "I can't have a dragon who is both tired and confused."

"Then explain some of this to me."

"I can offer you this. That these three are sisters doesn't need to mean anything. All the Oceanids are sisters, and while most probably work for Thaumus, not all of them do."

I started the car. "Let's get some sleep. I need to prepare for my meeting with Thaumus. If I were one to use figures of speech, I'd say this all stinks."

"I think you just did use a figure of speech."

That annoying remark guaranteed no conversation on the way home.

17

Chapter 17

Zeke kept his eyes closed throughout the morning drive to Santa Cruz. Despite his silence, I could tell he told the truth to someone. That meant telepathy, most likely. He pushed hard to arrange the earliest meeting possible with Thaumus, and the price of that would be his bosses holding a long telepathic conference call.

He opened his eyes when we reached the section of beach our directions told us to go. "I have a headache."

I eased my door closed. "Other than that, is everything okay?"

He didn't ease his door closed, and grabbed his head. "Yes. God damn, let's just get this over with."

Three large men in dark suits stood on the beach. I tilted my head. "They seem out of place."

He rubbed his forehead. "No worries. We hired security to keep this section of beach clear."

He tilted his hat as we walked by them to an end of the beach where sand gave way to low rocks. We were alone there.

"Okay, so where's Thaumus?" I asked.

Zeke winced and pointed at a crack running along the rocks, diverging from the coast line. He straddled it and faced the sea. "This way, son."

"We're going swimming?"

He held out his hand. "It's an invisible magic portal coinciding with the San Andreas Fault. Walk along the fault, heading into the sea, and instead of getting wet, you'll enter one very impressive mud room."

I'd been teleported before, but I'd never used a magic portal. My teacher in all things dragon and magic told me the advantage of portals was they work on as many people or things as you can fit through them. The disadvantages were expense and fixed end-points. Undesired people and things can pass through them from time to time if you don't keep them well hidden or guarded.

I took a step into the water but instead of getting my shoes wet, a different set of scenery flashed about me. Rock walls rose like giant brail scribbles on two sides. A smooth sand path lay between, stretching out as far as I could see. The chasm ceiling sat beyond the range of clarity, but light danced on it as if on ocean waves.

Seeing Zeke beside me, I asked an important question. "How does Thaumus keep just anyone or anything from wandering in here?"

Zeke set into a long stride. "We best get walking, or we could be in this trench for hours."

I kept pace, but I tugged on his arm. "Portal end-points are fixed. That seems like an awfully wide-open place for one."

"That's not true of this one. He can adjust its end-point to any place where a fault-line intersects a geologic feature."

"But, I was taught that adjusting portal end-points isn't possible."

"Normally, yes, but titan magic uses the Earth as a focus."

"So, if your portal end-points are on your focus, you can move them?"

Zeke sighed. "Son, I'm a former general, not some sorcerer like Harold the Dread. You should ask him some time."

He used the name of my teacher, a former friend who betrayed my trust. My hands stiffened. "Does my file also include the things I'm most likely to get upset about, or did you skip such warnings?"

He held up his hand. "Calm down, son. I should have known

better, but what I meant to say was I'm not the right person to ask about magic theory."

We walked a good fraction of a mile. The end of the path still evaded us. Though Zeke brought him up, I saw no point in thinking about Harold. He left Earth shortly after the wedding and I doubted he intended to return. He was little more than a bad memory.

I, on the other hand, was not a bad memory. I was here on Earth, and the rest of my kind as far as I knew were not. That brought up another question. "Okay, Zeke, why did the Olympians tell dragons to leave the Earth but let the Titans, of all things, remain?"

"Ah now, son, that's a political question, something I'm much better suited to answer than the nature of magic. Unlike your kind, the titans would lose their magic if they left the Earth, and the Olympians couldn't bring themselves to be so cruel. Funny how war can sometimes make you care about your enemies."

"But what's the point of the Olympians and dragons leaving Earth if the titans end up running everything. Won't that set up the same problems we're trying to avoid, with the titans interfering too much, just instead of the rest of us?"

"Most of the titans are imprisoned in Tartarus, the better ones in Elysium. A few like Thaumus perform useful tasks, like supervising the other remnants, those who remain for various reasons."

"Like the harpies?"

"Yes, and many other earthbound remnants, related to the sea, who aren't powerful enough to pose a threat to power-structures, but who still need kept out of trouble."

"What about the Oceanids?"

Zeke lowered his volume. "His wife's one, and she does what she pleases. Her sisters are no more subordinate to him than she is. Technically they're under his purview, but in-laws, you know how that works."

Yeah, I know how that works, and that with a stupid brother-in-law. I figured I should be grateful Hunter isn't a woman and there weren't a few thousand of him or her or whatever.

The Oceanids continued to defy my efforts to understand their role in things, other than it stinking. Ah, but the Empusa, they were a remnant too.

"And the Empusa, what titan is responsible for them?" I asked.

Zeke rubbed his forehead. "Good thing my headache is finally going away. That's a complicated one. One of Thaumus' sisters supervised them until she died."

"Who keeps them out of trouble now?"

"The Children of Galinthius are overseeing them until they choose a new matriarch or patriarch."

"They get to choose?"

"My bosses owe the late Titaness in big way."

I shook my head, resigned to the stupidity of political gesturing. "Okay, then how did she die?"

"An unbalanced desire for revenge brought her to a tragic end."

The path ended and what looked like a living statue of Poseidon with a towering Oceanid beside him stood in front of us; she eyed me as if she knew me.

Chapter 18

The Titan pointed the butt of his telephone-pole-sized trident at me. "So, this, Ezekiel Roe, is the dragon who wishes to speak with me?"

Zeke turned to me and mouthed something, three syllables, and removed his hat. "Yes, his name is Aiden."

The first syllable was simple enough that even a non-lip-reader could get it, 'no,' but considering he didn't give him my last name and 'last,' and 'name' could fit his lip motions, I guessed that was it, 'no last name.' Of course, it had to be it. My Irish last name from my unwittingly adoptive parents, though not my real father's name, sounded like it, one of many long and tragic tales of error in my past. Zeke didn't want to give Thaumus any clues as to who my father is.

Though tempted by the titan's appearance, I refused to bow to him. Instead, I greeted him as an equal. I nodded. "Thank you for seeing me."

I didn't like the way Zeke took a step back from me. Thaumus, for his part, peered. "What sort of dragon are you that you speak to me like this?"

A simple answer would tell him too much. My father and I were the only two of our kind. The titan's Oceanid wife's knowing stare reminded me of the other reason I didn't want them to know. I wanted to retain the advantage I had with a certain Oceanid not knowing my ability to catch lies. I used what had become my go-to tactic, distraction. "Your fair wife knows what sort of dragon I am."

Zeke's eyes widened. He shook his head. Thaumus turned to his wife. She blushed. "I only know what my sight tells me. His power is sufficient to be your peer, my beloved."

Clearly, I implied something I didn't intend. "I regret if I caused any confusion. I merely meant I could tell she has special sight to see my power."

Thaumus placed his trident across his lap, freeing his hands to go to his hips. "Dragon, I'll forgive you your blunder if you do me this one small favor."

I held my tongue, hoping that without my query as to what his desired favor was, he might be less bold. He finished his thought. "Tell me what sort of dragon you are?"

No clever tactic availed itself this time.

"I have to refuse to answer," I said.

Thaumus stood. "You what?"

I knew this could get ugly, but I saw no other course.

"I have to refuse, "I repeated.

Thaumus held up his trident.

Zeke flung his arm across my chest and stepped forward. "Mighty Thaumus, part of Aiden's conditions for being on Earth is for him to keep a low profile. For him to identify what sort of dragon he is would be to boast, and that would not be in keeping with this condition."

The titan lowered his forehead. "He must not boast, you say?"

"Yes," Zeke answered.

Thaumus sat again, resting the end of his trident on the ground. "Then next time, dragon, when you address me, call me sir."

I nodded.

He raised his eyebrows. "So now, dragon, who will call me sir so as not to boast, what is your business with me?"

With little time to wallow in humiliation, I answered him. "Sir, you sent two harpies to protect the life of Hunter Asta. What interest do you have in the politics of a witch's coven?"

Like his wife before, he blushed, only he forced it. "I saw the young man swimming in the storm and he impressed me. I had inquired about who he was, and my sources discovered the plot against him."

His wife stared. Her reaction was sincere. He had her fooled but not me. I couldn't help but to grin over the irony. "So, what are you saying is the reason you sent the harpies?"

"Why to save him, of course. Good thing that Charly Chord changed his mind at the last minute."

A curious mix of truth and lies worked through my mind. He did send the harpies to save Hunter, but somehow he lied when he said Charly Chord changed his mind. He knew something about why Charly stopped short of using Imhullu on Hunter and didn't want me to know.

My own sense of self-preservation spawned my next question. "Sir, between you and your sources, what do you know about the weapon Charly Chord seemed about to use on Hunter Asta?"

"It's a magic weather machine."

Unlike Charly, Thaumus lied when he said it. He knew it was something more, but I couldn't be sure how much more. I turned to Zeke and attempted to communicate my concern non-verbally.

Zeke cleared his throat. "As the representative of the Children of Galinthius, I will add this. We are actively investigating this item, and should you discover anything more about it, please let us know."

Thaumus turned to his wife. "I'll be sure to remember that."

He told the truth, but about what? He made no actual promise beyond remembering the request, but considering who made it, the Children of Galinthius, the Olympians' semi-autonomous secret police, I hoped for his sake he'd do what they asked.

He turned to me again. "Anything else, dragon, who will address me as sir so as not to boast?"

"Yes, sir. One last thing. When your harpy spoke to me, she referred to you as 'the god of the seas.'"

He laughed. "You'll need to forgive her. Some of my followers like to flatter me."

"Very well, sir, but as someone who is required not to reveal my status, I can remind you to take care not to entertain the idea of you having greater status than is actually yours."

Steam rose from his ears as he stood. "I assure you, dragon, that I follow all the rules of my agreement with the Olympians, and I don't need you to remind me of what those rules are."

His words were true in all of that. I nodded. "Thank you, sir, for your time, and thank you for your honor."

Zeke grabbed my arm and pulled me though the portal into the chasm pathway. "Let's hurry out of here, son, before he decides to move the endpoint to an Antarctic mountain or worse."

"Do you think I made him angry?"

Zeke ran down the pathway. "Isn't an understatement a lie, son?"

I kept pace. "Not if it's a question I want the answer to."

He huffed. "All I know is, between his ego and yours, that place was about to explode.

Chapter 19

At a time so ancient it preceded the Titans' forbearers, a battle raged in the heavens. There, Tiamat, the mother of all dragons, fought to kill civilization still in its mother's womb. A mysterious storm-god sent his son, equipped with Imhullu, a weapon said to be the winds themselves, to slay her, and he did. So, goes the story.

The irony of who and what I am, a dragon of order, the son of order, now faced with the task of resting Imhullu from a hack warlock and a Titan's child, sickens me.

My stomach kicked with fire like the poison legends claim must run in place of blood in me.

The legends were wrong on that point; such is the nature of legends. Truth sails on a sea of misconception. Like poison, my blood brought grief to the foolish. Like poison, I had no choice in that. I acted according to my nature, but I bled like a mortal. People got to choose the truth they'd rather face—the grief or my human heart.

Fortunately, the county holding Zeke's gun and freedom in jeopardy got around to discovering they shouldn't have. The Children of Galinthius were best off not knowing my plans until I could finish most of the violent parts. It served me well to let Zeke catch up with things away from me.

John could know from the start, in fact I needed him to. His feelings were mixed. "I'm happy to see you're back to being a dragon, but Charly changed his mind about killing Hunter."

"This isn't about Hunter. It's about Imhullu."

John's smile faded. "You mean it's about you?"

"I can't lie of course, but what it's about besides me is more important. Thaumus knows too much about it to let it be so available to him and Charly and the Oceanid's ignorance about it makes it way too dangerous to just let them wander around with it."

"Shouldn't we first see if they might be willing to just give it up?"

I loved John's faith in humanity and Oceanidity. I borrowed some of it from him on occasion. "We will do that, and while we're at it see if they'll tell us where they got it, along with any other helpful information we can gather."

We caught them at Charly's apartment in Cupertino. I saw annoyance get forced off his face when he recognized John. "Oh, it's you. What brings you this way?"

John shook his hand. "Charly, this is my friend, Aiden. Can we come in for a couple minutes?"

He showed us in. "Melina, we have company. A coven member."

The Oceanid rose from the couch when she saw me.

"This one's not from the coven," she said.

"His name is Aiden. Aiden, this is my girlfriend, Melina."

She looked at me like I forgot my clothes. "You're a dragon."

Charly's eyebrows raised. "Honey?"

"He's a dragon."

I put my hand on the doorway. "Does this mean I'm no longer welcome?"

Charly grinned in apparent delight. "Seriously? You're a dragon?"

I nodded. "Am I still welcome for a couple minutes?"

"Charly, send him away."

"John, where did you find a dragon?""

John put his hand on my shoulder. "He needs to ask you about that thing you wore on your arm at the coven meeting."

Melina cuddled up to Charly. "I'm telling you, send him away."

I could tell by the lack of discomfort inside me, he didn't want me to leave just yet. I took the chance to ask my questions. "Who gave you that magic item?"

He pointed at Melina. "She did."

"And, Melina, where did you get it from?"

She stepped between her boyfriend and me. "I'm not going to tell you. Now, Charly, for the last time, send him away, now."

I let my eyes glow purple. "Charly, you don't know what forces you're playing with by having that item. You need to give it to me."

John stepped between us. "Aiden, you can ask that question more politely. Please, Charly and Melina, can we have the item? If you cooperate with us, I might be able to get him to compensate you for it."

She turned to Charly. "Just tell him to leave and he probably will have to. We don't need to negotiate with him."

Charly lost his smile. "This is getting too intense. I think you'd better leave, Aiden."

She guessed correctly of course. At that point I did have to leave.

We drove back to Milpitas.

"There you go, John. They had their chance."

John shook his head. "We could probably have bought the thing from them with an almost unnoticeable portion of your hoard, but no, you had to jump right to demanding they give it to you."

"I don't believe it belongs to her. I can't buy something from someone if they don't own it."

John leaned on me. "Then at least give me a couple days to try and talk them into giving it up."

"I'm sorry if the reality seems cruel to you, but we are in the next phase of this. They put themselves there."

John buried his head in his hands. "Oh my god, oh my god."

I patted his shoulder. "You wanted me back. This is what you get."

"I never thought you were this way."

His new-found fear of me made me shiver. "I frighten myself sometimes."

He dropped his hands. "So, what's next?"

"We need to find a way to draw them and Imhullu to a place with relatively few mortal eyes."

"Do I have to be there?"

"No, you have to not be there."

He tapped his window for a quarter mile before asking, "You're going to kill them?"

"Once I have Imhullu, I'll leave whatever's left of them be, but that Oceanid seems pretty determined."

"I'm going to have blood on my hands."

"You killed that Empusa at the church. What are you talking about?"

"That wasn't human."

I shook my head. "I hate to break it to you, John, and you know coming from me, I really mean that, but Empusa, dragons, Oceanids, Titans, even those cats Zeke works with that I've told you about, they're all human."

His jaw dropped. "So it won't be my first time?"

"Pray that I can get Imhullu without it being your second and third."

Chapter 20

I made a mistake that almost passed unnoticed. My plan to take Imhullu from Charly and Melina overlooked a significant weakness of mine. Ambush was not my thing, even if I worded it differently. To draw someone out required either deception, something I didn't do, or their agreeing to a request, something they'd be unlikely to do. My mistake almost passed unnoticed because I barely asked myself the question as to how to draw them out, when fortune smiled on me.

As I drove from Cupertino to Milpitas, John noticed the tracker Zeke put on Melina moving. Apparently, whatever the tracker was, it eluded her notice since the last coven meeting, and she, at least, had left the apartment. If she headed up the east bay like she had the last time, there'd be a stretch of road close enough to a large landfill that we might be able to force her there, and I could get this deed done.

Instead, she drove east through the core of San Jose. We followed anyway. I hoped for the off chance she may yet go somewhere with few mortal eyes, and she did, Alum Rock Park. A few more people than a landfill, but the terrain could hide a lot.

By the time we reached the parking area, her blip showed as up the trails toward an overlook on the south side of the ravine. I tapped John's shoulder and got out, leaving the car running. "Drive this to my house and wait for me to call you."

He stayed on the passenger side. "So soon after we left them, so convenient, don't you think this could be a trap?"

I tapped the roof. "All the more reason for my favorite car and my best friend not to be here."

Black clouds filled what had been a clear sky, bringing darkness hours early. John slid behind the wheel and started the engine. "I don't know about this, Aiden."

Lightning struck a tree on the rise, close enough that the thunder met the flash. I peered at John. "You better get going."

As he drove off, I realized part of me wanted him to be right and that a trap did await me. I almost couldn't lose. A bad trap could help me get Imhullu and a good one could reunite me with Vedi.

People rushed by. Rain pelted the ground with a sound like a bass snare drum, and pelted people, stinging their flesh. Steam rose into a ground fog. I ran against the flow of runners until the last passed me, and I took flight.

Conjuring a storm like this in the east hills was a good way to get my attention. I guessed they planned for me to be drawn here from Milpitas, and to have only started this way from there when the storm began. They wouldn't expect me to already be on the trails. Being earlier than they planned could work to my advantage. Eyes glowing, claws and wings out, I flew to where I could see the overlook. Where else would someone using Imhullu to draw me out be?

The driving rain and darkness conspired to conceal me. I only needed to take care with my eyes, trying to keep the appearance of their purple glow fleeting.

Another glow in that darkness persisted. Imhullu shown—an island of light. It showed Melina's face like a storyteller with a flashlight by a campfire.

I only glanced, but she noticed me. In a day for me to not think things through, it occurred I didn't know if she understood Imhullu's potential. Survival inspired quick thinking. I shouted to her. "Shall we set the stage, Enki?"

Enki was the name of the storm god's son who slew Tiamat. If she knew what Imhullu really was, she'd almost assuredly recognize the reference. I studied her reaction.

I could tell she heard my words. I completed the scene by taking on full dragon form, less my full size, as that would be lost in the low visibility. Scaly metallic walls, while ominous appearing out of nothing, lack imagery.

She stepped back, and I could tell the name Enki meant nothing to her. This emboldened me.

I decided to strike out and get things over with quickly. Folding back my wings, I fell on her, or rather I attempted to. She raised Imhullu before I landed and a wall of wind met me like a stone wall and pushed me back.

Rolling off it, I flew out and around, hoping to get behind her in the dark downpour. The Oceanid had little trouble keeping track of me and raised Imhullu my way again. This time she shouted 'tundo' and the wind-wall struck me much faster and harder, planting me deep into a hill-side.

The dirt and rock falling around me frustrated rather than hurt me. It shouldn't be this challenging. I also hated the thought of Alum Rock Park's hill-sides pocked with transit-bus-sized holes, and I doubted my restoration powers could reverse damage to the terrain. Hillsides aren't structures.

The falling dirt left a hole for my eyes to see the Oceanid, probably a consequence of the magic that keeps me clean. For once she didn't know my exact location. I welcomed the reprieve, but if I dug my way out, even a near-sighted mortal could detect me.

I could have been content to wait in the ground for her to lower her guard, but the torrent started to cause mud-slides. If I didn't do something soon, the entire park would be destroyed.

Tiamat would have protected the park because of the trees, but she would have hated all the trails and benches, not to mention the paved parking area. Ironically, my only concern was the civic elements, the very ones she never wanted to exist. In both of our cases, our decisions would be guided by the least of evils.

I took full form; the hole I sat in became a place to plant one of my hind feet. One of my forepaws landed down the path from the overlook, keeping my torso from meeting the ground and crushing the Oceanid.

She screamed and slid down an erosion channel into the darkness below. The absence of light to contrast her with meant something important to me. A glow beneath my breast told me the rest. I needed to return to human form immediately.

The dark storm began to leave as quickly as it arrived I abandoned my size to have hands again. Imhullu lay at my feet, ignobly leaning against a tree trunk. I picked it up, taking care not allow it to entwine my arm with its ropes, and got out my phone.

I needed a ride, a clean-up crew, and a lot of explanations.

Chapter 21

Imhullu, it turns out is the king of all proverbial hot potatoes amongst the Olympians and Children of Galinthius. Not only does no one want to be left holding it, but they don't want anyone even remotely powerful to have it. Instead of this potato buzzing, it makes the one stuck with it too powerful to be trusted.

That meant that until Oliver could come pick it up and place it in some mysterious deep Olympian storage, it posed a big problem. I couldn't have it, Zeke and his boys couldn't have it, and we certainly couldn't let a Titan have it. Placing it in a bank would make it the property of whoever's box got used and no weaker being could be allowed to possess it for the very reasons so well demonstrated at Alum Rock Park.

We needed a place to keep it where mortals would be unlikely to find it, and where fault lines and ley lines don't cross. Thanks to my past encounter with a powerful goblin who tried to get me killed, I knew of just such a place.

So, we put Imhullu in a box, handed it to John and had the children of Galinthius arrange for his teleportation to and from. I had one important piece of advice for John. "Remind the cat that you're mortal and you'll need to transition through the pressure change from here to the Himalayas."

"They don't need to be reminded of that, son," said Zeke.

He spoke the complete truth as far as he could tell, so I shook John's hand. "Then don't remind the cat. Better not to risk offense."

John gave my hand an extra squeeze. "If I knew getting you back to you would mean I'd be transporting a doomsday device into a giant tomb, I might have just stuck to my graduate studies and let you mope."

He told a lie, but as usual for John, a good one. He smiled and vanished. I guess the cat wanted to get on with it.

I too wanted to get on with something, finding out who wanted the truce between me and the Empusa to fail so badly that they slow-killed one and leaned his body against Maria's door. Zeke arranged for me to meet Kern, the high ranking Empusa with an Oceanid girlfriend.

Zeke gave me directions to a parking garage in Oakland and told me to go there at midnight. The sign said they closed at midnight, but the guard waved at me as if he knew me. He didn't, but for some reason he believed he did. He opened the gate and yelled at me with a smile. "Go on through, sir. Third level."

When he said 'sir,' he meant it like the superior sir, not just the customer service sir. I wondered what sort of individual he knew who drove a 1971 Scamp and so deserved to be called sir.

A silver Jag sat in the middle of the third parking level flanked by two dark grey vans. As I pulled up, dark suits filed out of both vans, six men to a side. I resisted the impetus to park in a space and instead stopped my car opposite the Jag, about thirty feet away. Out of both sides of the Jag stepped Kern and his girlfriend. I too got out and he walked to the front. "Aiden Ferris, the dragon."

I nodded.

He smiled sheepishly. "But we don't know what kind, do we?"

"You know Thaumus?"

He turned to his girlfriend. "Sisters talk."

"Then how's Melina doing?" I asked.

Her eyes turned black. "Unless you promise me you won't hurt her, I'll tell you nothing."

I'd never seen that before, but I figured Oceanids must do that when they're angry. I gave her the most calming answer I could think of. "While I can't make that promise, I can assure you I'm happy she's still alive. I didn't want to kill her if I didn't have to."

Kern gave his car's hood a knock. "I didn't agree to meet you so you could try to intimidate my girl. I'm told you have some questions for me, so let's have them."

I walked close to him so I could speak without all of his well-dressed guards hearing. "All during the time our truce was being worked out, someone was trying to stop it from happening. Do you have any idea who that might be?"

He grinned and studied me. "You? One of your friends?"

I shook my head. "No. Clearly not. I wanted the truce and I was with my friends."

He jabbed his finger into my chest. "Don't you say 'clearly' anything to me. You're a dragon, one of those so privileged as to not be left behind, and even now, that you're on Earth, the Olympians give you license to hide your identity. There's nothing clear about you."

"Don't you think it's suspicious somehow you found yourselves at war with a coven of hacks?"

He pointed at my face. "You have nothing to say that interests me, because you have no idea what it's like for the Empusa."

"Then why did you agree to meet with me?"

"I didn't agree so you could tell me anything. The only good reason for you to be here is so you can listen to me. So, shut up and listen."

This was the closest to a conversation with an Empusa I had to that point, so I nodded and waited for him to say what he wanted to say. He shook his finger. "You dragons collected your hoards and left the planet. The Olympians took the most talented mortals and they left too. You left us with nothing but a world deprived of the magic it deserves. And when our matriarch tried to get us justice, you thieves came and murdered her."

He believed what he said, even though I didn't. I didn't see a point in just denying it to him.

"Have you talked to the Children of Galinthius about any of this?" I asked.

He stepped back. "Dragon, I don't know what you're here for, but I'm warning you. When they come to wipe us out, I'm coming for your mortal friends. That is what you need to hear."

I held up my hand. "Wait. Who do you think is coming to wipe out the Empusa?"

He glared. "All of you."

My welcome ended, and I had to leave. I thought I just encountered a more destructive force than Imhullu. I couldn't put a word to it or describe it, but whatever it was, it was there.

Chapter 22

Kern believed he told me a lot of things I needed to hear, but he told me more than he probably intended. His words didn't come from evasion and he sincerely cared more about his people than he hated me. He didn't say it, but he saw no reason to lead me away from the issue. I could safely assume the answer to my biggest question. No Empusa he knew of tried to kill the truce.

His belief in an impending genocide against his people also lacked guile. From that I concluded; however, honorable Kern may have been, we couldn't do anything for each other. Somehow, in his mind, I could only be a problem for him.

I called Zeke and told him about my experience. He said nothing to encourage my hope that Kern's view of others might be unusual for Empusa. Curiously, he evaded showing relief at my conclusion Melina the Oceanid survived her Alum Rock experience.

"Is that so?" he said.

I couldn't let that go. "What do you know that I don't about her?"

I lost the connection. I can't detect deception from the behavior of phone connections, but I can find their timing suspicious. Rather than drive home, I went to Hunter's apartment. With John some-

where in the Himalayas, I had to get my coven news straight from
the top, however much we hated each other.

A small crowd had gathered around Hunter's red Miata. Sure, a
red Miata is likely to attract a few extra looks, but not like that, and
not in the parking spot it's used for over a year. I pulled up and the
gawkers parted enough for me to see. Black rubber confetti occu-
pied the place where whole tires used to be. Even more ominous,
something cut through his fenders in several places, and one cut ran
up the hood and kept going into the windshield.

I parked and ran to his apartment. I found no more gashes
along the way or in his apartment, which I found open. A man
walked up to me. "Are you a friend of Mr. Asta's?"

"I'm his brother-in-law."

"Do you have any idea what's going on with him?"

"I was hoping someone here knew. Why's his car cut up?"

The man pulled out his cell phone. "You think I should call the
police?"

"Did anyone see him leave?"

"Yeah. A pretty boy with a sword took him to a van and they
drove off with him."

"And you're asking me if you should call the police?"

He shrugged. "He has a lot of LARPer friends who show up in
hoods and stuff, so I wasn't sure."

"By all means call, but before you do, did anyone see anyone
else in the van?"

"Yeah. A real pretty blonde, or at least I think she'd be pretty
without the bruises on her face."

I left the man to call the police, so I could go home and call
Zeke. He picked up talking. "Hey, son. Sorry about the phone going
out."

"No time, Zeke. Hunter Asta has been taken away at sword
point by a pair meeting the description of Charly and Melina,
complete with bruises."

"But, a sword, son? Someone would have to be awfully good
with a sword to keep your brother-in-law under control, and Charly
Chord isn't."

"I'm guessing it's magic in some way. His car's been sliced up, fenders and all."

A moment of silence followed. "Hello, Zeke? You still there?"

"Yeah, son. Just another one of those telepathy induced headaches."

"So, what can you and your boys do for me?"

I heard him sigh. "I'm sorry, Aiden, but my boys aren't going to do anything in this case."

"They're not? Oliver would and that's who you're substituting for."

"My bosses are telling me that since this has nothing to do with the truce, and it seems to be a fight you picked for yourself with those two, you're on your own."

"What about you, Zeke?"

"Son, I can help you with my free time, but I don't have much of that right now. I'm doing my usual job on top of standing in for Oliver, and even with that, without my boys, I'm just an old general well past my time with a desert eagle."

"Whatever you can do, please do."

"Son, to use a phrase I think appropriate for your desperate need to save a cruel thick-headed warlock, 'I'll hold your beer for ya.' Try not to make it too appropriate."

I hung up. I knew the implications of the phrase, 'hold my beer,' and I worried I might get a lot riskier than to hold a lit firecracker in my hand or try to jump a river in a pick-up truck. I hated Hunter, but I loved his sister more.

I drove up near the observatory and waited under the stars for her voice. It transitioned from distant and indiscernible to clear more quickly than before. She sounded panicked. "They're going to kill him, Aiden. You need to save him."

Not sure if she could answer, I asked, "Where is he?"

Pain saturated her voice. "In a crack, beneath the earth."

"He's buried alive?"

Her voice shot back and faded at the end. "It's like an under-world, where plates meet."

"Like at fault-lines?"

87

She didn't answer. Clouds gathered. I knew the answer to my question. Despite her chaotic essence, Vedi got A's in all her classes. Plates meet at fault lines, and something else I know of meets there too, Titan portals.

A busy night of driving took me to the cave on a beach near San Francisco. Ironic, I thought that my love of Vedi should cause me to go there. The cave welcomed me, of course. The Oceanid met me as I entered, too close for comfort, as had become usual. "Oh, you can really get rough, and oh so big."

"So, you've spoken to Melina?"

She grinned. "She got what she deserved. When do I get mine?"

"She seems to have captured my brother-in-law and taken him to someplace underground."

She pouted but insincerely. I guessed she already knew I wasn't there for sex when I walked in. "Melina may be foolish enough to try and make a god of her hack witch of a boyfriend, and foolish enough to anger you, but she's not foolish enough to tell any of her sisters the details of her plans."

"I didn't think it would be that simple. I came here hoping you could get me a meeting with Thaumus."

She walked toward the back of the cave. "I can do that for you."

"Thank you."

She looked over her shoulder. "What will you do for me in return?"

A warm chill ran down my spine, like when Vedi first put her fingertips into my pants in high school. "Uh, I'll definitely owe you a favor."

She turned away. "Don't worry. I don't consider your seed that cheap, but I'll think of something. Give me your phone number and I'll give you a call when I've got the meeting you want set."

Chapter 23

Sandra called me the afternoon of the next day. At least that's what my phone identified her as. She sent me back to Santa Cruz, this time, to the aquarium.

Thaumus wanted to meet me inside. I tried to guess how a ten-foot Titan could fit in the observation area, let alone be low key. I walked around and searched the tanks when I heard his voice. "Aiden, good to see you."

He stood six feet tall and his Hawaiian shirt made him an over-weight tourist with a long gray beard. He sincerely thought it good that he saw me, surprising considering our last meeting.

"Good to see you, sir."

For me, it was good because I needed his help. He grinned like a Santa Claus on vacation. "No need for 'sir,' Aiden. Call me 'Tom.'"

I wondered if his sudden cordiality might be part of him keeping a low key during our meeting, but I had a hard time reading the degree of his sincerity. "Okay, Tom, I need to ask you about caverns and portals and such. I'm not sure this is the best place."

He patted me on the back. "No worries, Aiden. These people are here to see the fish, not listen to us, and anything they may happen to catch us saying will just be weird talk, nothing unusual in California."

His confidence in this exceeded mine, so I walked us to a place where most people had their backs to us.

He creased his forehead. "Allow me to apologize for my previous inhospitality. My late sister would've sent her Empusa to make me pay for such mistreatment of a visitor."

"I accept your apology but I'm afraid I don't have much time. Can you help me find Hunter?"

"Sandra told me that was why you needed to see me. I already know where he is."

I grabbed his arm. "Can you give me directions to get there?"

"No."

I raised my voice. "No? If you know, why can't you tell me?"

He grabbed my shoulders. "I can't give you directions that will get you there because the place is inaccessible from the surface. Instead of directions, I will let you use my portal."

"How soon?"

"I'm told they're performing a ritual that requires three days of ritual before the sacrifice. I can get my portal to run from where you last entered it to one end of the cavern network. I'll have it ready for you at nightfall today. That should give you enough time."

I had to trust him, but I still tested him. "You say you're fond of Hunter, Why not save him yourself?"

"This place is so far inland that it's in my late sister's domain. That places it outside of my jurisdiction. I can't go, but I can get you there."

He answered honestly, but I still needed another question answered. "They had to use a Titan portal to get there themselves. How many of those things are in use?"

He shook his head. "Few, but more than one I might think. In this case, I'm guessing it was my sister's portal."

"So, the Empusa are involved?"

He shrugged. "Perhaps, but the Oceanids have their ways of gaining access to things."

Again, I had difficulty reading the degree of his sincerity, but honesty, at least, dominated those words. I guessed Titans, being ancient, must have seen too much to always be certain when they speak.

As the sun set, I rushed to where the fault ran into the ocean. I found Zeke waiting for me. Considering his boys weren't willing to help me find Hunter, I wondered how or why. "Zeke, what on Earth?"

He took off his hat. "Or the sea, son. You and Thaumus are working together now?"

"We seem to be the only two people alive who care about Hunter Asta."

He pointed at me. "Have you ever seen any story in mythology where a male Titan became stricken by a male human?"

"No, and I know he's not being completely honest about what he sees in Hunter, but I need his help right now."

"You and Thaumus are each a lot of power and issues for folks like Oliver and me to keep in line, but we manage. The two of you working together, however, could result in a kind of synergy we don't want, more trouble than we already have. It's not wise, son."

My jaw tightened. "Zeke, then what else am I supposed to do, let Hunter die?"

He put his hat on and closed his eyes. "I know you don't like hearing it, but the balance of things in the universe would be improved, and your truce with the Empusa would be a lot easier to maintain."

"I can't let him die."

I didn't want to tell him exactly why, but I couldn't let Vedi down. He gripped my shoulder. "Listen, son. The Children of Galinthius will be more than happy to help you deal with Charly Chord and Melina afterward, but you must not work with Thaumus."

I turned away. "And what if I work with Thaumus?"

His voice took on a dramatic pitch. "Bad news for someone who wants to remain on Earth."

His pitch staked out a strange area between truth and lie, and his words lacked clarity of meaning. He threatened me and yet he didn't. I found that more frightening than if he had threatened me outright.

The clear night sky whispered, *"Aiden, you must save Hunter."*

I turned to Zeke. "Did you hear that?"

He shook his head. "Hear what, Aiden?"

I took a step toward the water. "I can't let her down."

He yelled after me. "Aiden, if you go through that portal, my bosses will want you gone, and I won't be able to protect you from them."

My skin crawled at his words, all honest, though only the last part made a difference. They all meant I could find myself staring alone at the vastness of space and wondering what speck, if any visible, is where I came from, ultimate loneliness, unable to die, unable to leave. The thing is I suspected his bosses had wanted that fate for me, but that Zeke could no longer dissuade them, that gave me a reason to stop walking toward the portal.

I turned around. "Zeke, my friend, make sure our friend John gets back from the Himalayas okay."

That said, I backed into the portal.

Chapter 24

The giant brail scribbling of the walls seemed more like immense snakes floating against them. The chasm hadn't changed since I last walked it, but I had. The ceiling beyond view hovered in dark mystery. How could Vedi's voice command more in me than order? I didn't know, but my course drew me like a falling rock to the ground.

The sand path ended in stone and dirt. A natural cathedral rose before me, lit from below. The light emanated from a canyon-sized crack, running down the center of the floor. The whole structure turned into the distance, with forks in all directions, some obvious and others suggested by shadows.

Vedi's description of the place as an underworld was fitting. The ritual requiring three days of preparation before the sacrifice could very well match the time I'd need to find it.

I peered over the canyon's edge to see where the light came from. A floor made of lava. I pondered the significance of a flow of lava deep down a fault-line, but I couldn't find a theory before a scream changed the subject.

Far up the canyon, I saw a cloaked figure falling in. A male voice up top yelled, "leave me alone."

I ran toward whatever was happening. A large group of figures in green cloaks, like the ones Charly and Melina wore to the last coven meeting, surrounded someone or something.

One advantage of sensing sincerity is in situations like this. I can tell if someone is truly distressed, and the surrounded one was. The cloaked ones had long knives and lunged in unison like a drop of water hitting a pond, only in reverse.

I couldn't reach the fray before their blades came down. Two more of them were thrown the twenty or so yards necessary to send them falling and screaming into a molten demise, but the rest found their target. That scream started and stopped in less than a second. I arrived to see a bloody pile of flesh, barely recognizable for what it had been a moment before, a human form.

The cloaked ones spoke in unison. "Praise Hecate. We cleanse her temple."

I thought Thaumus should have warned me the preparations for sacrificing Hunter might involve stuff like this. My hands hardened as I struggled to hold back my claws. "What did you just do?"

I could see only hints of their features through the openings in their hoods. They each held some of their victim's flesh in their hands. One of them answered. "An innocent had to die. Hecate provided us with him. Praise Hecate."

The others nodded. I usually respect sincerity, even from evil people, but not mixed with this much perversion. I released my claws along with my wings and let my eyes glow. "Your evil exceeds any mastery of magic you are ever likely to achieve."

I rushed into the crowd and grabbed the speaker by his neck, and using it as a handle, swung him at the others nearby. His neck snapped, and I knocked some of their blades out of their hands. Others stuck in his flesh as they attempted to block.

Most still stood and rushed at me. My shirt turned to shreds. They were quick for hack-witches.

I raked with my free hand as they came and went. Blood spewed into the air from multiple angles. I tossed away the corpse in my other hand, and his hood came off, revealing why my opponents were so quick.

A pain in my middle started to bend me. I, at first, thought it good fortune that my opponents, those still able to move, retreated. For that moment, I remained confused as to why I bent in half. In the next, I remembered what the hood revealed. The corpse had become dust in my hand. Of those I raked, three were dissolving, while others struggled to keep their gushing wounds from touching the ground. As they lost their struggles, they too became dust and joined the earth.

The fate my life on Earth kept my father from experiencing had fallen on me. These hooded people weren't the coven's hack-witches. They were Empusa. I, the son of order, just broke the truce, which was my word.

A shadow casted on me, but all around the light met no interruption. The shadow didn't cast but rather emanated. A cold inside me spread slowly but surely to my extremities. I studied my skin, wondering how I could be stone cold all the way through and still be alive. The shadow grew darker and darker until I could see only a silhouette of pitch black against the ground and air. I became like a hole in things.

I spoke to see if I could. "I am order and I have become disorder. I must not exist."

Another voice came out of me as if to argue with me, Vedi's voice. *"Hunter needs you to save him."*

I mumbled through the stiffness setting in. "But, Vedi, I'm finished."

"No," she answered.

Warmth rushed over me like a crashing wave. The shadow left me, and I sat up. For the sake of order, justice could not be delayed. I yelled at the voice. "What wickedness is this? If you're Vedi, how is it that you can speak to me underground now?"

She didn't answer. I guessed I hallucinated. That meant the wickedness had to be inside me. I buried my face in my hands. "No, no, no, no…"

A sound of rolling stones interrupted my chant. Bloody bits of flesh rolled across the dusty ground and gathered in a mound where the surrounded one had been. The mound of bloody flesh turned into a gray-haired man. He grabbed a green robe from the ground to replace his destroyed clothes.

His eyes shown electric arcs when he noticed me. "You there. You could've gotten here sooner. It would've saved us both a lot of trouble. "

All I wanted at the time was to get back the brink of non-existence, so I could finally fall through. Justice demanded it, but another hallucination tried to distract me. "I'm not supposed to be here still. I'm a dragon of order who broke an oath. Leave me alone so I can find my way to the void."

He walked over and sat next to me. "Well, aren't we a pair? We both want to die and can't."

He spoke literally about himself and figuratively about me. I could die, with a great deal of force and/or magic, but such things were far from my reach. I wondered how he knew.

The pain came back along with the cold and the shadow leading to total darkness of my being. The man, not a hallucination, put his arm around me. Not only did he pull his chopped-up body back together, but he held on to my cold and void-bound body. "You are pretty useless, aren't you? You may as well be gone, but you're not."

Again, the warmth came back like a crashing wave. He agreed with me. "Why?"

"Why are you useless, or why are you not gone? Both are most unenviable states."

Chapter 25

I couldn't go into the void, so the cleanest resolution of my shame evaded me. I thus still needed to find and save Hunter. Slowly, my mind climbed out of the hole I threw myself into, using questions like hand-holds.

How could Vedi speak to me in this cavern with no sky? I had no way to know, or if it really was her voice. With that, I sat up.

If it was a hallucination, how could it have so well served her wishes? Perhaps my overpowering desire to not let her down contrived it. I got to my knees.

Who or what is this man sitting next to me? I would ask him as soon as I could stand up. With that, I reached my feet. "I am Aiden, a dragon, and you?"

He remained seated and wagged his head. "I'm Epimetheus, a Titan triply cursed, to never die, to never forget, and to always understand all I remember."

I needed one more question dealt with before I could go anywhere. What exactly did my fallen state mean to my capabilities? I turned to Epimetheus. "What do you know about dragons who violate their nature? What can they still do?"

He lifted his head. "Now that's an obscure question, one anyone but I would've forgotten the answer to."

He resumed his concentration on the ground, treating me to a long silence.

"Well?" I prompted him.

He ran his finger through the dirt. "You should be able to do anything you could before, only now you are turned against yourself. Did you really need me to tell you that?"

"Then before I do myself in, I need to find my brother-in-law and save him becoming the final sacrifice in this ritual."

His face contorted with my words but relaxed with a smile as I finished them. "I was worried you might tell me something I didn't already know."

"You know why I'm here?"

He jumped to his feet. "Thaumus wants this Hunter saved from the sacrifice and since you arrived by his portal and attacked those disguised as coven members, it all follows."

My head hurt trying to figure out how everything I told him would follow from the rest, but I could tell he spoke the truth.

He put his hand on my shoulder. "You were tricked, young dragon, by whom, I don't yet know."

"The Empusa?"

He shook his head. "I'm afraid I'm going to have to learn some more."

He didn't use a figure of speech when he said that. The idea of learning more did frighten him, and he did believe he had no choice but to do so.

"Why do you have to learn more in this? I could go on without you."

He laughed. "Here I get to pretend I'm my brother and pretend to know the future. You will not leave me without asking me if I know where Hunter is, and my answer will require me to go with you."

"You mean you know where he is?"

"Yes."

"You could just give me directions."

"Not if I want to be sure you find him."

"And, why should you care?"

He straightened his back. "Titans have honor too. You avenged my murder, so I owe it to you."

"But, is it murder if you come back to life, having never actually died?"

"They intended to murder me, and you believed yourself an instrument of justice when you killed them. That's all that matters to my honor."

I saw problems with his reasoning, but I didn't want to talk him out of leading me to Hunter, so I didn't challenge it.

"Can we start right-away? I asked.

"Absolutely. We can get there in half a day and have five times that much time, but why not be cautious?"

He led me along the lip of the canyon. The lava below occasionally popped, and a bubble would appear on its surface. When not keeping track of Epimetheus' back, I found myself entranced by the red river of molten rock.

I began to recall a time before I knew what I was, and two flying creatures tried to drop me into a recently poured concrete foundation. They knew I'd end up submerged in it and unable to get out, encased for near eternity, a fate worse than death. Such would be the fate of either of us if we fell into that river.

The lava leaped at me, and I heard Epimetheus. "No, dragon, no. That won't even kill you."

I realized the lava wasn't the one leaping. I had jumped. I sprouted my wings, but the lava's distance gave me too little room to pull up, so I reached for the canyon walls, taking as large a full dragon form as could fit. I jammed my thorax into both sides with an unsettling crack, not my ribs, but stone.

Lava scalded my belly. Boulders and shards fell on my back. I dug into the walls with all four sets of claws. When the last of broken bits of the walls had fallen, I flapped my wings. The first flap only caused debris to fall off me, but the second began to lift me, though against my claws, anchored in the walls. One more flap as I pulled out of the walls and I moved up and out of the canyon, landing on the edge.

"What was that?" I exclaimed.

"A part of you wants to kill you, dragon, like I told you."

"This is what being turned against myself is going to be like?"

"Until you either kill yourself or cope, though being encased indefinitely in stone would have been a terrible way to cope."

I returned to normal human form. "I guess I should stay away from the canyon's edge from here on."

"Perhaps not, dragon. Your subconscious now realizes that option won't kill you and it doesn't want you in a state where it can't kill you."

"So, it will try to kill me in another way?"

"You mean you will try to kill you in another way."

"When and how?"

He winced. "Do I look like my brother? I don't know the future."

The stupidity of my question hit me and I smiled. "Your words, Titan, are not very comforting."

"They seldom are. Welcome to my life."

Chapter 26

The violation of my nature caused my personality to split, one not wanting to let Vedi down, and the other not wanting me to continue living. Both focused on avoiding things. Each presented me with something incomprehensible, letting her down and continuing as the contradiction I'd become.

Epimetheus led me deeper into the cavern complex. We passed through an area filled with stalagmites and stalactites. In a futile effort to lighten the grimness of our circumstances, I recited a memory device. "Stalagmites might but stalactites must hold tight."

He sighed. "Ah, that would be a mnemonic right?"

"A memory device."

"Yes, a mnemonic. I wish I had a use for those."

The beginnings of my depression only met encouragement to deepen from his attitude. I probably should have apologized for being insensitive, but my own problems dominated my thoughts.

To use the terms of poker, a game I'm awful at, he saw my mnemonic and raised me what could have been a geology professor's lecture on stalagmites and stalactites. I could tell he knew the information in it mattered less than his opportunity to pass the time, like whistling a tune, like whistling past a graveyard.

My mind wandered as I studied the spires, especially the ones pointing up. A pain in my thigh and a bloody cloth wrapped tightly around my leg, cutting off my circulation, surprised me. I recognized it as a piece of a dress Vedi wore one night in the Himalaya's. The cloth wasn't real, just a memory of a time I almost bled out, but why so vivid?

Vedi saved me that night, one of many reasons I couldn't let her down. Reality clapped like thunder, but too late. My chest approached the point of a stalagmite at a velocity my self-destructive side had maximized by starting from the top of the cavern. Before I could roll to a side, it entered my chest dead center. I took full dragon form to avoid being wedged apart, but I could not save my heart from damage.

I lay impaled on the stalagmite. The pain defied description, the sort of thing one can't remember because their body refuses to. I felt myself rising and thought it the effect of losing so much blood.

Epimetheus shouted. "Dragon, again, you're not dying."

I rose because I regenerated, and as I did, my wound became smaller, forcing me up the stalagmite. The same stalagmite that punctured my heart held back the bleeding enough that it didn't outpace the magic repairing me. My self-destructive side could take impaling off its list of ways to kill me.

Vedi's champion still lived, but had to look pretty pathetic rising up a stone pole like part of a run-down merry-go-round.

Epimetheus didn't laugh. Instead, he shouted, "Whoa."

Three Empusa came at me, blades out. One's eyes were cut and missed an arm from the elbow, one hobbled, and one hopped on his only leg. The residue from the previous fight came to see if they could finish me off. I guessed the healthy ones must have left them behind when they retreated.

The Titan planted himself between me and them. He spoke with a tone of authority. "You don't want to touch him."

The hobbling one stopped and held the others back. He cocked his head. "Why wouldn't we want to finish the one who did this to us?"

"Because he is healing and the same magic that prevents your regeneration is acting on him now. If you touch him while he's being healed by it, its current level of intensity will kill you."

The hobbling one put his arm around the one-legged Empusa and spoke in his ear. "Go see."

He hopped forward, and Epimetheus moved to intercept him, but, one leg or not, he still had his sight defying swiftness. A swipe of the one-legged Empusa's blade gashed the Titan's leg and sent him to the ground.

He hacked at me, but my scales ignored his blade. Undeterred he jumped on my back, probably in the hope of working the wound, a good plan. It could have worked if it didn't require him to place a hand on me. I stopped rising for a moment and he screamed through it. He turned cold like ice and dust fell from where had been.

The hobbling one cried, "No," and ran off. The remaining one took a moment to find the way he went and followed.

Once off the spire, I returned to my human form. "When did you know they'd die from touching me?"

"When I saw their wounds hadn't healed. At that point all the deductions came to me, falling on me like crushing boulders as they always do."

I pointed at his leg. "And whatever magic keeps putting you back together, no matter what, why doesn't it keep them from healing?"

"I'm a child of the earth and so are they. We channel our magic differently but it's the same magic, so to speak."

"And the magic that runs through me?"

He smiled and shook his head. "You don't need to have the mind of Epimetheus to know that one, dragon."

"So, Empusa's regeneration is stopped by contact with dragons? You'd think they'd know something that critical to them."

He returned to leading me through the cavern. After several steps I pressed him. "Why wouldn't they know something like that?'

He raised his hand. "I only answered your question about why the magic in me wouldn't harm them in that way. I didn't say yours does what it does because you're a dragon, only that it can because you're not a Titan or other remnant."

"So, any non-earth magic could do this to them?"

"No."

"Dragon magic?"

He shook his head. "You see the quandary. All I know is it can't be earth and it's not all dragon, and I don't even know for sure it's dragon at all."

"But how can that be?"

He peered over his shoulder. "I only know what it isn't. Don't try to get into my head in hopes of anticipating my hypotheses. You won't like it there."

Chapter 27

Drops of water clopped in obscure places as we traveled past the stalagmites. For our part, we moved as quietly as we could. The Empusa may have retreated, but we suspected they followed us, waiting for another chance to avenge their dead and their persistent wounds.

We came upon a place where two boulders leaned against each other to form a bridge across the canyon. Rock-dust floated where the far one met its side of the gap. Epimetheus approached with no sign of hesitation. I broke our silence. "Are these safe?"

He turned to me as he stepped onto the first boulder. "I've used them before."

The second boulder slid a couple of feet down the canyon wall. A cloud of rock-dust flew out. He stepped back to the edge but failed to reach it before the second rock followed its slide with a free-fall.

His eyes opened wide. I reached for him and he reached back, but the boulder turned, moving him away. The motion of the rocks preceded our reactions. Epimetheus and the boulder fell.

I dove after him. Unfortunately, the same force of gravity acted on us and he had a head start. My wings sped me up. I pushed off the canyon wall that jutted out, gaining more speed, but I feared I wouldn't catch him before he and the boulder plunged into the lava too deep for me to reach him.

The first boulder to fall hit the lava, clearing a momentary glimpse of the river-bed, deep enough to swallow up Epimetheus but not much more. One last chance to save him from a fate arguably worse than death presented itself.

Trying as best I could, I aimed low on the canyon walls and roared. The walls rumbled. Their irregular percussion added to a bass horn blare. The stone dissolved into shards and boulders, sliding into the molten river.

Epimetheus' boulder combined with the rest, some splashing before and others after. The entire chamber shook and bits and pieces of rock, along with a few less than tight stalactites, fell and rolled and planted throughout.

A boulder slammed me to the others before it, where I managed to get out from under. My eyes glowed, allowing me to find the Titan's hand amidst the rubble. I dug him out, but not before the lava encased one of his legs. In full dragon form, but small enough to fit between the canyon walls, I lifted him out. Lava clung to his lower leg like a cast.

He sat where I put him and winced. "As soon as this cools, knock it off for me, will you, please."

I nodded but shook my head. "You know more than anyone I've ever met. How is it you didn't know better than you did there?"

He strangled his knee and rocked. "Sometimes I know too much to have room for foresight."

"Does your brother have the same problem with learning from the past?"

He laid his head on his knee and closed his eyes. "This burns so much that I'm tempted to ask you take it off at the knee."

"I've seen you'll grow it back with ease. Why not?"

He raised a hand. "No. I think the pain of it being torn off and growing back might be worse. Let's leave it for now."

I scanned our surroundings for motion, but I only detected water drops and an occasional late settling rock. I sat. "Do you mind if I ask you another question, or would you rather I leave you to your pain for now?"

"I don't mind at all, dragon. By all means, distract me from it if you can."

"You told me my self-destructive side won't be able to find a way to kill me in here."

He opened his eyes. "And, you're worried that was my limited foresight speaking?"

"No offense intended, but yes."

He managed a smile. "Not all predictions are foresight. Some, as that one is, are based entirely on past observations."

"So, you're not being foolish when you say with confidence I can't kill myself in here?"

He looked about. "I'm not being foolish when I say that, but that doesn't mean you couldn't achieve with help."

I kept him talking as the hot rock around his lower leg cooled. He told me about his brother and himself, how the stories in myth about them were full of inaccuracies but the truth was no less amazing.

As he spoke I noticed one dark area of the ceiling that wasn't there before I roared. Directly below it, a mountain of debris rose from what had previously been flat cavern floor. I pointed. "Is it possible my roar caused the cavern to open up to the surface?"

"While that is an awful lot of fallen ceiling there, I doubt it."

I turned. "You doubt it? In other words, it's not a conclusion based entirely on observation of past event?"

"You can go scout it out if you wish. You don't need to stand guard over me. The worst that could happen is that I get chopped into pieces again."

He spoke a shrouded truth I recognized as passive-aggressive. I didn't need to protect him while he worked through his lava ordeal, but he wanted me to.

"I prefer to stay with you until you can walk again," I said.

The dark hole in the ceiling still commanded my attention. I wondered how high above the cavern floor it went and longed to hear Vedi's voice again. What advice would she give me if she could? If Epimetheus was wrong, I could potentially see the night sky through that hole.

I couldn't. The next thing I knew, I had flown up the hole, found its top and flung myself to the ground. My self-destructive side applied all my knowledge of physics to maximize my eventual impact, an angle to get me past the mountain of debris, and mid-air adjustments to my mass and area. Like the point of a spear weighed in tons, my one-hundred-and-eighty-pound self was too close to avoid impact, evade anything, or even take a larger form.

To make matters worse, an Empusa hobbled into my path and pointed his blade at me. He clearly wanted to help my self-destructive side.

28

Chapter 28

Empusa quickness could still surprise me. The one who hobbled into my path did so at a speed I couldn't have managed, but the half-blind one knocked him away and took his place, blade pointed at me, all in the last second of my fall.

The hard stone floor delivered its punch in a glove of shattering bone and splattering flesh. My own bones shattered, but my flesh retained its integrity. I lost track of the blade in the collision and started sorting through a long list of thought defying pains for one resembling a punctured organ.

I panicked when I realized I couldn't breathe, but two ideas calmed me. I don't need to breathe, and any way, I didn't want to inhale the dust that used to be the Empusa I landed on.

My bones snapped back together. I opened my eyes to the bottom of a hole. Above me, stone drug against the ground. Dust settled about my forehead. I panicked again, kicking about as if I could grab the top with my feet and pull myself up with them. Someone grabbed one of them, and Epimetheus spoke. "I've got you, dragon. I'll pull you out of there."

"Where's the blade?" I asked.

He let go of my foot. "Stay still and I'll look."

His hand moved about my middle. "Here it is. Hold on. I'll pull it out."

"No," I shouted.

He laughed. "Why do you say that? It's not sticking in you. You crushed it."

He pulled back his hand and I heard something light hit the ground. He grabbed my ankle one more time and pulled. Again, stone drug on the ground.

"What's going on up there?" I asked.

He dropped me. "The other Empusa."

Another voice spoke. "You're the one who deceived us."

A blade cut the air and Epimetheus cried out. "No, not again."

I turned myself in the hole so that both my feet and hands were above the rest of me. Rocks fell on me as Epimetheus struggled not to fall as well.

"I will bury you and your dragon together," said the Empusa.

The Titan pushed himself out of the mouth of the hole. "I didn't deceive you. Do you think the dragon would tolerate me if I had?"

My bones and tendons needed more time to align, causing pain to fight my efforts to stand right-side up. If Epimetheus fell in, with me in my current state, the Empusa could bury us. The pain fought me with every inch of progress as the two above me argued.

"You're trying to confuse me," said the Empusa.

"Those green robes you wear made the dragon think you were from the coven. Whoever told you to wear those is the trickster."

"You think I'm stupid? You're good at lying, now prepare to die."

"Empusa, I am the Titan Epimetheus. There is no room for lies in my life."

"And why should I believe you are who you say you are?"

I spit out a mix of blood and words. "He's not lying."

"Why should I believe the dragon who ruined my leg?"

"Because he's tried to kill himself for breaking his truce with you, and you have witnessed him do this twice."

Metal clanged the ground. "Forgive me, Titan."

"Who made you wear those robes, Empusa?" asked Epimetheus.

"I don't know, but it wasn't Kern. We were told it would make Kern happy if we took care of this without him having to tell us to."

Turned right-side-up, I climbed out the hole I made. The Empusa fell over the back side of a rock, trying to hide. I stood and dusted myself off.

Epimetheus limped over to me. "Aiden, promise him that you won't hurt him."

I shook my shoulders. "After being tricked into breaking the truce, I have no intention to promise anyone anything, but at least for now he's safe with me. We seem to have a common enemy."

The Empusa got up. "Whoever tricked us, yes."

"And you don't know who asked you to wear those robes and attack Epimetheus?"

"Someone told someone who told most of us. Some of the ones who returned to Kern know who it was."

I sat to put him more at ease and to think about what he told me.

He sat but well out of my reach. "You need not worry. Whoever it was will surely be punished severely, once Kern finds out."

Epimetheus planted his stone encased lower leg in front of me. "Break this, please."

I obliged him with two chops of my hands. He winced and stumbled back to a seat of his own. "And how will they know they've been tricked if you didn't know until I told you?"

The Empusa and I seemed to share amazement at Epimetheus thinking through the pain.

"A good question, don't you think?" I said.

He pondered the ground. "Yes. They only know they broke the truce by attacking your friend. Until I return, they'll not want to tell Kern anything."

I leaned back. "As soon as Epimetheus and I have recovered, we will take you to Kern to explain."

"As long as he doesn't kill himself first, Aiden. Like you, he is bound by magic contract to his honor."

The Empusa waved his hand. "No need to worry. Now that I

know I've been tricked, I have a clear path to redemption by finding the deceiver."

I shook my head in disbelief. "Why can't it work that way for me?"

The Empusa glanced at me. "Probably because you don't serve a collective like we Empusa do. By seeing to it that the deceiver is punished, I serve my fellow Empusa. For you, it would only be revenge, not noble enough to counter your failing."

I grimaced. "Well, that's it then. I can't join a collective."

He raised a finger. "But there is another way we use to achieve redemption in cases like this."

"By all means share."

"I dread the thought of you using it. It's very unpleasant."

Honesty and fear echoed in his words.

"Why mention it to me then?"

"In hopes of redeeming myself for sending my friend to attack you when you were impaled. It was not a violation of my honor, but it was disgraceful."

"Okay, so here's your chance, tell me what it is."

He shook. "Let me gather my thoughts so I can tell you without error. If you choose to try this, I will stand back."

Chapter 28

As my tendons worked into their places, tightening, and loosening like strings on a guitar being tuned, I asked the Empusa about the way to restore me to my nature he mentioned. He stood and took four steps back. "I will tell you, but first allow me to tell you my name. It may become quite important to us. My name is Praxis."

For most, telling someone their name is an act of courtesy or convenience, but he meant it as an act of caution. He saw himself as risking his well-being to help me get right with my dragon nature. I nodded. "Mine is Aiden."

"Isn't there a title you'd prefer?"

"If you must call me something else, call me dragon, but please tell me about this way to redemption that doesn't require a collective."

He bowed. "Very well, dragon. The way is for you to make the world around you an altar, upon which you make the most reverent of offerings."

"And how do I do this?"

"Whatever your nature asks of you, do more, no matter what it takes, do more. Never hold back. Destroy compromise and temperance in the fire of your zeal."

I wanted this to be a way for me to get back to the way I was before I broke the truce, but it all had to make sense. "The first part of that makes sense to me, but 'destroy compromise and temperance,' really?"

He nodded. "Compromise and temperance serve a pure heart but feed all that's wrong in a corrupted one."

He meant what he said. I shook my head. "This goes against all Oliver taught me."

He closed his eyes. "I know of the one you speak. I have nothing but respect for the Olympian with a writ to stay, and I'm sure he's right about such things, but your heart is corrupted now, your nature is violated."

I queried Epimetheus' face for advice. He tested his leg, nothing more. I scratched my head. "I see little opportunity for things like compromise and temperance in these caverns, so why not? Starting now, whatever my dragon nature asks of me, I will do more."

Praxis bowed. "And I will try to stay out of your way, dragon."

We walked on with Epimetheus ahead of me and Praxis several paces behind. I kept track of the time since my decision. This approach had to be tested. How long could I keep my self-destructive side at bay?

To begin finding out, I restored the broken bits of metal on my wrist back into a watch. I checked it at one-minute intervals because my nature suggested every five. At first, I was off a few seconds, but my precision increased until after two hours I was spot on. More importantly, my self-destructive side only managed a suggestion that I roar to bring the caverns down around me, a fleeting thought, and one that never controlled me.

"I think this is working," I said to Epimetheus.

He peered over his shoulder. "I wish you well but this idea of making the world an altar worries me."

"Something based on past observation, or are you trying to channel your brother?"

He turned and continued to lead. I regretted my words. "I'm sorry, Titan, that was cruel of me. Please forgive me."

He stopped and turned. "I forgive you, dragon, even though I took no offense in the first place, but do you see?"

"See what?"

"What might you have done if I hadn't immediately forgiven you? What would this process have led you to?"

"I don't know."

"Think then, because it matters that you do."

"I may have promised you to never insult you again."

He pointed at me. "Aha. And you said yourself that making promises is dangerous for you. Do you see now?"

Part of his point landed with me, the part I agreed with. "I need someone to try and catch me before I do the wrong thing while trying to do this more than my nature asks of me stuff."

He turned his head, so I could see him grimace. "I'll do that for you, dragon, but I wish you were employing another process for your redemption."

Twelve hours passed without a single self-destructive thought. Epimetheus took us to a cave he knew of for us to get some sleep.

"We're about twelve hour's walk from the altar and the sacrifice is set to take place in two days. I think it's best we be rested before then."

I agreed and followed him in. He snapped his fingers and logs lit ablaze in the middle of a fire pit. The logs had been arranged to lean against each other, like supports of a teepee, but not as evenly spaced as they could be. I set myself to correct that. That fire burning my hands expressed my zeal for order as I took it beyond what was asked of me.

Praxis walked outside the fire-pit. "You and I, dragon, are the same."

I blew on my hands, waiting for the burns to heal. "The same?"

He bowed. "Forgive me, dragon. I should have said we have similar motivations. We are obviously not the same."

"Yes, choose your words much more carefully."

Epimetheus leaned back. "Dragon, are you always so picky about the use of embellishment, or is this your world altar in use?"

I hadn't thought about going beyond my nature, but I had.

Embellishment annoys me, but until then I had never ordered someone not use it. "I'm not sure. It is a little scary to think I may not always know when I'm doing it."

He took a deep breath. "At least you're aware that there's something to be frightened of. Praxis, you there?"

"Yes, Titan," he answered.

The Titan looked at me as he spoke to the Empusa. "I've been thinking. When you said the one who tricked you said Kern would be pleased, how exact was your meaning?"

Praxis stopped his pacing. "What do you mean by how exact was my meaning?"

"I mean do you think the one who tricked you was one who would know what pleases Kern?"

"Yes, Titan. Why else would it be put that way, if not?"

Epimetheus nodded. "So, dragon, who do we know who Kern's subordinates would trust to know what pleases him?"

I pointed. "His Oceanid girlfriend."

"Yes, of course," said Praxis.

I turned my finger to Praxis. "If you Empusa don't tear her to shreds, I will."

Epimetheus blinked and shook his head.

Chapter 29

After eight hours of sleep, we set out on the last leg of our journey across the cavern complex. The path stopped being a path. The large caverns stopped, and bedroom-sized pockets took over. Fork followed fork, on and on. If not for Epimetheus and Praxis knowing which choices to take, it could have taken weeks to get through.

At one fork, where the choices were between up, left, and down, a voice came from behind us. "I hope you three know how to get back to the altar."

I recognized it from high school, one of Vedi's friends, Kristine. What was she doing down here? Based on the brown robe she wore, she was in the coven. No surprise, after I thought about it. The coven was full of untalented want-to-be witches, so why not one of Vedi's friends from high school? It was also no surprise that she'd have wandered off. Kristine did that a lot in high school.

"Kristine?"

She dropped her hood. "You're that boy who had a crush on Vedi in High School."

Time seemed to stop for Kristine. Her face was still covered in white paint, where it wasn't pierced by metal rings or studs. Her green hair rounded out a look Vedi was fond of. How I fell in love through it all, I was still not certain to that day.

"How'd you get out here?" I asked.

She walked past Praxis and contorted her face when she had a clear look under his hood.

"Well?" I prompted.

She smiled. "Aren't these caverns amazing? Who would have known they were right under Santa Clara?"

"You got here from Santa Clara?"

"Through the basement of some software company's office, how else?"

I know rhetorical questions shouldn't be answered for the sake of not inviting suspicion, but I made a tiny offering to my nature on the world altar. "I came here through a portal near Santa Cruz."

Epimetheus grabbed my shoulder. "Is this wise, Aiden?"

She pondered. "Wow. This place is even bigger than I thought it was."

I grinned at Epimetheus. She already believed in witchcraft and I never knew her to be bright, so whatever I told her seemed unlikely to matter. What she could tell me did matter. "More to the point, Kristine, how did you get lost?"

Her face contorted. "The people I was with left me behind when I stopped for a smoke."

My nose told me marijuana. "Come with us then. We're headed that way."

She walked beside me. "So, I know she married you and all, but never knew you joined the coven."

"I haven't."

"So why are you here?"

"To save Hunter."

"You know I'm just saying, but you always were a killjoy."

Epimetheus turned and grabbed both my shoulders. I turned. "You consider wanting to save someone's life being a killjoy?"

She looked at me like I told her I was best friends with the Easter Bunny. "Charly's not really going to kill Hunter. It's all just symbolic junk."

"No, it's very real," said Praxis.

She nodded. "Uh, yeah, it's real in that we're summoning someone with it, but no one's going to die. Charly wouldn't do something like that. He just wants to be the new coven leader and Hunter's not popular."

She believed herself, incomplete logic included. "So, who is he summoning?"

"Someone named 'Silly.'"

Praxis cleared his throat. Epimetheus repeated the name under his breath and shook his head. I held up a finger to make sure I had her attention. "So how is it that a summoning that involves a sacrifice should work without the sacrifice actually being killed?"

She shrugged. "I don't know, but Charly's not going to kill anyone. I think I heard Melina say something like that to her sister."

I turned to Praxis. "What do you think about this idea of a fake sacrifice?"

"Dragon, there's no such thing as a fake sacrifice."

Epimetheus shook his head. "His name is Aiden, Praxis."

Kristine lowered her eyebrows and turned to all of us in turn. "Dragon? Whatever. You know that Melina's been pushing Charly to get rid of Hunter and take over. If you ask me, she's the one who actually wants to run the coven."

"You don't say?" I said.

"She's been changing how we do things ever since Charly brought her in. Vedi wouldn't have had any of her shit. I wish she hadn't died."

I choked out the words, "me too."

Kristine seemed to have thus far managed to live her life, certain of many things, knowing people, but not the things. Some things she'd know, but only when she wanted to. The rest she was confident in even though it wasn't so.

Fortunately for her, I'm a dragon of order, not discernment. Her inability to see the evil before her caused no requests of me.

Unfortunately for my throat and gut, I was a man in mourning and everything about her seemed to rip whatever figurative bandages I had off the wound. The way she adorned herself reminded me Vedi. Even what she lacked between the ears reminded me of her by the stark contrast.

I pointed Epimetheus onward and we resumed walking. Three more small caverns in, Kristine touched my shoulder. "Aiden, I'm sorry. I should've realized. You're being her husband and all. I'm so stupid."

I wiped a tear from my face. "Melina and her sister talked about the sacrifice with each other?"

She blinked as if I might change when she opened her eyes again. "Yes. I overheard them during one of my smoke breaks."

"It makes sense that they're both behind this."

"Behind what?"

Epimetheus stopped. "Young lady, I see you have a kind heart."

She rubbed my back. "I try to."

He pointed at Praxis. "You see that man there. He's not having an easy time walking. We may all get where we're going faster if you'd help him."

"Why haven't one of you?" she asked.

I smiled. "It's hard to understand, but he doesn't want me near him and Epimetheus here is the one who knows how to get back."

She started back to Praxis and stopped. "Okay, but just one question. When did Baby-Boomers join the coven?"

"Ask Praxis," Epimetheus told her, and she moved back to him.

I walked beside the Titan. "I wanted to ask her more questions."

"She's told us enough."

"But she may know more of use to us."

"You know more than she should be told."

Chapter 30

Kristine surprised me with how she took to helping Praxis along. She wrapped her arm around him and he leaned on her with each step. Praxis surprised me too with a never seen gracious smile toward her.

Epimetheus tapped my shoulder, so I would stop staring. He smiled. "While the Empusa can be quite harsh, Aiden, they're all about the etiquette of traveling and showing kindness to those who travel, especially those with a burden."

"All about showing kindness? I don't see how that translates into them running around like vampires, killing innocent people."

He held up a finger. "It's far better to need no rules than to need to enforce them."

I didn't welcome his confidence in that. It meant I had to think outside of myself. If he was going to force me to do that I figured I should do it aloud. "You're saying their need to enforce certain rules made them the monsters they are today?"

"It's not that simple. It's also the orders they were given and the methods they came to employ."

I tried to laugh. "So, there's still hope for me?"

He paced ahead, keeping track of the ground. Was he taking my question in jest seriously? Because of his non-answer, I was. I caught back up. "Is there hope for me?"

Condemnation readied to pounce and dread filled my stomach, but he smiled. "It's the first great deduction of mine that doesn't burden me. There is always hope."

Relief replaced dread, my steps seemed lighter. That word, 'hope,' caused me to remember part of the Greek classics. "Pandora, your wife, she let out hope, right?"

He peered over his shoulder. "Unlike you, my wife, Pandora is not someone I need to mourn."

He confused me. "She's alive?"

He shook his head. "No. She was never a person."

"But how did that myth happen?"

"It's a long story, but Prometheus predicted that if we composed an allegory for my curse of deduction, people would think they knew enough not to look further. You see, Pandora is my mind and the demons let out of the box are all the dark truths I deduce."

As someone being hidden from most of the universe, I've tolerated convoluted ways to keep people from asking the wrong questions, but one thought disturbed me. "And Zeus had nothing to do with it? You lied about him burdening humanity?"

He stopped. "No, dragon. The original version of the story didn't say anything about Zeus, or who gave me the box. The false accusation was not my doing."

"So, enforcement of rules isn't the only thing that can become monstrous over time?"

He furrowed his brow. "That allegorical box is full of truly terrible things indeed."

Because we stopped, Kristine and Praxis got too close for his comfort.

"Is there a reason why we're not moving?" he asked.

"You're right to ask, Praxis. We shouldn't waste time."

I patted the Titan and we resumed walking. Praxis and Kristine fell back to their usual distance.

Epimetheus asked me about Vedi, which surprised me, considering his aversion to learning new things. He believed the information could be important if we were to save Hunter. He didn't want to know about the goblin engineer who tried to kill me or the sorcerer who betrayed me, only about Vedi. I found it difficult to tell him what he wanted to know without mentioning my father, but he seemed to sense I avoided something important for him not to know, and he was more than happy to let me.

When I finished, he rubbed his head. "I don't know, Aiden, how you and this descendent of Chaos' chief acolyte could ever have married, but I know you wouldn't lie."

"So, do any deductions fall on you?"

He threw his arm across me. "Yes, but not about Vedi. Quick, hide."

We ducked around a bend in the rock. Three Empusa in business suits came up behind Praxis and Kristine. Praxis tugged at her hood, pulling it over her forehead. He then dropped his own.

They shouted when they saw him. "Praxis! We came back for you."

He hugged each of them. "Good to see you brothers. What did you tell Kern happened to me?"

The tallest of the three pulled up Praxis' robe, revealing a black gash from his hip to his thigh. "You're still not healing. What sort of demon-spawn are we dealing with?"

I almost leaped out at them, but Epimetheus held me back.

Praxis pulled his robe to cover his wound again. "Not a demon-spawn but a dragon."

"Yeah, we know who it was."

"So, what does Kern think of this?"

"He doesn't exactly. He only knows we were routed by something. We dare not tell him we attacked one of the dragon's friends, even if we were tricked into doing it. He's angry to no end as it is, and he insisted we go find the survivors."

"I'm it," said Praxis.

The taller Empusa studied Kristine. "You, and who is this?"

He pulled back her hood.

She smiled. "Hi, I'm Kristine. You three work at the software company?"

Praxis jumped between her and the other Empusa and showed his fangs.

They took a step back and pulled out blades. The taller one pointed. "What is this, Kern? Are you working for the ones who deceived us?"

Praxis growled. I sensed desperation in the communication. He had no confidence in his ability to protect her from three of his own kind. My own concern for her caused me to leap from my hiding place, wings, and claws out. I too lacked confidence and hoped I could frighten them off.

To be honest, I'm not sure which of us had been more effective, Praxis or me, but for at least one of our efforts, it worked. They moved with other worldly speed into the caverns behind us.

Kristine only witnessed the Empusa running away. I put my wings and claws away before she turned. "Did they just run off like really super-fast, or did I get some bad pot?"

Praxis faced me. "Things just got worse, I think."

"As a general rule, things always do," said Epimetheus.

Chapter 31

We traveled from where the three Empusa left us and my thoughts worked their way to the Titan's ears. "In a few hours, we may be close enough to the altar to do something about it."

"I can't predict the future, but it seems likely," he replied.

"Of the two behind us, one is now distrusted by the peers I need him to explain things to, and the other thinks I'm a killjoy for wanting to stop the sacrifice."

"Only because she doesn't believe it's real."

Sometimes people say what they want to believe but aren't sure of. In our minds the difference between truth and desire can be subtle.

"Do you know that?" I asked.

He shook his head. "I'm not a mind-reader, dragon, but she seems to have a heart and I know of nothing about her that would suggest she'd have anything significant to gain from Hunter's death."

I knew what he meant by "have a heart," but my world-altar state made it like sour milk to me. "All living humans have hearts, Titan, and at least two I know of want Hunter dead."

He raised his hand. "She is kind. Charly Chord and your

mother-in-law would be unlikely to be helping Praxis move along if they were here."

His change from confident sounding wishful thinking to qualified guesses on the same subject should have satisfied me, but in my state, it didn't. "So, you're guessing where her loyalties will be when we get there? I need better than your guesses, and I especially need you to make it clear when that is what you're doing."

He cocked his chin. "I am the Titan Epimetheus, once the confidant of Zeus and still would be if he had not left Earth. Now tell me, dragon, besides a big immortal lizard, who are you?"

"I'm the one you say you owe it to help save my brother-in-law, and you know dragons aren't lizards. Once again you lack precision. Your disregard for the truth is something I can't afford."

I knew I was being a disrespectful jerk. If Oliver saw me then, he would doubt if I was worth his efforts. Yet, despite me knowing the nature of my behavior, my world-altar state demanded it. The analogues water drop of my will struck the sea of my compulsion, subsiding ripples were all that remained of my ability to do less than the extreme.

Epimetheus stopped to glare. "I speak more truth by calling you a lizard than I do by being literal. If I speak less truth to please you, what would you be asking me to do?"

My eyes glowed and he smiled in defiance. I raised my voice, no longer caring if Kristine or Praxis heard us. "How dare you suggest I'm asking you to lie."

He met my volume with his own. "Suggest, you say? Answer the question. If the literal has less truth in it than the figurative, and one intentionally uses the literal instead of the figurative, what is being done? Is it not a deception of sorts?"

Praxis hobbled quickly up to us. "Titan, don't do this."

Kristine stumbled, no doubt caught by surprise when the hobbling man she helped to walk, darted ahead. "Whoa. You shouldn't move like that."

Epimetheus held Praxis back. "You two, stay out of this. It's between Aiden and me."

I assumed they'd do as he asked so I continued. "You are

twisting virtue into vice. What happened to your claim that you have no room for lies in your life? You seem to have plenty, and I can't tolerate it."

Kristine hadn't backed away. "Aiden, please, he's just an old man. Be nice."

I turned to face stupidity incarnate. It seemed high time she knew no one played games in these caverns. "That there is not just an old man. That is a Titan and if you'll notice my eyes, you'll see I'm not mortal either."

Praxis grabbed her shoulder, but she pulled away. "You have glowing contacts, so great LARP costume, but I still don't like it when you yell at him like that."

I sprouted my wings and flapped them at a wingspan a LARP costume would be unlikely to manage. "This isn't LARPing, Kristine. None of it is. Charly really intends to kill Hunter. I need you to stop acting stupid and accept reality."

She scowled like she'd tasted the contents of an ash-tray. "You're an asshole, Aiden, and you should apologize to the old man."

The thought of apologizing for asking him to tell the truth burned like a hot coal against my forehead. Before I realized of my own actions, one of my claws flew at her face. Epimetheus got between us, so it landed against his neck instead. To my horror, my claws passed almost all the way through. His head fell, dangling from what flesh I hadn't torn through. His body collapsed.

Kristine's scream reverberated through several sections of cavern, and she chased it. Praxis ran off after her.

My will came back to me. I placed Epimetheus' head back on his gushing neck and waited for it to reattach. When the bleeding stopped, and his eyes noticed me, I said, "I'm becoming a monster."

He placed his hands on his head. "And I owe you an apology. I intentionally brought this out of you, but I didn't anticipate the risks to our mortal traveling companion. I should've been more direct and less clever."

"Well, you made your point. This world-altar stuff is turning me into a monster I don't want to be."

He stood. "What are we going to do about Kristine?"

"We'll have to find her and talk her into rejoining us. Those Empusa will kill her if they find her."

"And how are you going to do that without risking killing her for something she might say?"

My answer became my new motto, my new miserable motto, "distance."

33

Chapter 32

I could forgive someone for thinking I have a magic sense that allows me to see through solid objects or out the back of my head. In fact, it's just excellent hearing combined with a dragon's level of mental discipline. I would first detect the patterns of what's normal in a place, after which any sound outside of those patterns jumped to my attention. I set out to use that to find Kristine.

I counted off fifty steps in the direction she ran. After a few seconds, I had the patterns down. A single creature was behind me, probably against a rock. I walked out further while listening for the creature's motions. Whoever or whatever it was followed me.

Every fifty steps I'd stop and my follower continued following me. One quick scurry gave me a good hint as to what I was dealing with. Another sound like the tearing of a suit coat made me almost certain. I wondered where the other two were and weighed potential consequences.

Poor Epimetheus could be chopped to pieces and come back from it, but Praxis and Kristine didn't even have my regenerative abilities. I quickened my pace.

At my next stop, a fork lay ahead of me, left, right, or down. My ears told me of the persistent Empusa behind me. I hated the idea of making a random choice with a two-thirds chance of being wrong. An error at that point could mean Kristine's death, one I chased her to. The thought made me cringe. Indecision paralyzed me. I wanted better odds.

A subtle sound emerged, settling rock-dust, sliding down the cavern walls nearest the left fork. Something had disturbed it, Kristine, I hoped.

The left fork led to a large cavern without the canyon's light. One step in, my dragon eyes found Praxis. Kristine's crying told me she was near him. I listened for the one following me, hoping all three of the suit-wearing Empusa might converge so I could deal with them. Instead, I heard him scurry away. Two other scurrying sounds from inside the cavern moved away. The only anomalous sounds were the words between Praxis and Kristine.

"His head came off," she said.

Praxis shushed her. "It's all right. He's okay."

"He can't be okay. His head was knocked off."

"Epimetheus is a special Titan. He'll be okay when we return to him. Come with me and you'll see."

"No! Aiden will be there."

After one more listen to make sure it was only the three of us there, I spoke. "Epimetheus is okay. He's waiting for us to come back so we can move on."

She jumped. "Stay away from me."

"That's my plan, to stay away, but we all need to follow Epimetheus to the altar."

"No. You're a monster."

"Praxis can explain it all to you as we go. Remember when I told you he doesn't want me near him?"

"No. I don't want to, not with you."

"I understand and I'm sorry about what happened. Epimetheus and I have forgiven each other. Now, as for you, those guys in the suits are still lurking around."

"They are?" said Praxis.

"At least one of them followed me here. I heard what was probably all three run off just as I got here."

He rubbed his chin. "Considering what they suspect me of and Kern's displeasure with them, they probably thought we'd lead them to the deceiver."

I stepped back. "Whatever they're thinking, I know they're a lot more inclined to hurt you and Kristine than I am. We all need to get back to Epimetheus."

Praxis rubbed her back. "He's right. You're safe with me. We'll follow as we have been, a ways behind him."

We got her moving and returned to Epimetheus who continued leading us toward the altar.

When we reached another large cavern, one with a canyon running through it, Kristine called my name. "Aiden, Aiden Ferris, right?

Epimetheus' shoulders lurched like she hit him with a rock in the back. I sighed. "Yes, that's my legal name."

"And one more than I needed to know," said the Titan.

Kristine continued to yell. "You went to elementary and middle school with John Eisenbach. How long have you been...?"

"Don't yell," I said.

She left Praxis to catch up with me. "Did Vedi know?"

Epimetheus grumbled. "Oh, no, no, no."

He wasn't answering her question but rather exclaiming his displeasure at another deduction falling on him.

"Yes, even before I did," I answered her.

Praxis reached out. "Kristine, don't bother him. Please come back here with me."

I raised my hand. "She's not bothering me; that is for now, but, Kristine, you'd be wise to stay with him."

She did so in time to avoid an angry outburst, but it wasn't from me. Epimetheus' face turned red. "What did your father do? No, don't tell me, but how? Oh, don't tell me that either."

"I tried to keep it from you," I said.

He shook. "No wonder you wander the Earth. This is a terrible secret. It's a wonder there aren't Olympians that want you dead."

Kristine caught up with us again, though not in all ways. "Dead? If Charly really wants Hunter dead, I think I know why."

Praxis called to her. "Kristine, no."

She waved him off. "Aiden's not angry. I can tell. It's okay."

"That's not what Epimetheus and I were talking about, but while you're up here, tell me what you think Charly's reason for wanting Hunter dead would be."

"Melina told her sister that once Charly becomes the coven leader some guy will let him keep his magic toys."

"Magic toys? You mean like the weather machine?" I asked.

"Yeah, but Melina lost that one and Charly's pissed at her over it. He told her she had to replace it."

"Have you seen any of the other toys?"

"Yeah, there's a sword, a ring, and an old wooden statue."

She held one hand over the other about two feet apart.

I pointed. "The statue's about that big?"

She nodded. "It's supposed to be special because it used to belong to Troy or something like that."

Epimetheus grabbed his head. "It just gets worse. I don't think I needed to know that. Please, young lady, go back with Praxis."

I smiled and she dropped back. I turned to the Titan. "Any idea who could be bribing Charly?"

"The Oceanids have a way with manipulating people, especially men. I wouldn't be surprised if Melina's pulling the proverbial strings for both Charly and this source of magic artifacts."

I recalled how well she used Imhullu against me, so quick to detect and answer my moves, and able somehow to amplify the attacks she used. Her ignorance of what Imhullu is may be the only reason I survived. She sent Charly somewhere else during all that, and that means she planned. She has a scheme that has been accounting for me all along.

I nodded. "She may even be pulling my proverbial strings."

Epimetheus offered me no response, no speculative rebuttal. He just continued to lead.

Chapter 33

As we got near the altar's chamber, we needed to get Praxis in front of Kern. I hoped he could convince him of his Oceanid girlfriend's trickery.

Praxis directed us into a cavern. Shadows obscured its entrance and darkness followed into the interior. He lit a conveniently placed oil-lamp, revealing a pile of green robes on the floor. "My group found this place shortly after Kern brought us here. We designated it as our place to store things out of sight from the coven."

Epimetheus picked up a robe and pushed his hand through a rip. "And now it holds the robes you were tricked into wearing?"

Praxis nodded. "I guessed as much. They're avoiding telling Kern out of fear, but they want the evidence if and when they have to."

"So, why did we stop here?" I asked.

He selected a robe from the pile. "My friends aren't going to make it easy for me to get to Kern. I'll probably need your help."

"I won't be welcome near him."

He pushed the robe toward me, taking care to stand behind it as if it were a shield. "You only need to get me to the edge of his camp. You can watch from there."

"I can't deceive either."

He gave the robe a shake. "Wearing this robe won't be deception. It will just be a way to avoid unnecessary panic."

"Deception."

"Only if we tell someone you're not who you are, and I promise you on the honor of my people, I won't do that. If anyone asks, I will tell them who you are. To say, by the way, this is the dragon, is far better than to talk to blades."

Epimetheus placed his hand on my shoulder. "Put it on, Aiden. I promise I won't use it to deceive anyone either."

My state made it more difficult than usual to accept their reasoning. I needed more time, so I asked Kristine. "And what about you?"

Her eyes wandered between us, and she spoke with an animated exhale. "Whatever."

Her choice of words gave no assurance, as did her character, but the semblance of a commitment resided somewhere only a dragon like me could see. My mind, however, near the brink of rational dysfunction, became convinced. I put on the robe and pulled up its hood. "And what about my extreme reactions?"

Praxis traded out his robe for an undamaged one. "I know better than to offend your nature and so do Epimetheus and Kristine."

I worried circumstances might make that less than simple, but he led us out and I kept my reservations to myself.

As we traveled, Kristine and I kept our hoods up. Me, for obvious reasons and Kristine out of a more general caution.

We came to an entrance to a cavern the size of seven stadiums. I say that because the floor of the cavern had a stadium-sized circle of Greek-styled pillars in the center and six similar circles around it. The middle one stood on a platform of interlocking monolithic slabs that bridged a lake of lava. The outer circles each connected to the inner one by arching walkways.

Praxis led us down along the cavern's edge. Two of the outer circles, on opposite sides of the center, had tents pitched near their pillars. Dozens of men in dark business suits mulled around in the one we approached.

"Don't you guys have anything else to wear?" I asked Praxis.

He turned. "Normally we wear suits to hide the shapes of our bodies, but down here we do it out of respect for the one being summoned."

"And who is that?"

He turned back to the path ahead. "I won't be the one to tell you that."

Kristina tugged at her hood. "Silly? What kind of name is Silly? I mean, that's who they say they're summoning."

"Scylla, a cousin of mine, so to speak," said Epimetheus.

I tugged on the Titan's sleeve. "Why can't this Scylla just use a Titan portal?"

"Because she's in Tartarus."

Oliver taught me about Tartarus, a place the Olympians imprisoned all the intolerable Titans and remnants.

I laughed. "Well, it looks like Oliver will owe me one after this."

Praxis glared. "Everyone except me will have to be quiet as much as possible from here."

I nodded.

One of the Empusa approached us as we neared the pillars. "Praxis, where have you been and why are you wearing the robes of those LARP witches?"

Praxis grabbed his arm. "My clothes are tattered. There's been an incident we need to tell Kern."

He leaned in. "Shouldn't I warn the rest of the guards first?"

"It's a betrayal. Kern needs to know the details as soon as possible. Take us to him now."

He studied Praxis, and for the first time I wondered how exactly Praxis thought I'd help him get to Kern. My hands stiffened. The Empusa took Praxis by the wrist and drug him.

Praxis called to us. "Keep up."

Epimetheus leaned into me. "This is going better than I expected."

I agreed but didn't like the attention we gathered as we passed through the camp. Four figures in green coven robes had to stand out in the Empusa camp. Some started to follow us. A crowd of suits gathered around us. They didn't murmur like a crowd of normal humans would, but I could sense curiosity motivated them more than anything else, though something like hate came a close second.

A voice shouted in front of us, the taller of the three we chased off earlier. "What are you doing? Don't take those schemers any further."

The guard stopped. "Schemers? Praxis told me he needs to tell Kern of a betrayal right away."

The taller one pointed. "Take off their hoods. You'll see."

My hood came down with a jerk and sudden release. They released me because whoever it was recognized me and decided better of pulling me off my feet. Kristine didn't fare so well and hit the ground with a crack and thud.

I stood over her and they backed away from me. I wanted Praxis to give some idea as what he expected me to do. He gave me nothing. Surrounded by angry Empusa, Kristine could be dead in a fraction of a second.

Chapter 34

The Titan stepped next to me. His voice boomed. "I am the Titan Epimetheus. My companions and I are not here to advance a scheme but to stop one."

The taller one came out of the crowd. "Don't listen to the one by whom suffering came to humanity. He is easily fooled. You remember Pandora and her box?"

I could tell he regretted the word 'easily.' I also recognized misdirection. "Are you saying you would not have been fooled by Zeus in that story?"

He received some concerned looks. I wasn't certain what the Empusa thought of hubris, but I could guess not well.

He shook his finger. "Story? He calls it a story? He doesn't seem to be the sort of dragon we've been led to believe. Remove them from the camp."

The guard pushed Praxis who, bad hip and all, stumbled and fell. My verbal fencing match failed because of a home field advantage. Soon, I'd have no choice but to leave, not being welcome. I picked up Kristine and gestured to Epimetheus. "Help Praxis. We need to go if they'll let us."

Epimetheus helped Praxis to his feet and the crowd began to clear.

"They seem to be oddly nice about letting us leave," said the Titan.

Even odder, I had no compulsion to leave. I stopped. Something anomalous happened behind me, so I turned.

Kern had arrived. "Ah, but he is the sort of dragon we've been led to believe he is. If he says it was a story, he must believe it was. Not that it is, but he must believe it."

I cringed at the implied insult but didn't miss the opportunity. "Kern, Praxis has a real incident of betrayal that it would benefit you to hear."

His Oceanid girlfriend passed through the crowd behind him and whispered in his ear. He cringed. "Well then, dragon, you and your companions should come to my tent so I can hear what you have to say."

The Oceanid grinned as we walked across the camp to Kern's tent. Epimetheus leaned in. "She shouldn't be happy about this, but she is."

I nodded.

On our way, I healed Kristine. She might have had some damage to her spine if not for my new found healing power.

Once in Kern's tent, we sat and Praxis told him everything, including how Kern's girlfriend, Ayla, had them wear the coven's robes which tricked me into attacking them. I confirmed his story.

Hearing this, Kern glared at her. "Leave me. It is only for Thaumus' sake that I don't kill you."

She fell to her knees. "Please, Kern. I didn't know that was going to happen."

"She's lying," I said.

He pushed her. "Leave now, before I change my mind."

As she rose, he pushed her a second time. She stumbled and fell at the tent's exit. She got to her feet, grinned at me, and left. Like her sister, she still had something going according to plan.

"My brother appreciates your mercy, but I'm not so sure I do," said Epimetheus.

"I still honor the truce in my heart. Is it still on?" I asked.

He nodded. "Yes. Now that the trickery that threatened it is revealed, of course, it is."

While relieved that the ones I cared about were still safe, I sensed my second self still there, hating me. That it was a trick didn't change that I broke my word. Kern must have noticed the expression on my face. "Ah yes, dragon, you don't benefit from having a collective to serve. You still suffer from this trickery."

"Yes. Does that bring you joy?"

"No, no it doesn't. Even though you killed some of my Empusa, I don't want you to suffer."

He spoke the truth, spawning a question. "It doesn't?"

"In fact, I want to help you."

"Praxis has already taught me about making the world an altar."

"Yes, the world-altar. That's a painkiller. I have a cure."

I rose. "I would be very grateful for such a thing."

He held up a finger. "As the clan-leader of the Empusa you killed, I can forgive you, and if I do, it will be as if you never did it."

I turned to Epimetheus. "Can his forgiveness free me from my self-destructive side?"

The Titan raised an eyebrow. "It can."

Kern smiled. "I ask just one promise from you in return for it."

I knew his magnanimity seemed out of place. He wanted something from me I dread giving.

"And what is this promise?"

"That you won't interfere with the ritual."

"But the ritual is part of a scheme by Ayla's sister and Ayla's probably involved. Why would you want them to complete it?"

"Because the Empusa need a powerful Titan to lead them and that's why we're here."

"But by the truce, you can't hurt Hunter."

"And we won't. The coven will. Then when Scylla is summoned I will be there to give her the Eset-Minerva scepter, making her our new matriarch."

"So, you honor the truce and Hunter still dies."

He pointed at me. "And you're restored, and you let a threat to the balance of the universe die. I don't see the downside of this for you?"

The tent silenced. Why did I need to save a guy who tied my best friend to a chair in the desert, or stole a homeless man's coat and ripped it? Why did I need to do that at the expense of my own life? Epimetheus gave me little hope of living much past leaving the complex of caverns; that was unless I wanted to become the monster the world-altar state was making me.

Kern grasped my shoulders. "I can't believe I need to beg you to let me forgive you. You can do thousands of years of good in the world if you just let Scylla be summoned."

"My dead wife's will is that I save her brother. Please let me think about this some more and come back to you."

He patted my shoulder. "Done. You've got time. The sacrifice isn't until tomorrow morning. Praxis, set up your friends with a tent outside the circle for them to rest in."

On the way to our campsite, Epimetheus whispered, "What are you doing?"

I whispered back, "I honestly had my doubts at the time, so I took advantage of them to get Kristine to a safer place."

"And?"

"I may not live very long."

Chapter 35

We entered our own circle of pillars; its emptiness drew us to its center. The indirect light from the lava made shadows dance, oblivious to us. The Empusa set up a tent for Epimetheus and me and another for Kristine. Praxis left with his own kind to their camp. Four became three.

We're on our way

I wished Kristine a good night and threw myself on the ground in my tent. Epimetheus stood, peering out its flaps. "I don't mean to be obtuse, dragon, but have you made your choice?"

The ground, however hard, invited me to sleep, and I didn't want a long conversation. "I told you enough to know. Now, let's get some rest before tomorrow."

"You told me you may not live much longer. I suppose my brother would know exactly why you said that, but I don't."

I rolled away. "I'm saving my brother-in-law's life for my dead wife's sake."

"And taking your guilt to the surface? I see."

I raised my head. "Epimetheus, please. I need all the rest I can get tonight. I don't need to be reminded of how bleak my future is."

"Oh, sorry."

He lay himself down and turned away. I considered crying myself to sleep.

"It may not be so bleak," he said.

With those words from a Titan who admits he's poor at predicting the future, we rested the night.

In the morning, I gave Epimetheus my plan. "I can't save Hunter in the world-altar state I've been in. I'd likely kill him for something he'd say or do, so I worked my way out of it last night with that delay of my decision to Kern."

He placed his hands on my shoulders as if to hold me down. "But what's to keep you from trying to kill yourself when you're needed to save your brother-in-law?"

"Praxis stopped back while you were still sleeping, and I gave him my answer to Kern's offer in the form of a promise. I promised him I will do all I can to save Hunter."

"And, what does this do?"

"My self-destructive-self shares my honor, so with the fulfillment of my promise in sight, it shouldn't interfere with me."

"Does a promise to do something unwanted work that way?"

The answer to his question would have been yes and no, but I didn't want to give it thought. I moved his hands and with parting grip released them at his side. "Friend, you've fulfilled your honor's obligation to me. I can ask nothing more of you from here."

You may not be able to ask, but as you declared me your friend, you can still expect."

The tent flap raised and Praxis came in. "She's gone."

"She?" I asked.

"Kristine. I wanted to say goodbye to her and didn't find her in her tent, so I looked around. She's nowhere nearby."

Epimetheus placed his hand on my shoulder. "She probably thought you weren't going to save Hunter."

Praxis pointed. "She did just that. She told me how upset she was last night before I left."

A lump hit the back of my throat. "I didn't intend to deceive her and didn't expect her to care."

I stepped out of the tent. The Titan followed. "What now?"

"We move within striking distance of the altar and wait for them to move Hunter there."

"And about Kristine?"

"Whatever horrors Melina intends to introduce them to, they're still just kids from the south bay. I don't think they'll harm her. At least not before I can get Hunter freed."

"Prometheus, is that you?"

He winked at me. I got his point. "Keep an eye out for us while we wait."

The two of us put up our hoods and walked to the next outer circle. We moved through the shadows until we neared the circle surrounding the coven's camp. The coven members started to move to the bridge that led to the center circle, so we ran across the clearing and joined the flow of cloaked youth.

At the bridge, Charly stood atop a crate. "Our day has come. Everyone to their places."

His face's ever-resident smile, larger than normal, shined as he waved them along.

He repeated his line twice more before someone interrupted him. "How can you be okay with killing someone?"

Kristine stood at his feet, her question a true query and not condemning. Charly's face matched her innocent concern but his intent didn't. "You're one of Vedi's friends, aren't you? Kristine, right?"

"Vedi was a good coven leader. How can you be okay with killing her brother?"

I continued approaching at the crowd's pace, weighing the merits of grabbing Charly.

He knelt. "Kristine, Ms. Asta told me about Vedi and Hunter. Remember those bruises she'd show up to school with?"

"Yeah," she answered.

"Hunter abused her."

He enlightened me, but not with what he said, but because he lied. I knew someone beat her. Probably someone in her family, but until Charly's lie, I hadn't been able to eliminate Hunter as a suspect.

Kristine believed his lie, but it didn't dissuade her from her goal. "Yeah, but still, we can't just go killing people."

Unfortunately, in a world full of evil, we may have to at times. I decided to grab him. While I didn't know exactly where to find Hunter, Charly seemed weak enough to me to tell me.

Of all my options for getting to him, pushing my way through the crowd in human form seemed best. Taking flight would have required my wings to knock several people to the ground, and taking a dragon form would have crushed people.

He saw me coming. "Aiden. How did you get here?"

"Don't lie like you just did to Kristine. Tell me where Hunter is."

He put his hand into his robe and vanished before I got close enough to grab him. Kristine waved her hands around where he had stood. "How'd he do that?"

Epimetheus cleared his throat. "That would probably be the ring you told me about, Kristine."

I jumped onto the crate and huffed. "Seriously? He escaped me with a worn-out trope?"

"No, dragon. The ring of Gyges isn't a worn-out trope. It's a curse upon whoever where's it."

"Okay, so can that curse help me here?"

He shook his head. "The curse is due to what he can get away with, not what others can do against him."

"So back to my first plan?"

Kristine grabbed my arm. "You're going to save Hunter?"

The Titan sighed. "That would be his first plan."

Chapter 36

Seven megaliths leaned against each other to bridge the lake of lava. Six, the size of houses, leaned in from the cliffs, combining their vectors to suspend the seventh, the size of a stadium, between them. The structure seemed improbable to me.

"Any idea how much weight this place can hold?"

Epimetheus raised an eyebrow. "I want to say these stones are too large to care about a few hundred people, but a couple creatures the size of ancient dragons, now that could be a problem."

"I'll keep that in mind."

"You should, considering who they're trying to summon."

"This Scylla's an ancient dragon? Funny Harold never taught me about her."

Epimetheus winced. "Why would Oliver get that sorcerer to teach you things? Has he lost his mind?"

"It's a long story of mistakes made when he wasn't around."

He shook his head. "More stuff I didn't want to know, but as for why Scylla wouldn't have shown up in your dragon lore lessons is because Scylla isn't exactly a dragon."

I squinted. "Not exactly but is?"

"You know how humans became dragons?"

"Yes, an extreme magic contract."

"Scylla is what happens when a Titan makes the same sort of contract. In her largest form, she is larger than any dragon alive."

"Larger than my father?"

"Easily."

"Good thing she's not going to make it here."

The coven wandered into their places around a stone altar like a drunk marching band. They each took a candle from a passing bucket. They formed an eight-pointed star emanating twenty yards from its center.

We didn't join, but no one seemed to notice. I guessed our green robes suggested we were with Charly and Melina.

A half-formed thought haunted me. I held up my cloak's sleeve to Epimetheus. "I'm beginning to wonder why they gave these green robes to the Empusa they sent after you."

"Why do you think?"

"I don't know, but they're suspiciously convenient for us now."

He leaned in. "You mean those two Oceanids may have wanted us to get here all along?"

"Does it make sense they'd play me this far so well, and not have thought about the robe colors?"

Kristina shook her head. "Don't think like that. You're scaring me."

Epimetheus patted her shoulder. "We're probably giving them too much credit. These are Oceanids after all, not some trickster god. Ayla's smirks were probably just her trying to plant doubts in our heads, or glee at the thought Aiden would accept the deal that would let her sister complete the summoning."

Logs tied together to form what looked like a giant upper case 'A' rose up over the altar.

Epimetheus rubbed his forehead. "Oh my, that hurts."

I tugged his sleeve. "Are they planning to crucify him?"

"No, it's just clear to me now how they're ritual is capable of pulling someone out of Tartarus."

"And it hurts?"

"It hurts me. Knowing how to pull someone from Tartarus was

burden enough, but knowing whoever is behind this is playing with the void? This deduction fell on me twice as hard."

The game being played teased me. The void, the place I tried first to go after breaking the truce, seemed to have a new appointment. Could the Oceanids intend to facilitate my other self's desire?

I pointed at the giant letter 'A'. "That has something to do with the void?"

"It's a dormant chaos portal. Most likely the ritual's purpose is to activate it."

Kristine's hood turned in my peripheral vision. "Why are we talking about this?"

I patted her shoulder. "I'm rescuing Hunter. Don't worry about that."

Charly appeared on the dais behind the altar. "So, how is everyone?"

His smile was more at home on a kindergarten teacher than the leader of a coven, especially one preparing for a human sacrifice. His coven would have been more at home at a gaming convention.

"It's all good," someone yelled.

"We're just kicking back," yelled another.

Charly held up both his hands. "You all remember the chants. Let's get them going."

A cacophony of voices rose up. I couldn't recognize a single word. The language was none I'd heard before, but I could still tell they're chanting was out of sync.

Epimetheus shook his head.

"What are they saying?" I asked him.

"They're butchering an ancient language, so it's hard to tell, but they're addressing Hecate and Nix."

"How badly can they mess this up and have it still work?"

He raised both eyebrows. "One of the first of my deductions in life was that these words almost don't matter. It's all about the group mind."

"So, Hecate and Nix, do they hear them?"

"Hecate, probably not. She's the goddess of mages and I'm not even sure she's still alive. But Nix, on the other hand, she's the goddess of the void or chaos."

"Chaos?"

He nodded to the giant 'A'. "They're forcing her to be involved."

"What kind of temper does she have?"

He grumbled. "I don't know, and I don't want to know."

The coven passed flames from candle to candle. Epimetheus and I exchanged stares. He smiled. "We're almost there."

I nodded. "Bring it on."

Melina appeared in front of the dais, latent bruises still on her face. She studied the crowd until her eyes came to rest on me. With a jerk of her head, she tossed her blueish-blonde hair to one side.

I glared.

She grinned and touched one of the legs of the 'A'. Blue fire ran up the log to the nearest intersection. There it filled the interior triangle before vanishing. The logs framed a pitch dark void.

I leaned into Epimetheus. "Is that an active portal to the void?"

He grabbed my shoulder. "Perhaps we weren't giving her too much credit."

Kristina whispered, "What are you talking about?"

"I've been lured into a trap."

She tugged on my cloak. "But we have to save Hunter."

I gave her shoulder a squeeze. "I will, if it's the second to last thing I do, which has become very likely."

"Second to last?" she asked.

"Melina knew what she was setting up from the beginning. Once I save Hunter, my self-destructive side will take me through that portal."

Chapter 37

Some rats can pass on traps, but this trap set out for me, gave me no way to go but in. Both my love of Vedi and my honor required me to save Hunter, and once achieved, my dragon nature, having been betrayed, would force me through the chaos portal into the void. From the moment the Empusa and I fought that battle spawned by deception, the two wicked Oceanids had control.

I resigned myself to my fate and determined to make the best of my final moments. The Oceanids knew saving Hunter would be my last grasp on this world, so they had to present him. When they did, I'd finish the task I came down here for.

Kristina tugged my cloak. "What are we going to do?"

I turned. "When you see me go to the altar, go to our tents. Hunter and I will meet you there."

Epimetheus raised his hand. "I'll be sure she gets there."

At least in all of this, I made a friend in Epimetheus. Kristine remained an acquaintance. Our common cause is what we believed Vedi would want. For that reason, I cared if she got out of these caverns alive.

We waited for Hunter to be presented. We endured the coven's incoherent chants. The cacophony came to a merciful end when the sound of grinding stone came from the altar.

Hunter rose out of the altar on a pole. Duct tape wrapped around him up to his neck, he looked like a gray plastic mummy. The shape of metal straps, like those that held pallets of lumber, bulged from underneath. His bloodshot eyes glared until he noticed me. Then I saw his face like I'd never seen it before. I couldn't tell if I saw confusion or fear, but for the first time ever, I pitied him.

Some of the coven laughed. I had to tell myself they probably didn't think Charly really planned to carry through. Anger still built up in me. Even if they thought it all a joke, how could they look at someone in Hunter's situation and laugh? Fortune shined on their wretched lives that day, that I abandoned my world-altar state.

Charly Chord, on the other hand, deserved no mercy. He climbed atop the altar and produced a blade from his cloak. With his back to me, he held the blade out as if to ask the rest of the coven what he should do with it. They chanted in unison, "kill, kill, kill…"

I took full dragon form, house-sized, and reared up. The chanting stopped, replaced by gasps. Some pointed, so he turned. His eyes widened, and his resident smile took its leave.

I pounced, but Charly and Melina left the dais before I landed. He vanished, and she ran out amongst the coven members. I growled at her cowardice, that she would shelter herself amongst those I didn't deem deserving of death. It was no matter though as I had my objective.

Hunter tilted his head. "You're here to save me, right?"

He asked a sincere question. Considering all the duct tape removal, I answered his question with actions rather than words. I tore up the pole with Hunter on it and took flight.

He yelled out, "Easy, Aiden, I think you broke one of my ribs."

His coughing told me he could be right, but I thought it better to heal him later than to delay his rescue. With one quick flap of my wings, I pressed toward our camp.

Ayla's voice lifted from the dais as if through a megaphone. She said the words of the previous chant, no doubt with more precision than the coven, and then added one more word, "tundo."

The last time an Oceanid said that word around me, I got slammed into a hillside, so I paid attention to my surroundings. A woman in silver robes jumped out of the portal and landed on the altar with a reverberating crack.

Hunter coughed blood with his words. "The summoning still worked."

For all their lies, the Oceanids truly intended to summon Scylla and didn't need Hunter to die for it to happen. They were getting everything they wanted, Scylla out of Tartarus and me soon to be gone, but why? I figured I wasn't going to answer that question.

I managed to spot Epimetheus and Kristine as we passed over. The coven split into two groups. A few remained near the altar with the Oceanids and Scylla, the rest ran to their camp. Epimetheus and Kristine approached the megalith bridging in the direction of our tents.

One object appeared out of place, a large raven. It flew in their direction. Its size could intimidate a mortal, but I suspected not a Titan, so I sped on to our tent.

I put Hunter on the ground and took human-but-clawed form. I stayed alert as I ripped at Hunter's wrappings.

The raven swooped at the two but the Titan back-handed it, sending it into a wing-over-wing roll. It managed an awkward landing. I couldn't figure out what it was up to until the bird changed form into Charly.

He staggered and fell to a knee. I had no doubt the Titan's blow had to hurt. Charly heaved a few times before noticing me. He smiled and tossed something out from under his cloak, a sword. He yelled something, and it lifted into the air and flew toward me. He pulled at a black cape and turned back into a raven.

The bird flew at Epimetheus, but this time pulled up before getting within his reach. He flew around and swooped again. In that time the sword had almost reached Hunter and me.

"That thing cut up my car," shouted Hunter.

Fear inspired him, and considering what had happened to his

car, I shared his concern. I sprouted my wings and wrapped around him. The sword waved about and swiped at us as though wielded by someone dexterous.

It struck at my wings that I dared not move for Hunter's sake. The sword's blows bounced off, no energy got through, but Hunter still yelled out as each blow landed.

Kristine arrived and screamed. Epimetheus caught the sword by the blade, apparently between its focus on Hunter and Kristine's scream, he managed to sneak up on it.

"A shameful waste of a relic," he said and snapped it in two.

The raven flew toward the altar and I finished removing the duct tape and metal straps from Hunter. I healed him and gave out instructions. "Epimetheus, lead these two to Thaumus' portal."

Hunter stood. "You going to deal with that Scylla lady?"

"No, I have an appointment with the void."

He cocked his head. "Did you say the void?"

"Yes. Epimetheus can explain. I need to go."

I took flight and he waved. "Say hi for me."

What he meant evaded me, but a lump grew in my throat. His ignorance of my pending fate seemed childlike; innocence from someone I've always known to be a world-class jerk. I fought back tears and darted toward the portal.

Chapter 38

On the way back to the chaos portal, I noticed Charly, the two Oceanids, and what members of the coven who had stayed with them. They walked back to the coven's camp. Their job done, for whatever purpose I didn't know.

The Empusa surrounded the dais. Kern approached the silver-robed Titaness with a scepter. The recent escapee of Tartarus was about to become the Empusa's matriarch.

I couldn't fathom the depths of Melina and Ayla's treachery, but I knew it had to go beyond destroying me. I wondered if Kern worried at all about it. I knew of his honor, but did he also possess logic?

I could have flown through the portal from the opposite direction of Kern's approach. It would have been the politest direction, the most likely to go unnoticed, but I thought better. Kern needed every reminder of the treachery behind the moment. I flew straight over his head and over Scylla's on my way into the dark triangle over the broken altar.

I left everything behind. Nothing engulfed me and nothing was cold. Everywhere, if that could be what one calls all the wheres that are nowhere, was cold, except for a sound, a warm sound. *"Aiden."*

"Vedi?"

"Yes."

"What's happening?"

"You're stepping on my feet."

"Vedi, I can't feel or see anything."

She laughed. *"We're dancing and you're stepping on my feet."*

"How can I dance if I can't see or feel?"

Another woman's voice, neither warm nor cold, spoke. "It's time for him to go."

The warm touch of Vedi's fingers brushed the back of my hand. *"Aiden, you need to do your part of the dance, not mine."*

"Be sure your feet are under you," said the other woman.

Light, air, and ground pounced upon me like a boulder about to crush me. Instead, it embraced me. A rock invited me to sit and I accepted. In contrast to the void, all matter becomes intimate.

Some green cloth and grey piles of dust near my feet told me where I was. I could reach Thaumus' portal in a short walk.

To my surprise, so could Epimetheus, Hunter, and Kristine. They hadn't noticed me as they passed by.

Kristine's white face-paint revealed she'd been crying. The tears left floodplains of clear skin from her eyes down to her jawline.

I walked up to her. "That must have been a lot of crying for such a short time. What happened?"

Kristine's eyes widened, and she punched Epimetheus. "You lied to me. Aiden's alive."

The Titan turned and winced. "I hate these caverns."

Hunter sneered. "So, you're not the iron dragon after all. You chickened out."

"No. I did go through the portal to the void. It just kicked me out to here."

Epimetheus grabbed Hunter's shoulder. "Don't question his honor."

Hunter yanked away. "Or you'll do what? I can take you."

Epimetheus pointed. "What I said was intended as a friendly warning. You can hate him, as I suspect he hates you too, but if you manage to be wise in anything, don't question his honor."

Hunter's head jerked about as if he could shake the Titan's words off. "Okay, Aiden, why did you just sit here? Charly could've come after us."

"Because I just got here myself. I'm wondering how you three managed to get her in only a few minutes."

"Two days, it took us two days," said Epimetheus.

"But how can that be? I was only in the void for a couple minutes."

He rubbed his head. "I suppose that could explain why we hear so little from Nix, some sort of distortion of time, but speculation is my brother's purview."

"Then why did you wince when you saw me? A deduction fell on you, right?"

"Yes, one did."

"And?"

"You're not going to like it."

"Since when do I have to like knowledge? If it affects me, please tell me."

"Very well. You tried to go to the void, the place where all corrupted dragons should ideally go, but Nix, the goddess of the void rejected you."

"So, the void is no longer an option for my self-destructive side?"

"I think it's bigger than that, dragon. Did perchance, she tell you why?"

"She told me to be sure my feet were under me."

He stared at me. "I have no idea what that could mean. She's the goddess of the void, sometimes called the goddess of chaos, and you're the son of Ferus, sometimes called the god of order. You're sometimes called the son of order, in fact, and she essentially told you to watch your step on your way out of the void?"

Hunter laughed. "That's heavy, but I could have told you. My great-grandfather couldn't get there, so what makes you think you could?"

Epimetheus looked Hunter up and down. "Because he's a dragon. Your great-grandfather was a conniving sorcerer who tried to invite himself, not to mention he wanted a two-way door. He was

155

downright uppity, if you ask me. Now, corrupted dragons, it's in their magic contracts. Of course, he should have expected to get in."

Kristine raised a finger. "Uh, why would you want into the void?"

I smiled. "No one should, but my self-destructive side wants me gone and that would have been the most honorable way for me to go, following the dragon contract."

She shook her head. "It just makes no sense to me."

"I guess you're blessed in that way. Now I wonder what the next most honorable way would be for me to go?"

We walked to Thaumus' portal and Epimetheus led Hunter and Kristine in. I didn't follow. Instead, I skirted canyon walls just above the river of lava.

Vedi's voice replayed in my memory. *'Aiden, you need to do your part of the dance, not mine.'*

If this is a dance with my precious Vedi, what were my steps supposed to be? I wanted to know but didn't. All I knew was that I intended to attack the product of treachery, this escapee from Tartarus. Scylla, being more powerful than even my father, would probably kill me, but at least in that, I wouldn't be stepping on Vedi's feet.

Chapter 39

I pondered the task of attacking Scylla. My effort aimed to anticipate my self-destructive side, but could I do it? Did my truce with
the Empusa forbid me? That side of me would know once presented
the option, so that became my plan. I'd address her and let what
happened after, happen.

I covered a day and a half of walking distance on the cavern
floors with hours of flight along the canyon. At the lake, I rose up by
the bridge between the Empusa's circle and the center one.

Scylla, the Titaness, sat on a throne of logs in front of the altar.
Sacrilege suggested itself to me but what divinity had anything to do
with this broken altar meant for a fake sacrifice?

Lines of Empusa filed in from the surrounding camps, each, in
turn, nodding to her. They came to show their respect to their new
matriarch. My reason for being there alluded me. Had I come to
die, achieve justice, or both?

I flew up to the nearest queue, hovered, and considered if I
should get into it or just get Scylla's attention. Kern noticed me.
"You don't belong here, dragon, go."

Such words should have been followed by an irresistible compulsion to leave, but not this time. "I know you don't want me here, but someone of higher authority must."

He glared just before studying the crowd. "Do you know any of the other high ranking Empusa besides me?"

"No. What's going on here?"

He walked up to my dangling feet to lower his voice. "If you must know, all the high ranking Empusa in the world have come to recognize our new matriarch, and since you don't know any of them, I can't imagine who would want you here."

An accented woman's voice boomed from the dais. "You, the one flying, go here."

That Scylla could speak English at all impressed me. She pointed to the ground in front of her, clarifying what she meant, so I complied and landed on the dais before her.

Her eye, not obscured by the lone lock of red hair amongst the flaxen, squinted. "You, the passed into the void one, how and why?"

"Nix sent me back."

She stood and shook her head. "No, the staying out one is not with Olympus."

I saw her as sincere but also fearful. She dreaded the thought of Nix being aligned with the Olympians so much that she couldn't accept it.

My next words, I found myself saying rather than having planned them. "Olympus is with me."

She thrust her hand against the back of her throne. "No, the one sent, I will not go back."

I became an audience to my words and actions. They came from me before I knew them. "I can't let you stay."

She studied me and grinned. "The one sent will fail."

My wings lifted me over her. Her eyes glowed red as I passed. I grasped the dark triangle's frame. It froze my hand and stung. She turned and snarled. My stinging hands threw the frame at her. I hoped to get it to land around her neck, bringing her to the void, but she grew too large for it to fit and the triangle bounced off her. It couldn't be that simple.

I guessed my self-destructive side must have been relieved to have not won, but the rest of me wanted her back in Tartarus. Her dragon form, if one wanted to call it that, deflected the portal so that it flew off, passing over Empusa who scurried to the outer circles.

She grew larger and larger, taking a hideous form. She had six heads on the ends of six long necks, eight giant octopus legs, and six extra maws around her middle. I flew toward the ceiling, hoping to stay out of her reach. She sprawled across the center megalith, the ends of her legs dangling over the edges on all side.

I could see how she might have been a menace to ancient shipping, but closer to home, I could see how she might kill the largest of dragons. My largest size is greater than most, but my body quaked at her presence. Worse yet, I took my largest size without thinking and my wings had no room for flight. I fell into the midst of her necks.

I wrapped my front legs around three of her necks. My hind legs struggled for footing amongst her eight. My tail flailed about the chasm at the giant platform's edge.

We wrestled, but she was stronger than me as much as she was larger. Her tentacles pulled my hind quarters toward her maws, which already turned what was left of the dais and alter into gravel.

She screamed as if in pain, but I could tell it was anticipatory pleasure. Was I about to be ground like hamburger? One of her mid-section's maws bit into my hind foot and I screamed in pain. My tail shot out straight and the portal fell into the lake.

The light from the lake stopped as if flipped off at a switch. Startled, she threw me away.

The airtime allowed me to take a smaller dragon form and I began to fly under my own control. A stream of blood flowed from what was left of my hind foot. I knew I needed to address that soon or bleed out. I can't regenerate from that.

Besides the large drops of my blood dropping on scrambling Empusa, my dragon eyes spotted two more interesting things in the pitch dark. One was why the lake's light went out. When the portal hit the lake of lava, for reasons I didn't know, the entire lake became one giant portal. Also of interest, a second supporting megalith slid into an awkward tilt.

I wondered if this could have something to do with why Nix sent me back, or was the situation just one more suspiciously convenient thing in the plans of Melina and Ayla? I knew in the case of the first, I should try to do my half of the dance, and if it was the second case, once again, I saw no way out but in.

My bleeding foot had to hold on. I darted in, evading her flailing legs, and passing my mouth close to one of the supporting megaliths, roared into the stone. Despite my best efforts to modulate the sonic attack to be local, bits of ceiling still rained down. I pushed off as the megalith started down. The central megalith lilted to the side and Scylla screamed, this time in fear.

My consciousness began to drain with the blood. I needed to make sure the platform would go down. Knocking out one more support should do it. I swerved around to reach it but one of her legs grabbed me. She sent me flying all the way to the cavern wall.

Blood shot out from the collision. My vision blurred, but not enough to miss two of her legs reaching across the chasm. Her mass lurched toward me. My tail wrapped around my wounded leg and squeezed to stop the bleeding as I rolled to the ground.

Landing, I had to get eyes on her again. A loud deep crack of stone reverberated through the cavern. Half of her legs reached for the edge. A death-wish propelled me into a roll toward her.

She screamed. My roll allowed me intermittent impressions of her falling with the collapsing platform. Two of her legs held onto the edge. I risked more blood loss, using my tail to steer a leap. I landed on one of her tentacle legs with all claws out, but her quickness matched mine. Her other leg wrapped around my neck.

More of my scarce blood flowed freely to the ground and mixed with some of hers. My claws did something worthwhile.

I forced her to let go. She fell, dragging me by the neck. I took human form as quickly as I could. It worked. She lost her grip on me and entered the void below alone.

I fell to the ground and grabbed my ankle to save what was left of my blood. I won that fight but a lot of disturbed Empusa rushed out to see the one who just sent their matriarch back to Tartarus.

Chapter 40

They swarmed to me like an imploding suit warehouse. I took human form and shouted. "She started it."

A blur stopped between me and the rest of the Empusa, Kern. He glared before turning to them. "What he says is true. Scylla apparently wanted to make an example of this dragon."

I nodded, and he continued. "This dragon who refuses to tell us what sort he is. He came to see our new matriarch who, I must add, was chosen because of her immense power. The results are before us. This dragon the Olympians brought to Earth and forbid him to tell us who exactly he is, this dragon defeated her."

I spoke in his ear. "Ayla and Melina set us all up."

He pushed me away and kept his side of the conversation to the crowd. "Ayla and her sister Melina are no longer welcome in the Empusa camps or any other place we settle, as is the case with you, dragon."

My hamburger foot burned, but my gut stung more. Unwelcomed, I needed to leave before anything else. I sprouted wings and Kern pointed to the cavern's exit.

I landed two small caverns past the Empusa encampment. My foot needed attention. The mangling required me to move flesh around with my hands, lest my dragon self-healing would leave things in the wrong place. Having a second healthy foot to compare to saved me from becoming crippled.

The pain softened, and I leaned against the wall. A woman's voice came from behind me, Melina. "Don't think you've paid for what you've done. Not even close."

Once again, she knew exactly what she was doing. My foot wasn't ready for me to launch at her. "What I've done? Haven't you planned this all along?"

"You broke up Ayla and Kern, almost getting her killed, and I still haven't healed from the bruises you gave me. A doctor tells me my nose will never be the same, even with surgery."

My hands hardened. "You tried to kill Hunter, and Ayla is responsible for killing Empusa."

"Don't change the subject. You wronged me and my sister in ways we can't forget."

My foot still burned but I thought it at a stage where I could move through it. "Everything I've done to you and your sister, you brought on yourselves."

I stood and turned to notice she had left. My foot protested, and I sat. "Your victims don't care about your nose."

She probably didn't hear me, but it made my foot feel better for me to say it. Once I could walk on it without wincing, I took flight.

Thaumus left his portal in place for me and I walked down its path to Santa Cruz. Two Titans and an Oceanid waited for me there. Epimetheus took my hand and patted my shoulder. "You made it out. Thaumus told me you would."

Thaumus, in his Hawaiian shirted human form, grinned. "Hunter left in a cab about ten minutes ago, and thanks to you, healthy and whole."

He looked sheepishly at his Oceanid wife. She glared at him but smiled at me. "I'm Electra. I understand two of my sisters behaved very badly. I am pleased that you spoiled whatever they were scheming."

My dragon senses told me she believed it to be true. I shook my head. "I'm not so sure they haven't gotten exactly what they wanted."

Electra glanced at Thaumus. "Then we shall look into it. Rest assured, dragon, they will be dealt with."

Thaumus stuck his large soft hand into mine. "Yes, Aiden of the dragon sort I don't know, Electra will deal with them, and she's not happy with them."

Epimetheus took me aside. "Do us both a favor and get me on a bus for Yukon before I learn things I don't need to."

"We have an appointment to make and I need my portal back," said Thaumus.

He and Electra vanished with a single step into the sea.

I waved at the space they left behind. "Everyone's acting like it's all a job well done and it's time to go home, but I'm about to do myself in. What's wrong with this picture?"

Epimetheus put an arm around me. "We need to dare to do things we don't want to do."

"What? You think I should just stop fighting it and do it?"

"No. I'm saying you should take advantage of the things you know."

"Like what?"

"You and your self-destructive side must share the same mind. Your self-destructive side won't try things it knows won't work, so anticipate, and research. The ways to kill you are very rare. The odds of you finding one soon is equally rare, but as long as the part of you that wants to live is earnestly looking, your self-destructive side is likely to wait and stay submerged."

"Leaving me in control and able to do other things like finding out what Melina and Ayla are up to?"

He patted my back. "Yes. Now get me a bus ticket to Yukon."

"Why Yukon?"

"I ran out of solitude in Manitoba."

I drove him to the bus station and bought him a ticket and shook his hand. "I am grateful for all the help you've given me."

He squeezed. "Expect me to write some time."

"You know my address?"

He laughed. "No. Expect a letter nonetheless."

"I can give you my address."

He turned away. "I don't want to know it and won't need it. Now get on with the important things."

I didn't want to think too much about how he could be so confident in his ability to get a letter to me without knowing my address. Too many of my theories involved my death. I didn't need the depression.

On my drive home, I compared the velocities I attained in the caverns to what I might achieve with my car. My physics and math knowledge did a decent job with the vectors, and I could assure my self-destructive-self it wasn't an option.

Chapter 41

I found John at his house.

He swung it open. "Aiden? Thumper told me where you went. Is Hunter alive?"

I stepped in and threw myself onto his couch. "Hunter's his usual jerky self, and back at his apartment by now. Now, who's Thumper?"

"That's the cat that took me to the Himalayas and back. He gave me a world tour on the way back. Great guy."

I leaned back and closed my eyes. "I'm happy that you had a good time, but my trip, well, I've got bad news."

The footstool's feet drug on the floor and John sat two feet from my face. "I've never heard you like this before. What could it possibly be?"

I told him about being tricked into breaking the truce and the implications of my self-destructive side. He didn't take it well. He leaned in and grabbed my forearms. "No, I won't let you kill yourself."

I grabbed his elbows. "You know I don't want to."

He wagged his head and teardrops fell to the floor. "But, damn being this dragon. Can't you just stop being it?"

"I am this dragon."

He threw himself around my shoulders and sobbed. "Of course, you are. I just wish you didn't have to be."

I held him, comforting both of us. I knew what he meant, and I wished it too at the time. He pulled himself off me and flopped into a chair. "What can we do?"

"My self-destructive-self will leave me in control as long as there isn't what seems like a viable means to do me in available."

"So, we keep sharp objects away from you? What?"

I leaned over and tapped his knee. "Other than one sharp object I hid in an obscure place thousands of miles from here, I doubt there are any that could kill me."

"Maybe you should tell me where it is, so I can re-hide it."

I shook my head. "Once you took off, my self-destructive side would probably tag along on any transport you took. For the time being, closer and less remote possibilities should be of greater interest."

He sat up. "What can I do then?"

"My hoard is full of artifacts, some of them magical. I want you to go and look through them to see if any might be able to harm me."

"And hide them?"

"No. You need to promise me now that you'll leave them there and contact me about them as soon as possible."

He stood. "Why would I do that?"

"Because if I know you'll tell me, my self-destructive side won't see a need to go there before."

He chopped at the air. "You're asking me to help you kill yourself?"

"It's counterintuitive, I know, but this is the only way I can keep control long enough to stop Melina and her sister from doing what-ever it is they're plotting."

"But, while I'm over in Slovenia, I won't be here to stop you."

"I've already added terminal velocity to my maximum flight speed. That's not enough. I also can't do it with a car. That leaves just whatever may be in my hoard and the dark blade I've hidden.

That all means at worst, I start traveling to the blade, and that would take most of a week."

"And what's to keep you from starting, say, now?"

"You can get to Slovenia in less than two days. I can too. Other than the desire to do myself in, my self-destructive side shares my compulsions. The hope is that as long as you're looking for the means of my destruction, I'll let myself deal with those who did this treacherous thing to me."

He turned his back. "You're asking me to promise to help you die."

"I'm asking you to earnestly look for a means in my hoard and waste no time in reporting back if you find something."

"This is hard, maybe too hard."

"John, you'll buy me time to stop something, something that must be awful."

"You'll know if I lie to you. I'm going to have to mean it before I say it."

I touched his shoulder. "Then mean it. I'll wait for you to mean it."

He cradled his forehead in his hands and I waited. He grunted. "I hate this, Aiden. I hate it, but yeah, I promise you I will look through your hoard as quickly and thoroughly as I can and report anything that might be usable to kill you, without delay."

He nailed it, a sincere promise. I could tell how much it pained him and that knowledge delivered a punch to my gut. I choked out words. "Thank you."

He packed his bags, and I drove him to SFO. I left him at the security gate with what would have been an awkward hug, but with this one, we didn't care.

"I love you," he said.

I gave him a parting squeeze. "You're truly my best friend."

I expected to see him again, but in a sense, he was already mourning me. I was glad no one ever asked of me what I was asking of him, to help me find a way to die.

A rare clear night sky sat over the valley on my drive home.

"*Aiden, dance,*" said Vedi's voice.

"I'm driving," I answered.

"*Melina and Ayla are hiding.*"

"I don't blame them."

"*Hunter will be safe for now.*"

"From Charly?"

"*His sword is broken.*"

"Vedi, when I die, where will you be?"

"*Aiden, dance.*"

'What does that mean?"

She didn't answer. Clouds entered the sky and rain fell. The patter of water saw me the rest of the way home.

I stood in my yard pondering an irony and a mystery as vapor rose from me. Vedi was in the void, but not alone. I was surrounded by matter and alone. I wanted to step on her feet, but she insisted I dance my own steps.

43

Chapter 42

A knock on my door interrupted a dream where I danced with Vedi. The sun peeked over the east hills, striking my house with a blinding ray, but I managed to make out the hat. I opened the door. "Zeke, why so early?"

"Word, son, got to Olympus about this Scylla incident, and they want my ass on a silver platter."

I ushered him inside. "How much does Olympus know?"

He sat and pointed his hat at me. "They know she escaped from Tartarus and the kid I'm supposed to be keeping out of trouble sent her back while my boys and I were picking our noses."

"Do they know I got tricked into breaking my word to the Empusa?"

He dropped his hat. "Do the Empusa know you were tricked?"

"Yes, the truce still stands, but they won't forgive me for breaking my word because they really wanted Scylla to become their matriarch."

He retrieved his hat from the floor and studied me like he might a rabid dog. "I guess we now know what happens to one of you when you break a solemn vow?"

"I now have something like a split personality where my other self wants to die."

"Damnit, son, I told you not to go there."

"Someone had to, and you and your boys were determined not to."

He turned away. "You realize my boys could have taken Scylla back to Tartarus as easy as landing next to her?"

"Yes, but they had no intention of saving Hunter or interfering with Empusa. Like me, your bosses were led to believe Hunter's sacrifice was part of the ritual. Considering that, it bugs me. Didn't it occur to your bosses that any ritual claiming to require a human sacrifice might be something too big to ignore?"

He chuckled. "You've only been alive what twenty, thirty years? Human sacrifices were common most of some of my superiors' lives."

"Now butts on silver platters will do, right?"

He took a long breath. "Son, I'm really sorry about your state of affairs and I feel like it's my fault."

I sat across from him. "I'm listening."

"I'm back to helping you stay out of trouble until Oliver returns, and all that stuff I said before you went through Thaumus' portal, it's nothing now, especially considering my bosses owe you one for taking care of Scylla for them."

"Okay. I appreciate that but what can you guys do about my death wish."

He rubbed the back of his neck. "I'm afraid not much, son, and I'm afraid Olympus can't do much either. If they could, no one would have had to hide you from your father."

I moved to the edge of my chair. "The Children of Galinthius have some influence over the Empusa. You think they could convince them that this whole thing is just these two Oceanids scheming? Then they'd probably forgive me."

He pointed. "There's a thought. Maybe after they've been caught, I could get them to fess up to it all, and then the Empusas may forgive you."

"They're amazingly clever, but how long could two Oceanids hide from the Children of Galinthius?"

"Well now, son, there's a thing. It's a jurisdiction thing. Thaumus and Electra are dealing with them because Oceanids are under his authority."

"Those two Oceanids have been playing everyone so far and I'm almost certain they're still heading to their endgame."

"Surely they didn't anticipate you defeating Scylla."

I stood. "I think they did. They set her up just like they set me up."

"Okay, son. So, what do you think they're driving at?"

I paced. "There's nothing transparent about their plans, just that they keep achieving the steps in it. Now, if your boys were to go after them, I can't imagine how they could plan their way out of that."

"They already have, it seems."

I grabbed my forehead. "Already have? How?"

"We offered our help and were refused. Unless Thaumus gives us the go ahead, we're not allowed, and Electra has insisted we leave it to her."

"Convenient, right?"

"Maybe if you had some idea what they're trying to do, I could ask again or go over the Titan's head."

"Or maybe I should get another audience."

"I don't know, son. I think you're giving those girls too much credit. I think whatever plans they had were tied up in freeing Scylla and you spoiled it all right there."

"Then why bring Scylla to a platform delicately balanced over a lake of lava?"

"Why go through so much trouble to get you to curse yourself?"

"The last time someone went through this much trouble to hurt me it was because they hated my father, but I don't think two Oceanids would know him."

"They probably just thought it would keep you out of their way while they worked with Scylla."

I shook my head. "No. They're summoning turned out not to need Hunter. They used him just to get me there."

"They wanted Scylla to kill you. It's that simple."

"And we're back to the precarious monolith that made it easy for me to defeat her."

"And, son, you still can't give me the slightest idea of what they're up to that they'd make all these things happen, including setting up Scylla for defeat after summoning her. Getting someone out of Tartarus is quite the task to intentionally throw away the results."

"Melina came to me afterward and told me I wasn't done."

"Okay, but what's she doing at this point. Until you can give me something, at least something as opposed to nothing, I have to leave this alone, and you should too."

"Zeke, this is all I have left to do, to find out what they're up to before I die."

"Son, I just don't see how this demands your time. You should be spending quality time with family and friends."

"Whatever they're up to, it's required so much effort and planning, and they've been so free to kill and destroy people along the way, it can't anything we want to happen."

Chapter 43

Melina and Ayla were in hiding, Zeke's people wouldn't look for them, and while Electra seemed nice enough and reasonably bright; I feared she was too late to the game. I alone possessed the advantage of knowing what we were up against.

The hidden cave near San Francisco remained the residence of the Oceanid, Sandra. My welcome there also remained, which helped me, considering her anger. "I want to tear her eyes out," she shouted in my face.

"Who?"

"But only after cutting her open. I'd want her to see that, and her beating heart after I tear it from her chest."

"Sandra, who are you talking about?"

"My sister Ayla of course. Can you believe she smiled and laughed when she told me what she did to you?"

"I can. Do you know that she and Melina are working together?"

She ran her fingers down my shoulder. Tears formed in the corners of her eyes. I had enough of people crying over me while I was still alive, and I found a rock to sit.

Her tirade continued. "I slapped both the last time I saw them. I would have done more if they didn't have me outnumbered."

"I'd like to catch up with them. Do you have any idea where they might be?"

She blushed. "I suppose if I can't have you, seeing you shred them might be almost as rapturous."

I pondered the room. She sincerely wanted her sisters shredded before her eyes. I noted a pattern with Oceanids. Getting in one's way is rage inducing. Sandra had another thing in common with them. I didn't know her endgame.

"Why did you want to bear me a child so badly that you now want your sister's dead for preventing it?"

She spun to face me. "My plans haven't been prevented yet."

"You have a cure for my condition I don't know about?"

She winked. "You know what they say, Aiden. Love conquers all."

Her turn of a phrase wasn't a lie, but as such things are, it wasn't true either. She had nothing but her self-serving desire to get in my pants.

"Time is against your plans," I said.

"And, so I want Ayala and Melina dead."

"You wanted to be the mother of a god or demigod. I understand that, but why so badly?"

"Why do you want to live?"

Up until then, I suspected Sandra wasn't too bright, but she turned the conversation back onto me and gave me a reason to pause. I didn't have an answer for her question and it bothered me, but my time was precious. "Can you help me find Melina and Ayala?"

"We don't need to. Electra is sending the Empusa after them. I told her not to worry about my feelings if she deals harshly with them."

Her confidence in the Empusa's ability to catch them seemed naive, but it wasn't that that struck me. "How did Electra draft the Empusa into this?"

"Thaumus gave her some."

"Thaumus? I'm confused."

"You didn't know? I would have thought he'd have thanked you for making it possible. After seeing what you did to Scylla, the Empusa came running to Thaumus to make him their patriarch."

"That happened fast."

She caressed my arm. "I don't mean any disrespect, but might your late wife have wanted you to father a child before you die?"

"I want to see Thaumus and Electra. Can you arrange it?"

She pouted. "I guess I'm just a receptionist to you?"

"My late wife still talks to me at times. If I say I like you, can you arrange me a meeting with Thaumus and Electra? It needs to be both."

"Ooh! 'Like.' At least I'm making progress. Yes, sure. I can do that, but they're busy taking on their new responsibilities, so don't expect it to happen tomorrow."

She began to be more useful than annoying. I kissed her on the forehead. "You're definitely better than Ayala and Melina."

Her eyes popped wide and she blushed. "If I get the meeting for tomorrow can I bear your child?"

"You don't believe you can, so there's no point in my answering that."

There was also no point in me asking her if she knew what her sister's endgame was. As a dragon of order, I knew she wanted them shredded, and thus she would have told me their plans if she knew them.

I needed to make the best of my time before meeting with Thaumus and Electra, and I asked myself if there was anything I could address before then. The void and all it came to mean to me came to mind.

I found Hunter at his apartment. Unusual warmth came across in his welcome. "Oh, it's you. I guess I should invite you in."

"Seen or heard anything from Charly?"

"What? Oh yeah, him. No."

Oh, good. Maybe I was done wasting time protecting Hunter. For the first time in our lives I needed something from him, so I needed to entice him. "You're sister's in the void. She spoke to me when I tried to go there."

He gave no outward reaction. "Uh, yeah. Figures she'd beat everyone there."

"Who'd be racing to the void?"

"My great-grandfather, my mother, my sister, they want to talk to Nix."

It made sense. "They think if they can talk to the goddess of chaos, they could become more powerful in chaos magic?"

"It's all gibberish to me. They could just think it's cool."

I had no confidence I could entice his help, but at that point, I may as well ask the favor. "Your mother is the only one of those three still on this side of death and the void. I'd like to talk to her about my experience. Can you get me invited to see her?"

"I don't want to."

"Who saved your life?"

"Would this make us even?"

"It would go a long way."

He grinned. "You're such a wimp. You can't lie, but this is a big favor you're asking of me. Keep that in mind."

It was a big favor, but I didn't think I'd have time to collect the rest of the debt, and I'd take what I could.

Chapter 44

I stood on the sidewalk in front of the Asta's house for half an hour. Mr. Asta crossed his lawn wearing a smoking jacket, leather patches on the elbows. He dressed up for my visit I guessed.

"It's a good thing the city considers you a favorite son, otherwise, where else would you stand?"

I laughed politely. "Is she ready to see me?"

"It took some doing, but I talked her into it."

He opened the door for me and spoke into my ear as I passed. "She's very upset. Try not to push her buttons."

We went upstairs. He led me down the hall and tapped a door. "She wants us to meet in Vedi's old bedroom."

Ms. Asta claimed the only chair in the room—by Vedi's desk. That left her old bed for Mr. Asta and me. Her face looked like a message of death. "Hunter says you think you've seen my daughter?"

I could tell she knew the word 'seen' made an otherwise true statement false. I countered with a correction. "I heard and felt her, but I couldn't see anything."

"I didn't know that a dragon of order can't see underground."

Considering I was asked not to push her buttons, she sure

pushed mine. "I see fine underground. It's in the void where I had trouble."

She winced when I said the word 'void.' I checked Mr. Asta's face and figured I'd better cushion that. "I think Vedi needs my help. I know it's a sensitive subject for you, but for her sake, I need your insight."

"Please, Marilyn, it's our daughter."

She gave her husband the same look she had reserved for me. "If I must."

One of her eyes looked a different direction than the other. "When Vedi was twelve, I came across the notes of one of my grandfather's projects. He wanted to summon Nix, the goddess of chaos. I set out to reproduce his work and Vedi helped me."

"I assume you weren't successful?"

Her wayward eye twitched. "No, we were successful. We got as far as he had."

"Any further?"

"We tried to get a chaos shard to create a portal with. We tried alchemy and summoning creatures to bring us one but to no avail. It was so frustrating."

"You two worked so hard to bring the goddess of chaos here, all while living only a few blocks from my house?"

The awful look on her face relented for a smile. "It would have brought me great pleasure to see her deal with you."

In case I forgot, she hated me. "Well, I don't know why now, but Vedi's in the void. I met her there."

Mr. Asta stood. "She may still be alive. Isn't that wonderful, Marilyn?"

"How could you have met her in the void? You're a dragon of order."

I passed on explaining to her that I have a ticket to the place because of my magic-contract-breaking. I didn't want her to know I did that. "I flew through a chaos portal Melina set up, somehow."

She shook a finger. "No, you must be mistaken. Nix would not have allowed you through."

"You're half right. Nix threw me out, but only after Vedi touched the back of my hand and spoke to me."

Her head joined her finger in shaking, but Mr. Asta grabbed her shoulders. "Marilyn, please. This dragon can't lie. Vedi must be with Nix."

The veins in her face and hands bulged. "I worked too hard to be shown up by my traitorous daughter."

"But honey, this means she's still alive."

Tiny arcs of electricity danced on and passed through her veins. I stood. "Ms. Asta, I could use your help to help Vedi."

With a backhand, she flung her husband into the wall. Arcs trailed like stretchy webs from him. He hit it hard but managed to say, "Honey, please help."

She yelled, each word clear and precise. "I don't want to."

"But, Marilyn, don't you love our daughter?"

"No, you sniveling man. Love is for the weak and ordered, not for chaos."

Blood on the wall told me he could be seriously hurt, and I moved toward him. She eyed me like someone watching the flame on a burning fuse. She went off when I got there.

She pulled the chair out from under her and threw it across the room. Electric arcs acted like strings, keeping the chair under her control. She swung it about like a huge flail. The chair and its trailing arcs passed through interior walls with greater ease than a wrecking ball. Support beams collapsed as the roof began to fall.

Mr. Asta cooperated with me picking him up, and I flew out the window. I landed so I could dispense with my wings.

"She's gone mad," he told me.

I touched the back of his head and something moved through me. It healed him.

The chair continued breaking out of the house, only to swing back in for more destruction. She moved down the hall and the chair pushed further along.

Mr. Asta sat on the ground. "That's not the woman I married."

She shouted indiscernible words. Her tantrum moved up to take out what parts of the roof hadn't fallen in. I wondered how she could gain altitude, considering she destroyed the second floor until the answer became clear. Enough material fell away for us to see her hovering near a gable. Her chair and trailing arcs chopped it up.

"I'll not be shown up by that little traitorous witch," she shouted as the chair dragged her off into the eastern sky.

I joined my father-in-law on the ground. "I doubt the Children of Galinthius are going to like this."

He turned to me. "Do they have anything like restraining orders?"

Chapter 45

My father-in-law and I sat on his back lawn, getting our heads on straight. His house renegotiated its relationship with gravity, now that most of its weight-bearing beams were gone. What remained of the roof and the second floor teetered and creaked. My confidence in the magical authorities did too.

"Now, with a moment to think, I'm not sure if Oliver would want me to contact the Children of Galinthius at this point."

"They'd locate my Marilyn in a snap and take her off to some remote place, right?"

"They've wanted to do that for a while now. This will be all the justification they need."

"And they'd be right to do so."

I paused to reset the mood. "You still love her?"

"I can't say. She's been saying little things here and there that made me suspect she was what we just saw fly over the east hills. She hates me and my children, her own children. I can't see how I could love that."

"So, you want me to go ahead and contact Zeke?"

He grabbed my knee. "No, Aiden. For Vedi's sake, you must not."

"For Vedi?"

"It just dawned on me. Vedi's in the void with Nix. Marilyn wants to use Nix to make her more powerful. If the Children of Galinthius catch Marilyn, she'll tell them about Vedi, and they'll hate that."

"But can they get to her in the void?"

"Based on what Marilyn told me, they're terrified of the void and of Nix. They're ever grateful she's stayed out of everything all this time."

"Then Vedi would be safe from them."

He grabbed my head. "We both want her to come back, don't we?"

I brought us both to our feet. "Yes, absolutely. In that case, you need to take care of your house somehow."

He smiled. "Unlike you, I can tell lies."

"And I need to find a way to contact Oliver without going through Zeke."

I took out my phone and found Sandra's number in my list of incoming calls.

"How are you going to do that?" he asked.

"Thaumus is now the Olympians' superintendent of both sea and land. You'd figure he'd have to have a pretty good way of communicating with them."

Mr. Asta left me to inspect the mound of broken brick, wood, and plaster that used to be his house. Sandra was able to tell me she set up my meeting for the next day, but she didn't have the address yet.

I wanted to find something, anything, I could do to advance my goals in the meantime. I drove into the east hills and drove for a while. If I managed to come across my mother-in-law, fine, though that would be a bit like catching the proverbial tiger by her tail, but what I really wanted was a clear sky for nightfall. This was California after all. There had to be a clear sky somewhere.

Clouds faded away at a field of brown grass. A dusty haze hid distant mountains, but I thought it clear enough. All I needed was night.

I called John, waking him.

"It's like four in the morning. What's up?"

"I'm about an hour to sunset, looking at a clear sky. You know this myth stuff. What might a clear night sky have to do with the void?"

"You're not planning to off yourself. Are you?"

"No, I can't make a night sky fatal to me. I'm just trying to make the best use of my time."

"Oh man. If you weren't in the state that you're in, I'd be pretty pissed with you right now."

"And I wouldn't be calling you right now, but my question could still be important to answer."

"Uh, yeah. The goddess of the void, Nix, is associated with the night sky because the ancients thought they were looking into the void when they looked at it."

"Well, the ancients may not have been too far wrong. Vedi is with Nix in the real void and for some reason, she can talk to me through clear night skies."

"Nix? You mean Nix is real? I thought she was a sort of myth of myths. You know. What an Olympian tells you when asked where they came from."

"You mean the myths say she's the mother of the gods or something?"

"Well, many cultures' mythology speaks of primordial gods and goddesses, often a chaos god is one of them. That's the case with Nix in the myths surrounding the Olympians."

"Scylla referred to her as the one who stays out."

"That makes sense. She's seldom if ever mentioned as having anything to do with happenings."

"So, if someone could involve her, they might achieve something significant?"

"If one's goal is chaos, who really wants chaos. We know Vedi ultimately didn't."

"Thanks, John. The sun is setting, and sorry about waking you."

I wondered if Vedi would still talk to me through the night sky after I visited her in the void. Our connection seemed fragile to me. I worried I might have broken it.

"Aiden, my mother's gone mad."

I hadn't broken it. "Vedi, I'm going to try and get a message to Oliver, and not tell Zeke."

"Thank you."

"Can you tell me where she might go?"

Her words faded in an out so all I heard was, *"Great-grandfather's home,"* and what sounded like *"Georgia."* I knew her great-grandfather lived in his entire life on another world. That made what sounded like 'Georgia' curious. I asked her to repeat herself, but clouds rolled in, and a thunderstorm chased me into my car.

While I couldn't stay wet for more than a few seconds, I still didn't like not being able to see through all the water drops in my eyes and steam in the air. Besides, I needed to head back if I hoped to get good rest before my meeting with Thaumus and Electra.

The storm struck me as flukish. Not only did it come out of nowhere, but it worked its way up to baseball-sized hail. One stone shattered my windshield. The restoration power I had developed came in handy. Otherwise, my car wouldn't have made it home.

That night I wondered what Vedi's words meant. If Marilyn Asta has some way of going to another world, I couldn't follow, and if she was going to Georgia, I didn't have a clue as to why.

Chapter 46

A man built a mansion south of San Jose, high in the hills where no trees grew, leaving it exposed to the sun. The integrity of his business plans fared no better than the mansion's paint, and he was forced to sell it at a bargain price. That price went unpaid for twenty-five years until the day before my appointment. Thaumus wanted a place to hold court and the remote mansion suited him. At least that's what Sandra told me.

All the driving uphill pushed my car's coolant system to its limit, which wasn't far. I popped the hood and one of my hoses had a hole in it. I guessed the previous night's hailstones did more than shatter the windshield. One must have bounced off the road and ping-ponged around the engine compartment.

Thanks to magic, I could mend the hose, but I couldn't create water. Only I traveled that road, allowing me to fly most of the rest of the way.

Painting and roofing crews climbed and crawled around the mansion's exterior as I walked to its entrance. One of the doors swung open. Thaumus stood grinning before me in Bermuda shorts and a Hawaiian shirt.

"Aiden. Come on in."

He led me past large empty rooms to a furnished one in the back. It had a view of the western mountains. "My responsibilities now include both sea and land."

I nodded respectfully to Electra, despite her success at appearing mundane in a blue blouse and tight jeans. "I don't want to interrupt your transition, but I'm afraid I'm in some need of a favor from Thaumus."

Thaumus put his arm around me. "I'm in a generous mood and especially for you, my dragon friend. What is it?"

The word 'friend' fell through a hole in his sincerity but at least his offer was sincere.

"My mother-in-law has gone berserk, destroyed her own house and flew off to the east in a mad rage. I don't want to tell Zeke about it before Oliver knows."

He moved his hand around like a toy plane. "You mean she magically flew off?"

I nodded.

"Ewe," he said.

"I figured since the Olympians are now counting on you to administer all things magical on both sea and land, you must have a way to get messages to them."

"Absolutely I do, Aiden, and absolutely I will, right-away."

His degree of honesty amazed me. I wondered if I should pinch myself. I also wondered why his arm still hung around my shoulders.

Electra gave him a stern look and softened for me. "Whatever made her go into such a rage?"

These two didn't need to know about the Asta's experiments with chaos portals and their goal of communing with Nix. I chose my answer with that in mind. "Jealousy."

"Jealousy of whom? My wayward sisters' managing to get their hands on a chaos portal?"

"I don't recall that being mentioned to her, but I told her I entered the void and Nix sent me back. She could have been jealous that I got to meet the goddess of chaos."

She studied me. "You had an audience with Nix? You surprise me. Very impressive."

Thaumus' face flushed. "Did she say anything to you?"

"She told me I couldn't stay and had to leave."

"You're a lawful dragon, right? You can't lie to me."

"I haven't changed in that regard since we first met. You know I can't lie, at least not knowingly."

"She won't let you stay there, and why would you want to?"

"You know what Ayla and Melina did to me. I'm supposed to be bound for the void now."

Electra cocked an eyebrow. "That, lord Thaumus, tells you what sort of dragon he is."

"And that would be?"

"He's not of law and good, as you suspected, and not of law and evil. He's only of order, not even law so much as its spirit, order."

"So, what does that tell us that Zeke and Olympus wouldn't want us to know?"

"I don't know, but it tells us he should know whenever we're lying to him."

The truth of their words relieved me. They somehow didn't connect what I was to my father.

Thaumus took his arm off me. "Then I should come clean, so to speak. I don't fancy men."

I hoped to bargain at this point. "If I don't ask you why you wanted to save Hunter, can you get Kern to forgive me?"

Electra slapped him. "You'd rather make me think your eyes were wandering to a young man than tell the truth to this dragon?"

He cowered out of her reach. "Electra. Please forgive me. I only wanted Hunter saved in the hopes that in so doing, Aiden would keep Scylla in Tartarus."

He turned and I nodded. He told the truth.

"Now that you're his boss, can you get Kern to forgive me, so I'll be freed of my self-destructive-self?"

He thought on my question. Electra pushed him. "Come on, Thaumus. You owe him that."

"I can't order him to forgive you as that would make it insincere and thus ineffective at removing your curse, but I can try to convince him."

188

"Thaumus," she growled.

He waved his hand like a white flag. "And I will, I will."

I stepped back, as more seemed to be between them than about me. "Thank you, Lord Thaumus."

I couldn't believe I just tried to butter him up with the title. It showed me how desperate I'd become. I lowered my head, not sure if it was out of shame or fear of my condition.

Electra's hand touched my shoulder. "Come with me Aiden. I'll see you out properly."

We reached the door and I remembered my car. "Do you have a couple gallons of water in a form I can carry back to my car?"

She went off somewhere and came back with two milk-cartons full of water. It was my turn to study her. "Thank you, and I could have carried those here for you. You're amazingly kind."

She handed me the jugs and huffed. "I want you to know, dragon, that those two sisters of mine will be dealt with very harshly, especially Ayla. You are like a guest on the Earth and don't deserve such treachery."

I walked out of sight of the work crews and became a large enough dragon that my wings could carry the water. When I got to the car and popped the hood, to my surprise, the radiator and over-flow were already full of water.

A note clung to the overflow with tape that read, "Sorry about the hail."

Nothing more was written, no signature. I told myself I didn't need another mystery.

Chapter 47

Hope lighted and flew off before I even gave Thaumus a chance to talk Kern into forgiving me, but I thought John might find more in knowing I tried, and not just biding my time before finding justice in Terra Del Fuego. That is where I hid the dark blade.

I gave him a call. "Hey, John."

"Aiden. Much better time to call than last time. I'm still in the hoard chamber, but I need to be making my way back to the hotel soon."

End of days or not, I had to ask. "The chamber gets cell coverage?"

"Yeah. I haven't found anything yet that could kill you, but I have found a mini-portal. It's like a magic dumbwaiter. I don't know where the other end of it is, but it gets full bars there."

"That's convenient."

"Convenience, oh boy. That's all I need, right? I don't need to be speeding up your death, but there it was for me to find."

"About that, I want you to know that I'm trying to beat this. I just finished asking the Empusas' new boss to see if he can get this curse off me."

"So, you think maybe I can come home before this inventory search is done? The Smithsonian has nothing over your ancestor."

"I don't have high hopes, but at least there was an angle to try and I tried it."

"Damnit Aiden, then why tell me?"

"I wanted you to know I haven't given up completely."

"Just mostly?"

"John, while I have you on the phone, I'll tell you this now. Set a few million's worth of artifacts aside for yourself as a gift from me. That way if I die, you won't lose everything."

"You idiot, Aiden!"

I had to note he didn't mean it literally or even as an offense. Someone not what I am might not have known that, but even in knowing, it still made me blink. "John?"

"You think I'm in this for your wealth, or for your power? Ever since that day in the third grade when my joy-buzzer backfired on me, I've been in this for you."

"That was just a sorcerer's spell to keep me from losing my temper."

"Aiden. I know that. That's why my joke didn't work on you, why no one got away with anything in any class you attended, but that's not what made me your friend. You, you did that."

"If I recall correctly, you did that. You kept knocking on my door after school until I called you my friend. You've been my friend ever since."

"If I die before you do, me being mortal and all, that's how it should be, but if you do, I'm a young man well on my way to a doctorate in a field I love. I'll survive, but without you, I won't be missing your hoard. I'll be missing knowing you're there to do what you do."

"That's why I want you to set those artifacts aside, so I can continue taking care of you after I'm gone."

"You're still missing it, Aiden. I caught a glimpse of it the day we first met and again that day when you plucked me out of the rubble in New York. It's like there's a cause that's chosen you. Being mortal, I may not live long enough to see what it is, but I don't want to live to see you die before you see it through."

Wind and an airplane in the background of his phone told me he left the hoard chamber. I wondered what I could tell him that he shouldn't already know. "John. Just do it as a favor to me. Set a few millions' worth aside for yourself and do all the papers on it you need to make it yours. I'll sign whatever's needed."

"Okay. I'm committed to setting that stuff aside and you're committed to sign the paperwork. I'll take that deal, but only because it assures me you'll not off yourself before we've both done our parts."

I ended the call as my dragon conscious demanded. "I hope that deal will make you feel better for the time, but I must say, I fear I don't see a cause beyond order."

The cruel coldness of it didn't miss my notice, but I couldn't encourage what I saw as a false hope. That would be like lying. A lump hit the bottom of my throat as I imagined John's reaction to the call ending as it did.

The Scamp purred all the way home and after dinner with Nikki, the woman who thinks she's my mother and may as well be, it purred back into the hills to meet a clear night sky. Near the observatory I talked to Vedi, a conversation always starting with her.

"You need Hunter," she said.

"Vedi? What?"

"My mother's gone mad."

"Your father and I have agreed to not tell the Children of Galinthius."

"They're going to find out. You need Hunter."

"What can Hunter do to help?"

"Tell him I need the shard."

"How do we get something to you?"

"Get the shard and it will become clear."

"What's going on, Vedi?"

A large cloud swept into the sky and showed no signs of leaving. I drove to Hunter's apartment. His being there amazed me. I figured he'd be out stealing from homeless people or one of his other hobbies.

He opened the door and waved me inside. "So, you're saving my life means I have to let you bother me at my apartment a lot?"

"I could normally think of much better things to do with my time, but Vedi gave me an instruction for you."

He slammed the door. "She wants me to dig her stuffed animals out of the rubble?"

"She told me to tell you she needs the shard. I don't know what it is, but she wants it."

"Of course, you don't know what a chaos shard is, legal beagle."

I laughed. "Legal Beagle isn't just the kindest nickname you've come up with for me, but I think the most creative. Now as for this chaos shard. She says that once you give it to me, things will become clear."

"Uh, okay, follow me to the graveyard."

Chapter 48

A witch and a dragon walked into a graveyard at night. I've got no punch-line for that as it wasn't that kind of joke. The joke was on me, the dragon. My mission depended on Hunter, a man I thought no one would ever trust with a task they wanted done right.

Just through a metal latticed entry arch, he put his hands on my shoulders and stopped me. "It's best you stay here until I get the shard."

"Why?"

"You don't want to know."

He started to walk away but stopped. "If you see a guard, talk to him."

Great. I knew enough then to grasp what he meant by 'you don't want to know.' Whatever he needed to do to get the shard required trespassing or perhaps worse. His plan to have me talk to any guards who happened along held a sort of accidental brilliance. Not only would it distract and delay them, but it would alert Hunter to their approach. Its brilliance had to be accidental because Hunter was almost completely unteachable and not bright enough to think all of that through.

Heavy stone drug on stone a couple times then footsteps came up behind me.

"You lost?"

A woman in a private security uniform shined a flashlight at me. This was to be the point in Hunter's plan when I'd start a conversation long enough to give him time for whatever it was I didn't want to know.

"No," I said. Not much in terms of word count.

She also wasted few words. "The cemetery is closed at night. You should move along."

I had no options. I moved to the street and she must have read my face. She moved past me into the cemetery to look around. Never use a dragon of order as a lookout when trying to sneak something out of a graveyard.

I figured the best I could do at that point would be to find a perch somewhere and watch. I looked for something to serve my purposes but before I did, I heard her voice again. "You're Aiden Ferris, aren't you?"

She came back.

"Yes, I am Aiden Ferris."

"The police are always telling me what a good citizen you are, and if you ask me, that's just odd. Who talks about good citizens? Kind of makes me wonder."

I spotted Hunter walking out of a mausoleum. Again, his plan, no doubt, would have had me keeping her talking long enough for him to escape notice. I had no interest in helping him deceive her, but her words required something from me anyway. "I'm compulsively honest and respectful of property and law enforcement. I guess that makes me a sort of freak."

"Uh huh. That makes sense, so why were you just standing in the graveyard?"

This woman needed a recommendation for real police-work, but for right then she wasn't making me happy.

"My brother-in-law and I came here because of a message from my dead wife."

Her jaw dropped. "Uh, did you say your dead wife?"

"My dead wife sent us a message."

She shined her flashlight into the cemetery, but Hunter stood just a few feet from her. She backed up. "Is this your brother-in-law?"

I walked over and grabbed him. "Yes, and we should be leaving now so you can do your job."

We walked away to her tilted gaze. Hunter whispered, "You just told her?"

I shrugged. "When all else fails, the truth can confuse as well as any smoke screen."

"You told her Vedi's dead. Don't you think she's alive?"

"Private or not, that woman's law enforcement so in their language, anyway, but I honestly don't know. Your father may be more confident than I am."

He nudged me. "Hold out your hand."

I did as he said. He dropped a piece of a metal familiar to me, the same metal the dark blade was made of. It was unmistakable, somehow black but at recurring glimpses, also gold. It was shaped like a flattened teardrop and about the size of a good skipping stone. It chilled my palm like an ice cube.

"Aiden?" asked Vedi.

Clouds hung in the night sky and Hunter stumbled along oblivious. "Is she talking to you?" he said.

"Yes. Vedi?"

"Good. Then Hunter's given you the shard. Tell him 'thank you' for me."

Hunter waived. "Tell her she's welcome and I'm headed for bed now."

I admired the mysterious symbols on the shards surface. "I take it these symbols make this piece of dark metal what it is?"

"Yes. A chaos shard."

I cringed. "Chaos? Why does it have to be called that?"

"Because, silly boy, that's what it is. My great-grandfather created two of them to try and commune with Nix."

I took a breath rather than throw the thing away. "Okay, so now I'm holding onto a chaos shard. What do you need to be done with it?"

"*Two things. First, you need to be careful not to step through any portals or allow yourself to be teleported while you're in contact with the shard.*"

"Why?"

"*Because, pretty boy, Nix doesn't want to see your face in her void.*"

"What? What do you have me carrying around?'

"*It will turn any teleportation, whether by portal or any other means into a trip to the void.*"

"Seems appropriately named, but okay, what's the other thing I need to do with this?"

"*You need to plant it on my mother.*"

"Give it to her?"

"*No. That won't work. She can't know she has it on her. Nix needs her to try and use a portal and end up in the void.*"

"You want her with you, but not me?"

"*Aiden, I want to be with you more than anyone else, but I'm stuck here.*"

"So, Nix wants her company but not mine?"

"*As so often, my beloved Aiden, you're only half right. Nix is going to put her someplace where she won't bother anyone, including Nix.*"

"So, how does that differ from what the Children of Galinthius would do with her?"

"*They must not discover I'm in the void.*"

I reached my car. "Okay. How do I find your mother?"

"*If you're going to beat a flying witch to Georgia, you're going to need to book a direct flight to Atlanta.*"

"If you had wings."

"*What's that, Aiden?*"

"Just an old airline slogan that jumped into my head. It seems especially silly right now."

50

Chapter 49

Last minute airline flights are expensive for folks without dragon hoards, bet even having one, it's not without a price I care about. People in certain government agencies take notice when airline travelers act strangely. Getting a last-minute flight to Atlanta from San Francisco is a little strange, but just one day after doing the same for an employee to Slovenia, that's a lot strange.

I spent the flight worrying I might be delayed by hard questions on the other end. The answer to what all these last-minute flights are about would not be easy for me. I can't tell them John's looking through my hoard. I can't tell them I'm chasing down a witch. I especially can't tell them part of me is suicidal. I've practiced strategies to avoid answering certain questions, but I'd have to hope whoever asks these isn't as good at cornering me as the security guard at the cemetery.

After landing in Atlanta and docking, I walked down the walkway to the terminal. I did my best to use my peripheral vision to look out for anyone looking like law enforcement. My heart jumped at the sight of a sign with my name on it.

A round man of humble stature held it. He wore a three-piece suit and two men with badges on their belts stood two paces behind him. It struck me as odd that law enforcement would use a sign, but the man's stature didn't seem to say Empusa either.

I stepped over to him. "Did Thaumus send you?"

He returned a cold look. "No, Olympus. Are you the one who broke the dragon contract?"

Uh oh. I wasn't expecting that. Our words thus far could have been the words of high tech people talking software-related business solutions and company divisions, but they were about something much more fatal.

"I am Aiden Ferris, yes."

He dropped the sign and I stepped back. I knocked into another departing passenger. A large smile flashed across the face of the man with the sign. He extended his hand. "That's the answer Aiden Ferris would give to that question. Pleased to meet you, son of order."

The passenger moved by, not giving me a chance to apologize, and I turned back to shake the hand of the man with the sign.

"I'm Dr, Gabriel Schalken," he said.

"What's Olympus want?"

He folded his sign and tucked it under his arm. "Come with me and I'll explain."

No sooner than had we started when the two men with badges stepped in our way. "Aiden Ferris?" said one of them.

Gabe waved at them with a shooing motion. "He's with me."

"One of your cases, Schalken? By all means. We wouldn't dream of taking one of those from you."

They cleared the way for us and we left them at the gate. I waited until they were well behind us. "You're Dr. Gabriel Schalken and Olympus sent you?"

"More accurately, I work for them. I'm the psychoanalyst to the gods."

Walking down the promenade, we were isolated in a sea of people going places—safe enough for us to talk.

"Zeus thinks I need to see a shrink?"

"I've been keeping an office here in Atlanta lately, and when I found out you were passing through, I thought I should see you."

"Zeus is here?"

He paused and patted my back. "Oh no. They almost never come to Earth anymore, and by the way, I answer to Athena. She's had me here for various reasons, but none so demanding I can't spend a little time with you."

"Well, then talk fast. I've got a rental car reserved."

"Cancel that. I'm going to be your chauffeur."

I halted. "No offense to you or Athena but I'm in a hurry."

He grinned. "To catch your mother-in-law before the Children of Galinthius do?"

"How could you possibly know that?"

"Olympus got your message about your mother-in-law going on a mad rage."

"But my message didn't say I was going after her."

"Correct, and nor did it say you're carrying one of Dak's chaos shards."

"You'd better have a really good explanation for how you know what you claim to know."

He looked about. "You said you were in a hurry and we're just standing here."

I grabbed him. "How do you know these things?"

"Athena can tell you what the weather in Japan is by watching someone buy a candy bar in Atlanta."

He studied my grip on him.

A voice in my head said, *'Trust him. Nix says she trusts him and Athena.'*

"Vedi?"

I let go. He brushed himself off. "Do you have luggage to claim or do we go straight to my car?"

We went straight to his car—an old silver Mercedes from the sixties, apparently the last decade the Olympians wanted to buy cars in.

"Where to?" he asked.

Vedi gave me directions and I passed them on.

Traffic leaving the city crawled, giving us plenty of opportunity to talk.

"I've met your father once," he said.

"How recently?"

"Back when he had to deal with Dak."

"You don't look that old."

"Working for the Olympians has amazing health benefits, but the reason I mentioned your father is that nasty dragon contract of yours."

"I've got two of me now. One, you're talking to and the other wants to kill me."

"Yes, that is quite the problem."

"You've got any solutions that don't involve my other-self getting his way?

"That's not how psychoanalysts work. I help you discover solutions on your own."

"You actually think you can remove a magic curse with psycho-analysis?"

"No, but we can strengthen your mind against it."

"Okay. Go. Do it."

"You're going to have to talk to me more than me to you, but we can cheat a little. Athena loves to speak in cryptic ways and she gave me something to tell you."

"What?"

"Your magic contract calls for a justice that requires you to die, but she says your death would be an injustice."

"Order must be honored. I must die for the sake of order."

"So, you're saying your death will achieve a greater good than yourself?"

"I am not as important as the order I have lived for."

"Athena told me you'd answer this way and if she were here, she'd remind you that only the one who can defeat death achieves a greater good through his own death. All others, though noble, are at best staving off a greater evil."

"Don't soldiers die for their country and achieve a greater good?"

"In battle. So, Aiden, where is your battle?"

Chapter 50

"My battle is inside me."

"And that, Aiden, is a good place to start examining yourself. How about we leave things there for the time being and talk about your father."

"Don't psychoanalysts usually like to start with mothers?"

"That's the stereotype, indeed."

"So, why not there first?"

"Because we left things with you thinking about the battle within you and if that can make your death productive. Now we're two men on a road-trip, and I thought you might want to hear about when I met your father."

"I do, but no matter how wasteful my death would be, it doesn't change the contract that binds me to it."

He wagged his finger. "Eh eh eh, young man, you're not on Dr. Schalken's couch right now. Let where we left it to swim in the back of your mind. Right now, we're two guys passing the time. How about I tell you about when your father and my paths crossed?"

I could no more press the older point than I could stay in a place I was unwelcome. "Okay. Were you my father's psychoanalyst?"

"No. As a matter of fact, I was on a sort of sabbatical. My

work with Ares hadn't worked out so well. He needed major magical medical attention and I didn't want to work anymore. Athena still believed in me and insisted I take some time to clear my head."

"If my father is anything like me, I can't imagine how meeting him could help in that."

"He is a lot like you, and I didn't seek him out. Like I said, our paths crossed."

"How?"

"Dak."

"You met him too?"

"I wanted to. Athena would not have approved, but my curiosity got the better of me. He was obviously a madman, and I wondered how madness and extreme power interacted. Sabbatical or not, I was compelled to find out."

"I understand compulsions like that."

A dimple formed on him. "More than I do, I'm sure, but yes, it's similar. I wanted to find a way to get ahead of the pursuit of Dak but instead, I only managed to see his final battle."

"That must have been a sight to see."

"He gave himself an immense dragon form, albeit a bit clumsy. Clumsy or not, it took three elder gold dragons to cut him off in a pass long enough for your father to come up and block off the other side. Four heroic mortals with artifacts and a powerful member of the Children of Galinthius were all involved, and I'm not sure with how much less they could have managed."

"Wow! I didn't know Dak became that powerful."

"Yes, and to think he didn't complete that one project with the chaos shards, one of which you carry on your person."

"I don't need to be reminded of the risk I'm taking."

He cleared his throat. "After the battle, your father found me. I thought I had hidden out of sight of everyone, but he knew I was there the whole time. He flew off, changed to winged human form and came back so that only I could see him."

"Did he know who you are?"

"Precisely. That's why he came to me. He wasted no time for

chit-chat. He just landed, shook my hand and said, 'take care of Athena,' and left."

"He knew something about her being in danger?"

Gabe concentrated on the road. "He beat me at my own game."

"He did what?"

"He knew that in me feeling sorry for myself I could potentially let Athena down."

I turned away. "Am I back on the couch now?"

"Oh no. You're not feeling sorry for yourself, Aiden. You're bound by a magical contract. You didn't foul up the counseling to someone so that they almost got themselves killed. You got tricked into breaking a promise. Those really are different."

"You're not totally sincere when you say that."

"Yes, of course. There are clear differences but there are parallels. I didn't intend for you to find an answer for your curse in my account, but I did expect you to look for one."

I accepted his explanation because it was honest, not because I understood it. I spent the rest of the drive imagining Gabe psychoanalyzing Epimetheus.

Vedi's directions took us to an abandoned farmhouse near the Georgia Mountains.

Gabe spoke right after shutting off the engine. "This is an interesting place. I'll be interested to figure out what it is about this place that Athena couldn't find it."

Vedi spoke. *"The basement has an outside entrance. Find it and take care going in."*

The situation seemed suspicious. I studied Gabe for non-verbal signals but found nothing unusual. He returned my stare. "Well?"

"I just led you to someplace you've been wanting to find?"

"It's okay, Aiden," said Vedi.

He pointed two fingers at me and then back at himself. "Check my words, son of order, we're on the same side."

"Nix tells me this place is as important to Athena as it is to her," said Vedi.

Between her words and his sincerity, my suspicions were more than dispelled. "Let's find the entrance to the basement. It's on the outside."

We found it around the house's backside. An exterior stairwell led to the door. I led the way. Vedi warned, *"Step in with care lest you enter a portal."*

I stopped at the door. "One point and one question."

Gabe almost ran into me. "What and what?"

"The point is that there's supposed to be a portal in here, so we should take care not to accidentally enter it. The question is how I can enter this place without an invitation from a resident?"

Gabe grabbed the door handle and moved me aside. "Athena and I have known about the portal. That's what we were looking for. We're still cleaning up after an incident and this is one of the last few items we have left to take care of."

I stepped back to give him more room with the door. "And as for my questions?"

He turned the handle and opened the door with his shoulder. Dust flew about as he stepped through the doorway. "This place was the property of a fugitive which I, amongst others dealt with. That means I have authority from Olympus to confiscate it and as of now, I have. Welcome."

I guessed he pretty much completed his business with the place, as in we found it. My business, or rather Vedi and Nix's, still lay ahead.

Chapter 51

Gabe found a light switch and flipped it. A naked bulb lit in the rafters. Cobwebs partitioned the room until I touched one. They flashed like negative images and vanished.

"You did that?" asked Gabe.

"Yes, passively, but making the light bulb work was someone else's doing."

"You wouldn't expect the light in an abandoned basement to work would you?"

Other things stood out in the basement, or rather they didn't. Nothing in the room competed with a glowing arch standing under a set of stairs to an interior door above. Nothing else took up space there. Nothing hid the portal. Nothing distracted from it.

The portal's gold-plated frame cried out to be burgled, prompting a question. "How long has this been here?"

Gabe rubbed the frame. "Well dusted. This is how one hides something from the mind of Athena, by not trying to hide it."

"Place a portal in an easy to access basement where it stands out and could easily be stolen by a curious looter?"

"Yes. And by being intentionally foolish."

I stood close to the portal. "Any idea what's on the other side of this?"

"A place near where your father fought Dak. You, of course, shouldn't go there. Some of those gold dragons still live in that land and they would be burdened to learn of you."

Strangeness emanated from the portal. "Is there a residence on the other side of this?"

"I suspect Dak's old lair."

"And he's dead."

"Yes, of course."

"Someone must live there now."

Gabe half-smiled. "Why do you say that?"

"Whoever lives on the other side of this portal considers me welcome. I sense it."

He coughed. "Uh, um, well, then you most definitely shouldn't go there."

"Besides the gold dragons that may realize whose son I am, why?"

"Try and think of the list of individuals, not on Earth, who could possibly see you as welcome. Take away various Olympians, who I can tell you it's none of them, and you'd be left with a very short list that includes your father."

"You think it could be my father?"

He wagged his hand. "I'm not saying that. It's just that we don't know, but we know enough not to find out."

I stepped back from the portal. It made him nervous, so it did the same to me.

"I wouldn't go there if I stepped through anyway."

"Ah yes. That shard you carry. Why do you?"

My mother-in-law is probably coming to use this portal and I'm supposed to plant the shard on her without her knowing."

"Someone has asked a great deal of the son of order. Are you going to trick her, place an item into her possession without her permission?"

I waited for Vedi to explain herself. In my hurry to get ahead of

Marilyn Asta, I failed to think how I could do things tantamount to either deceit or invasion of property.

"Aiden, you've got to find a way."

Gabe tapped the side of his head and grinned. "I may not be Hephaestus, but I've watched masters of magic gadgetry work enough that maybe I can try something."

"What's your idea?"

He held out his hand. "Hand me the shard and we'll see."

"Nix says to trust him."

I wondered since Nix's judgment had included asking me to do what's impossible for me to do, perhaps I shouldn't be too quick to trust her judgment in trusting Gabe. That convoluted thought ended with me dropping the black metal shard into Gabe's hand. I trusted Gabe myself.

He felt around the portal frame. "Aiden, see if you can find something we can hang over the portal and something I can attach this shard to it with."

"Is the plan the sort I'm best off not knowing?"

"Get me those things and we'll see."

I searched the house. I found two sheets covering furniture and brought them to Gabe. "The large one should be able to cover the portal and we could rip up the smaller one to make rope."

Gabe took the larger sheet. "This will do nicely, but I'm afraid rope can't be wrapped through the portal."

He climbed halfway up the stairs and leaned through the railing. "Stand beneath me and make sure I don't accidentally drop the shard through."

He placed the shard on top of the frame and balanced it there. The portal's frame filled with darkness and the sense of welcome stopped emanating from it. We carefully hung the sheet from the railing so that it obscured the portal.

He rubbed the dust from his hands. "Now we just need to get her to rush through without noticing it's become a chaos portal."

"How did you know resting the shard on top would make this portal into a chaos portal?"

"Contact between the mechanism of any portal by a chaos shard will make it into chaos portal."

"See, Aiden, we knew there'd be a way."

"Okay, everyone. How do we make sure she runs through without looking to see what it is?"

Gabe raised a finger. "Psychology, my dear dragon, psychology."

He laid out the plan, one I could play a role in and we waited for Marilyn's arrival. I crouched beside the door and Gabe stayed out by his car. We waited for over an hour before the sound of an unstable transformer approached and stopped.

"Leave me," came her voice.

"I work for Olympus, and I'm here to advise you to turn yourself into the children of Galinthius," said Gabe.

He told me earlier this should make her more determined to get to the portal. Footsteps approaching proved he got that right. The doorknob turned, and Gabe shouted something. "Teleporting cat approaching."

Our plans didn't involve shouting that, besides he spoke the truth when he said it. My part of the plan was to confront her when she came through the door so that she'd flee through the portal without looking. I knew I had to change that to something quicker.

When her wrist showed, starting to push in the door, I grabbed it and yanked her in.

She screamed. "Oh no, son of death, you won't stop me."

I threw her through the portal. The blanket fell around her and went through with her. The portal returned to its normal glow and I noticed the reason. The blanket's fall knocked the shard to the floor. I dove to pick it up. I knew what was coming.

Before I could reach my feet again, one of the Children of Galinthius stood on all fours in the middle of the basement, all white fur with amber eyes. A voice in my head, not Vedi's, a male voice spoke to me. "Where's the witch?"

I didn't want to answer so I did it the only way the son of order could, with silence. He closed his eyes in a way I recognized as feline for, 'okay, be that way.'

The ground began to shake and more of his words entered my

head. "I am Thumper, son of the late Rumbler, who was friends with your father. Where's the witch?"

His father had a unique talent, besides being their greatest tele-porter, he could cause earthquakes. His father and mine were good friends. What a pair they must have made.

The ground shaking threatened to take away my balance and I feared I might fall through the portal. "You don't want me to fall through that portal."

He whipped his tail about and closed his eyes again. My experi-ence with the cat form of a cursed sorcerer allowed me to recognize the subtle difference between the one that means, 'okay, be that way," and this one which meant, 'your way this time.'

The quake stopped.

"We've got her where we want her. Go ahead and tell Thumper."

"She went to the void. Nix tricked her into going there."

He hissed, but at the portal, not me. "Nix is active after thou-sands of years? Son of Ferus, stay away from the goddess of chaos."

"She's been making that easy so far."

Thumper vanished.

Chapter 52

Gabe stumbled in the door. "What was that?"

I finally reached my feet. "You shouted 'teleporting cat.' Don't you know?"

"The quaking. What was that?"

"I guess Rumbler's son inherited his father's talent."

Gabe inspected the portal. "This survived. Where's the shard?"

"I picked it up before he noticed it, I think."

"A wise precaution. Rumbler having a son with his father's talent isn't something the Children of Galinthius have shared with us."

He spoke with a curious confidence.

"You would know if anyone in Olympus knew this?"

"Athena would. For an Olympian, even not talking to her tells her many things, and such a major asset being available would not escape her."

"So, do you think they may be up to something?"

"If I had to guess, I'd say they're growing increasingly untrusting of Olympus. Hiding you on Earth and protecting the Asta's from them makes them nervous, to say the least."

"I don't trust them. They always seem to be working against me."

"Funny how you, the Empusa, and the Children of Galinthius can all be on the side of order, and yet you lock horns so often."

He hid a point for me in that statement, but I didn't want to find it. "I do what I do because I have to. I suspect they get to bend things."

He pulled out his phone. "I'm getting a good amount of bars out here."

"You calling in where the portal is?"

He started for the exit stairs. "Once we're on the road back to Atlanta. The cleanup crew doesn't need to be meeting you."

Vedi spoke to me as we moved to Gabe's car. "*I am so happy that you still have the shard. Talking to you like this is almost like being with you again.*"

I suspect Gabe must have read my face. "Keeping that shard allows you to hear her, doesn't it?"

"Yes. Yes, it does. She's happy I still have it."

He started driving. "She has a sense of duty like you do apparently."

"What makes you say that?"

"She gave you Nix's instructions which involved you giving it up."

Vedi interjected, "*Tell him thank you for me.*"

"She's grateful that you found a way to use the shard that didn't require me giving it up."

"Ah, yes, and you're most welcome, Vedi Ferris."

Gabe's deliberateness caused me to think about every little thing he'd say or do. I guessed he went out of his way to call her Vedi Ferris instead of just Vedi in some effort to remind me of who she is to me.

"I'm grateful too," I said.

A few miles down the road he made his call. I insisted he let me operate his phone for him, so he wouldn't be in violation of any driving laws.

After he finished talking to some woman clicking away at a keyboard somewhere, I whined some. "They're not going to help me with any of this."

"Oh, you might be surprised. Athena loves to solve people's problems all while not letting on she's doing it."

"No. I'm sorry. I meant the Children of Galinthius."

"Oh them. Of course. Silly of me."

"So, you think I'm right about them?"

"I'm not sure I can say that, as I don't know everything you're thinking about them, but it's probably a good thing you and I met."

"That good thing has something to do with them?"

"Athena and I have to work with them quite often, and we have a policy with them, even with her personal attendant, Theberaz. Keep them in the dark until we need them."

"Why? Because you can't trust them?"

"For quite the opposite reason, because we can trust them to do what they believe they must, no matter the cost."

"So, that should become your policy with me as well, I guess."

He leaned back and smiled as if to emphasize what he was about to say. "It's not."

Chapter 53

Gabe's answer bothered me. It should have encouraged me, but I'm a dragon of order. "Doesn't Athena see that I do what I believe I must, no matter the cost?"

"How does the son of order treat the property of the law-fearing?"

"I only enter it when welcomed by an occupant."

"Who welcomed you into the United Nations building?"

"Athena must know that. The Egyptian ambassador."

"Does such a welcome give you license to destroy the building?"

"They weren't so law abiding as a whole, and I needed to bring down the building onto the automaton in order to save the world from falling into chaos."

"What sort of laws were these leaders not abiding by?"

I studied my hands and had to ask myself why. Did I expect them to change? The same force that changed them into claws acted on them, but in the opposite direction. If they had been claws, they would have changed to hands, but as they were already hands, what could they become?

The easier question was Gabe's.

"The purpose of law is to maximize individual liberty to as many as possible," I answered.

"So, you concluded that laws that limit liberty are the opposite of laws?"

"Unless a greater evil is prevented by it."

"Thus, Aiden, armed with this reasoning, you justified destroying the United Nations building?"

"It was the right choice."

"Perhaps. I'm not here to argue that with you, but right choice or not, it wasn't what the rules you're magically bound to would have dictated."

"I didn't violate my nature. I was true to it, just as I've always been until those Oceanids trapped me."

Gabe concentrated on passing a car. "You didn't violate your nature in the same way using the opposing lane to pass doesn't break the law?"

"I suppose that's similar."

"You suppose?"

"Well, I'm not sure, but it sounds close."

"You can't tell a lie, even if it's really just a guess. That's the only way in which you're like the Children of Galinthius, the only way in which you will do what you believe you must without considering the cost."

"I am bound by the magic contract."

"But what exactly it means is something you've come to interpret based on concepts like liberty and choosing the lesser of evils."

"It's not a lie I am bound to."

He held up his hand. "And I'm not saying that, Aiden. You live by a noble cause, and you are bound to it. What I am saying is that you have found at times that your commitment to order means more than order itself. You have found that you have a greater commitment to its purpose than you do to its instruments."

"Yes."

My heart leaped as he took his eyes off the road to face me. He must have realized my anxiety and returned them to the road.

"Sorry. I've just never heard the word 'yes' said with such weight of meaning before."

Though his therapist nature made his sincerity unusually challenging to read, that line was clear. Discovery patted my shoulder and vanished.

"What was that?" I asked.

"What was what?"

"Was that what you were fishing for, the reason you wanted to meet me?"

"To help you discover your own answers? That's my goal with all my clients."

I rubbed my temples. "I guess I should thank you, but what answer have I discovered?"

He smiled and tapped his head. "You said it, I reworded it, and like only the son of order ever has for me, you confirmed it, making it yours. That, Aiden, is why I'm the psychoanalyst to the Olympians, because I make it look just that easy."

"Are you suggesting I might be able to get rid of this curse by finding a reason related to liberty or choosing a lesser evil?"

His smile left. "Now, I'm afraid, it's my turn to not be certain. In fact, it can't be that simple, can it? If you could just spin-doctor like a politician to devise some noble sounding reason why not being true to your nature would be the lesser of evils or greater serve liberty, one would have to wonder how dragons exist at all."

Confusion played with my soul, and I didn't like it. "So, what good is this answer that can't be used?"

"Oh, I didn't say it can't be used."

"But how, Gabe?"

"It's the nature of this counseling method I'm using, much like many others. There's a lot of rinse and repeat, and that is where we are."

"Torture me by having me arrive at useless conclusions and then seeing if I'm stupid enough to let you do it again?"

"No. Each time you move closer to the answers you need most. Sometimes you barely advance. Sometimes, like this one, you make a great stride. So, Aiden, we have an hour's drive to the airport. Shall we see how far we can get toward another destination along the way?"

I agreed. We achieved one hundred percent of our journey to the airport, and about sixty-seven percent of the other.

Chapter 54

Silence accompanied me back to SFO. Once Vedi heard the captain's speech from the cockpit, she told me the differences in time between the void and here discouraged her from listening in for the entire trip. She'd contact me on the other side but couldn't be precise in predicting when.

Paradox and irony flooded my mind. Silence isolated me, alone in a crowded airline seat. The organized matter and energy of the universe put on a show around me while all the company I could want existed in the void, a place where matter and energy have no form.

When we landed and pulled up to the gate, I remained alone in a crowd. Vedi didn't speak to me and no one stood holding a sign with my name on it. SFO's halls took me for granted. My stomach stood alone to prevent my heart from dropping to the Earth's core. I wanted Vedi back in my arms, or at least her voice back in my heart.

Past the security area, I spotted a familiar face. Isolated from the recent journey, my response missed correct proportion. I raced over as if to embrace. "Mr. Asta!"

He stepped back as if to dodge but smiled. "Aiden. John told me what flight you were coming in on."

Vedi's voice entered my thoughts. *"Daddy? My Daddy is there?"*

I pulled the shard out of my pocket for him to see. "Vedi seems thrilled to hear you again."

He reached out as if to touch it but pulled back. "Oh. She can hear us through that?"

"Yes, but only I hear what she's saying in return."

He paused and then led me over to a wall. He held a spiral-bound notebook to the wall and wrote on it. "You see that?"

The writing read, "Marilyn and Vedi's void project notes."

I started to read it aloud, but he hid it from me before I could. "You don't read everything out loud, Aiden, do you?"

"No, most of the time."

He pointed where I kept the shard, then at his eyes and at the notebook. He shoved the notebook into my hands. "I want to treat you to the Italian grill downtown."

I caught on. He didn't want Vedi to know I was about to peruse her notes. As much as I believed in Vedi's love for me, wisdom held my hand. Until I knew why he thought it best not to let her know, it made sense to go along. Besides, the sandwiches at that restaurant were amazing.

After dropping him off at a motel, I took the notebook home and began to read. Much of its contents required wizardry to comprehend, but I gathered a few things here and there.

One section looked a lot like algebra, but it clearly wasn't. Apparently, there were some elements of void travel in every form of teleportation.

"Did you enjoy your dinner with my dad?"

I closed the book before I realized she couldn't see it. "Yes. Yes, I did. I rather like the lamb sandwiches there."

"They taste and smell too much like liver to me."

I could picture her contorted face. I re-opened the notebook. "Out of respect for your pretty nose, I would not have ordered it if you were there."

The next section read of something I had a painful familiarity with, what material dark blades were made of. Chaos shards are made of the same and forging the stuff into blades or to have runes depressed into them is a magical task only a handful of artisans in the universe can achieve. Harold, my lore instructor, taught me all of that except for the existence of chaos shards.

"You think my nose is pretty? What ya doin?"

She turned from cute to paranoid on a proverbial dime. I flipped through the notebook to see how much I had left un-pursued. "Reading stuff related to what Harold taught me."

"I thought you didn't want anything more to do with him."

"I don't, but unfortunately that can't include everything he ever taught me."

"Oh, okay. Don't mind me. I'll let you read."

Of all the less than literal uses of language, my wife saying something like 'don't mind me' is most irritating. I think it means I'm supposed to feel guilty about something, but one advantage of being a dragon of order was that I had an especially good excuse to take it literally if it served my purposes to do so.

The section on the magically forged metal also included draw-ings resembling my physics notes on magnetic fields, only these were magical fields. Apparently, whatever magic was applied to turn one magical metal into this one tightly aligns the atoms in it, and this causes the metal to take its shape. Vedi and Marilyn wrote a warning for themselves extra-large and underlined. It read, "Don't let them touch!" Apparently, this would cause their fields to cancel each other or something.

Vedi's interrupted my admiring of the crude drawings in the notebook. *"Daddy said, 'you don't read everything out loud.'"*

"What?"

"At the airport. He said that to you, and I didn't know why. Now you're reading something related to what Harold taught you. Are you reading something daddy gave you?"

Blast my required honesty sometimes. "Yes."

"And what might he have given you that would be related to what Harold the dread sorcerer taught you?"

"Something related to magic."

"The house was destroyed, and daddy must have fished through the rubble and found something he wanted you to see. What is it?"

I flipped through the pages seeking out something that might be useful for me to know, one more thing before Vedi would put a stop to my search, something that could tell me when and if I'd get her back. I saw a drawing of Dak's dragon-like form, a fat lizard and skipped by, but the most interesting place yet unseen was a gap where a group of pages were torn out.

"Aiden, what is it my daddy gave you?"

Time was up.

Chapter 55

Her answer claimed my next words. "The notes you and your mother made while trying to commune with Nix."

"Destroy them Aiden. Read no more. There are things in there you must not know."

"Vedi. I'm trying to understand why you've been taken away from me."

"If you don't kill yourself, you'll know in time. Now, destroy those notes, please."

"What good does knowing or living do me if I never get you back?"

"There's something I can tell now if you just destroy those notes."

Her sincerity drove me to almost stumble in my rush. I shredded them, threw them into my fire place and lit them ablaze. "They're burning up in the fireplace now."

"You made no copies?"

"It's the only one. I hope your father doesn't ask for it back."

"They're mine to burn. Now, you're making sure they're burned up beyond recovery?"

"Yes. I'm your honest anti-scribe. Now, what can you tell me?"

"Aiden. Nix likes you."

"What does that mean?"

"She sees in you someone she can work with and she has long sought a champion of order to achieve common goals with."

"But how can order and chaos have common goals?"

"How did you and I marry?"

That was a long and complicated story involving some things I'd left undiscovered because their leads pointed to rage. I changed the subject's course to answers I wanted. "Will we be together again?"

"If you don't kill yourself first, but you must be patient."

"I'm good at patience, but my self-destructive side can't be held at bay indefinitely."

"Your freedom from your curse could be found by finding the one responsible for you having it."

"I'm right here."

"No, Aiden, I mean the one that tricked you."

"I suspect the Oceanids haven't been seen since Melina taunted me on my way out of the caverns."

"Thanks to Dr. Schalken's help back in Georgia, you now have the help of a gifted wizard."

"I do? I didn't catch that."

"Me, silly."

I've never gotten used to the idea that I married a witch. "Oh, yes, of course. I don't think of you that way."

She sighed. "Well, however you think of it, we can start by finding out how they left the caverns."

"Might Nix know that?"

"And what would make you think that?"

"They had to use teleportation, either direct or through a portal, and all teleportation involves travel through the void."

"How much of those notes did you read, Aiden?"

"The parts that looked like physics to me, you know, about teleportation and dark metal. You know, Vedi, that part could have been handy in disposing of that dark blade in Tera Del Fuego."

"And that's all you read?"

Fear marked her concern. I tried to calm her. "That's all I read before you made me destroy the notebook."

"Okay, good then. It seems little if any damage has been done."

"Speaking of damage, Vedi, we could have destroyed the dark blade instead of leaving it hidden in Terra Del Fuego."

"I'm so sorry, Aiden, but we only had two shards and only you know exactly where the dark blade is. Otherwise, I would have been inclined to sacrifice a shard to destroy that thing."

This was one of those moments in our early courtship where I would have sent her away, and there were many of those, but not this time. I forgave her working behind my back on a project I'd consider anathema. "Vedi. Let's forget this and get on with our work."

"Nix and I watched the Titan portal the Oceanids came in with, the same one the Empusa used. They didn't leave through it."

"Epimetheus, Kristine, Hunter, and I used Thaumus' Titan portal, so I don't see how they could have left that way."

"They didn't use a chaos portal. Those are especially easy for Nix to keep track of."

This reminded me of sitting with her at the outdoor lunch tables back in high school. We thought through magical mysteries then too, only this time she was beyond my reach. I reached out anyway. "I miss you, Vedi."

"We don't have time for tears pretty boy."

She said that but something in her voice told me my tears weren't the only ones involved. I pushed out words. "We need to get more information about what happened after I left the Empusa camp."

"Yes, Aiden, so we can track down the ones who've done this horrible thing to my precious dragon."

Before recent events, I would have needed Zeke to get me a meeting with the Empusa, but now I could get one through Thaumus, and perhaps with better reason for them to cooperate with me. I gave the Oceanid by the sea south of San Francisco a call. She assured me she would set it up and get back to me.

After I hung up, Vedi asked, *"Who is she?"*

Some may have thought it foolish, but quick honesty was the best course to me. "An Oceanid that wants to bear my children."

"What? And you're not cooperating with her wish of course?"

"No, of course not. You know me and my loyalty to Oliver."

"Hmm, and your faithfulness to me?"

Oops. "Until recently I thought you were dead."

"Good thing for this Oceanid that I'm in the void."

"Indeed."

The phone rang. She called me back. The meeting was set between me and Praxis. He must have coped with his injury. He'd have to climb out on an unfinished highway bridge to make the meeting.

"Two days from now," I told her.

"In the meantime, I can get us back to the cavern to look around."

"Nix can teleport me or something?"

"Nothing that simple, Aiden."

I gave her a chance to finish explaining but she didn't. "Okay, Vedi, what complexity is going to get us there then?"

"The Titan portal the Empusa used."

"It's still connected to the cavern?"

"It will when you get to the other end."

"The basement of a software company?"

"No. Inside a bank vault."

Chapter 56

As I often forgot I married a witch, she often forgot she married a dragon bound to respect private property. She usually caught herself more quickly than I did.

"*Oh, my. Aiden. I didn't think that through, did I?*"

"Is there another portal we can use?" I asked.

"*No. I'm afraid that's the only one available to us.*"

"So, I, the son of order need to get into a bank vault. I don't suppose I could introduce myself to its owner and convince him or her to let me in."

"*I wish she'd be that easy to persuade, but she'd want to know why, and she wouldn't believe your honest answer. I'm so sorry. I didn't think when I should.*"

"She?"

"*Yes, Aiden, Eva Knudsen. You know some women are wealthy and powerful enough to need entire bank vaults to keep stuff in.*"

"And this one is keeping one end of a Titan portal in hers?"

"*She manages the Empusa's financial resources, which are quite large, and she's not going to trust you. I'm afraid we'll have to wait for a later opportunity to get into those caverns.*"

Something occurred to me. "She's built up all her wealth by managing things for the Empusa?"

"Her family has for generations, along with various other remnants, including a few Titans."

"Hmm. Maybe, Vedi, we don't need to wait after all."

"If you're thinking of asking for her services, I don't see how you can tell the truth as you do all the way into her vault."

"You're right about that. I don't sneak or trick, but I see something about her business that could get me where we want me to be." I got out my phone.

Vedi anticipated. *"Her business is legal, Aiden. I don't see any way you could justify breaking in."*

My finger found the saved number. "It's the fact that her business is legal that can help me, that and the magical nature of her clients."

Zeke answered. "Aiden?"

"Hey, Zeke. I've got a favor to ask of you that I'm pretty sure your bosses won't mind."

Vedi interjected. *"Remember not to tell him about me."*

"If my bosses won't mind, I'll do it, son. Just name it."

"Eva Knudsen has one end of Thaumus' late sister's portal in her vault. I know the Empusa have been using it, so your boys would probably not want to be caught nosing into why it's there, but at the same time they probably want to know."

"I'm not sure I'm following you, son."

"Your bosses, the Children of Galinthius owe it to the Empusa's former matriarch to take care of the Empusa, and you know from the incident with Scylla that the Empusa may possibly be getting into trouble. They should want to know what's going on with this portal, why it's in that vault."

"I can let them know and if they're interested, as you're suggesting, they'll probably send me."

"Except, Zeke, the Empusa are starting not to trust the Children of Galinthius, like anyone else associated with Olympus. If instead of sending you, I go, the worst that's likely to happen is they think I'm up to no good toward them again, and they're paranoid enough to think I'm capable of enough guile to get there without your help."

"Okay, I see that, but why do you want to look into this? Something to do with your curse?"

"I think there may be answers to be found on the other end of that portal."

"Okay. Fair enough, but what exactly do you need me to do?"

"Ask Eva Knudsen for her permission to inspect her vault. Don't tell me how you justify that but send me as your inspector."

"How long do you need to use the portal and come back?"

I needed a way to ask Vedi that question without letting Zeke know I had an accomplice. "So, how long do I need to use the portal and come back? Good question, Zeke. Let me think for a moment because that's important."

"*With you flying, six hours,*" said Vedi.

"Six hours should do," I said.

"That's a long time to justify locking you in and keeping the security cameras from revealing your absence, but I've pulled off tougher deceptions, err, I mean blackouts."

My stomach turned. "If you're going to lie to someone, don't tell me. I mean you can just cause stuff to malfunction, right?"

"Yes, and I will try to do it just that way."

His honesty settled my stomach. "Okay, so you're going to call me when you've got me cleared to go in?"

"Expect my call, son."

I ended the call and bragged. "See, Vedi. There's a way for this dragon to get into that vault."

"*Pitiful and impressive at the same time.*"

"Ha ha. Now for another big question. How do I pass through that portal with this shard on me and get anywhere but the void?"

"*Ask my father for a glyph pouch. They're little bags you can put a glyph or rune into that contains its effect inside it. They're quite common amongst witches. Just keep in mind that I won't be able to talk to you when the shard's in one of those pouches.*"

Her father and I just found three pouches in the rubble of his house when Zeke called with the go-ahead. "You're set. I'm texting you directions to the vault's location. If anyone asks the purpose of the inspection, you can honestly tell them you're following up on a tip about a potential security breach. This is true."

He laid out his words so that they clearly defined the lines between their truth and any potential deceit.

"Zeke, I consider you a true friend."

Vedi had been silent for a half hour. I dropped the shard into one of the pouches and walked to my car. I'd take it back out once I reached the caverns.

Chapter 57

I trusted Nix's timing because my self-destructive side hoped she'd miss and send me to Terra Del Fuego or some other place with death readily at hand. She didn't miss, but the result resembled my self-destructive side's hope.

After traveling down a marble path lined by impossibly tall Greek pillars I stepped through the portal at the other end. I thought the cavern walls shot up around me, but I sprouted wings in time to avoid swimming in the lake of lava. I avoided a fate worse than death for someone who could not be consumed, only encased for eternity.

Landing near one of the outer circles, I pulled the shard out of its pouch. "What kind of portal placement was that? I stepped out over where the central megalith used to be."

Vedi didn't answer. I figured she had to be up to something other than listening to me. With weird time differences between the void and everywhere else, I could only keep talking as if she listened until she did.

"I guess I should fly around and see if I notice anything interesting."

A flight about the pillar circles revealed only that the Empusa cleanup well after themselves when they break camp, and the coven, in contrast, are litter-bugs.

"Nothing of interest seems to be in the altar cavern. I guess I should head toward where Thaumus had his portal?"

"Go to the place where Melina taunted you."

"Good. You're listening. How long have you?"

"I just started. Nix says she's sorry about the portal placement. It was the easiest place to put it since a large chaos portal had been there before and she knew you could fly."

"How much effort would it have taken to put it somewhere safer?"

"It would have taken more time than you gave us."

I arrived at the cave where Melina taunted me. "Okay, Vedi. I'm where you told me to go."

"Good. This is a place where we know she'd been for certain. Can you recall the exact place she stood?"

Even though she stood behind me, out of sight, my senses knew precisely where. "I'm there now."

"Okay, Aiden, this next part's tricky. We need to work together to cast a simple spell, well two, sort of."

"I can't cast spells."

"You can't, pretty boy, but we can. Grip the shard as tight as you can in one hand, place the other on the ground where you know she stood, and tell me when you've done this."

The shard's hardness hurt my knuckles to squeeze it. My other hand touched the cold dust. "Done, Vedi."

"Now repeat after me. Revelare."

"Revelare."

Spots appeared on the ground in the form of two shoe-prints.

"Can you see where she was standing?"

"Yes. It's glowing."

"Good. Now say, Revelare in tempore."

"Revelare in tempore." More shoe-prints glowed. They revealed a trail. "These glowing prints will lead me to where Melina teleported out of the caverns?"

"So, it worked? We managed to cast those spells?"

"You're suddenly surprised?"

"Well, don't get full of yourself, dragon boy, and follow that trail."

I followed the trail deep into lightless areas of the caverns. "Do you think they could still be here?"

"I would doubt it."

A thought occurred. "I can see here because I'm a dragon, but what about Oceanids?"

"They can't, not underground like this."

"For Oceanids, they sure have a lot of things going for them they normally wouldn't, don't you think?"

"I'm not so sure, Aiden. They're very persuasive. They just need to know the right individuals to get them to give them whatever they may need."

"Like something to see in pitch dark?"

"That would be a small thing."

The trail of glowing shoe-prints ended in a small cave. "End of the trail," I told Vedi.

"Is there a portal there?"

I swung my hand with the shard in it about. If it found a portal, it would become a chaos portal and its cold sting would reveal it. I found nothing. "No portal, Vedi."

"No portal now, but Nix should be able to tell me about the portal that was here."

The wall where the trail ended told me more than Nix would likely achieve. "The trail doesn't end in here. There was a cave in."

"Oh, my. Maybe their scheme, whatever it was, ended ignobly with a well-deserved tragedy."

I dug into the rubble and the trail's continuance. The rocks and gravel annoyed. My desire for order fought my need for expedience. "Oh, for a goblin engineer, I never thought I'd hear myself say."

"I hear your struggle, pretty boy. If she's dead, I want to know it as much as you do."

The annoyance gave way to tedium as the debris I cleared from the trail of shoe-prints needed to be moved to other caves. Hours passed as I labored.

Air whistled between rocks ahead of me.

"What is that?" asked Vedi.

I kept hauling rocks. "I don't know what could possibly cause air to move like that down here."

"Be sure you have a good grip on the shard."

I grabbed the next boulder and the piled-up debris raddled away from me. Dust flew into the air before leaving. A wind sucked at my clothes and hair before my feet abandoned the ground.

My wings served as stabilizers but nothing else. The sucking wind controlled me. I tried to fly against its pull, but the air ignored my efforts. I tried to see where I was going. My sight, though effective in pitch dark, could not see through clouds of dust and larger flying bits of stone.

"What's happening, Aiden?"

A glow awaited my arrival. "I think I'm about to pass through a portal."

"The pouch, Aiden, the pouch!"

I reached for my pocket but the wind's intensity threatened to tear the shard out of my hand if I spared enough fingers to use the pouch inside. "Tell Nix, I'm sorry, but I'm paying another visit."

"What? No Aiden."

"It can't be helped."

Chapter 58

The void greeted me with its biting cold. I couldn't tell if its previous darkness remained.

Vedi held her hand over my eyes. Her other arm embraced me. "Put the shard into the pouch or you'll never get out of here."

I wrapped my wings around her warmth. "Why would I want to leave your arms?"

She whispered. "*Do you have more than one pouch with you?*"

"No. I have two spares at my house."

"*Then you'll need the one you've got. Place the shard in it and keep your eyes shut.*"

I put the shard into the pouch. "I don't understand."

"*You will in time.*"

I pulled her against me. I clung to her body like an island of life in a sea of death. "How long will this last?"

"*A little over a minute.*"

"Then what?"

"*You'll come out a chaos portal on the Earth's surface.*"

"Can we ask for more time before that happens?"

"*The longer we wait, the further out the portal will be from the one you came in with. If we wait any longer, you may not come out on Earth.*"

"For a goddess of the void, you'd think Nix would have more..."

"*Shush, Aiden. You need to go now.*"

Cold concrete substituted poorly for Vedi's embrace. My eyes opened to a claustrophobic's nightmare, a dark concrete box. I pulled the shard out of the pouch. "Do you know where I am?"

"*My grave, most likely. Whatever you do, don't roll sideways. One of the sides is the portal.*"

"Okay. So, how do I get out of here without damaging property?"

"*Braking through at either your feet or your head should get you out, and then you'll only be damaging our property, no one else's.*"

"True." A couple taps, and kicks and careful listening and I knew which wall to break.

"*Are you okay, Aiden?*"

I punched through the wall by my head and crawled out. "This is a little humiliating but I'm fine." I placed my hand on the broken wall and restored it. No one saw me leave the mausoleum as far as I could tell, but another detail haunted me. I called Zeke. "Hey, Zeke. Slight problem. I've ended up back in Milpitas without returning to the vault."

"Believe it or not, son, I accounted for that possibility. I can even tell you how without upsetting your belly."

"Thanks again for the help. I'll be sure to tell you what I end up discovering at the end of this."

"I'm going to tell her we found the security breach and are looking into fixing it, and that's what's happening, right?"

"At my end, anyway."

"Um, yeah, I understand you feeling that way, but can you tell me what you've discovered so far?"

"If I learned nothing else from Epimetheus, it's not to share speculation with anyone who might want to run with it."

"Alright, fair enough, son, but is there anything that isn't speculation you can share?"

"Yeah. Melina left the caverns through a different portal than the ones we were already aware of."

"A wizard's?"

"Speculation again, Zeke. I'm not going there."

"Alright, son, then you'll let me know when you know more?"

"As soon as it's practical."

"And the rest of us less honest folk would just say yes."

I laughed, and the call ended.

"Vedi. Can Nix tell us anything about that portal?"

"She was distracted by your dropping into the void. Otherwise, she probably could have told you who it belonged to and what's on the other side, but as it is, she can only tell you it's a Titan portal."

"Another Titan? You think perhaps this other Titan could be the mastermind behind all of this?"

"Or another successful seduction of one of theirs. Why are you inclined to think the Oceanids couldn't be the masterminds?"

"It's not sexism, if that's what you think. It could be elitism though, but primarily it's just that I don't want to think that something there are thousands of might each be capable of all of this."

"Dare I say fear?"

"Maybe terror, Vedi."

"I want them dead. Is that an act of fear?"

"Yes, Vedi, it is, but not all fear is bad."

"Nix tells me that in two days she can arrange a portal back to the caverns, so we can find out where that portal goes. That is if it doesn't get reconfigured by its owner before then."

"In the meantime, I have a meeting out on an off-ramp to nowhere."

Sandra texted me instructions. At night, two police squad cars waited for me to pull up near where the closed ramp began. The concrete barriers had been temporarily moved aside for me to drive through. The policemen, I didn't know, acted as if they knew me and waved me through. One of them shouted after me, "Drive carefully, sir."

Playing with people's minds must be a talent the Empusa have at their disposal. The police that knew me, the Milpitas police, tend to think well of me, but these state troopers have no reason to know me.

I turned off my headlights and drove slowly. A few paces from where the ramp stopped in mid-crossing to someplace the state's money failed to reach, stood a familiar face. I stopped the car and got out. "Praxis. How are you doing?"

He limped up to me. "I'm still not healing from the wounds you gave me."

"It's not because I don't want you to. You know that?"

"Yes, and I try not to blame you. It's just an honest answer, the kind I know you demand. Speaking of which, you have some questions for me?"

"Yes. As you'd imagine, I'm looking for the Oceanids that did this to us."

"And I wish you well in that, you and Electra."

"Electra seems trustworthy. What do you say?"

"She's my lord's wife. What else could I say? But, yes, I trust her more than the rest of her kind."

"I asked because I value your judgment and know your sincerity."

"Thank you, dragon."

"Now for the real reason for us being here. I've discovered that besides Thaumus and his late sister's Titan portals, there was a third Titan portal connected to those caverns. Do you know whose portal it was?"

"Does Epimetheus have a portal?"

Vedi told me, *"No."*

"No, but I was hoping the Empusa would know about the third one. Thus our reason for being here."

Praxis stumbled oddly, moving most of the distance to the end of the ramp.

I grabbed his coat-sleeve and pulled him away from the edge.

His eyes widened. "Something grabbed me and tried to pull me off."

Vedi shouted orders into my head. *"Pick up some dirt and the next time he gets pulled on, throw it into the air and shout, revelabo stultitiam."*

I scooped some sand from the ground and gripped Praxis' arm with my other hand. "Stay with me."

Wind muffled and yanked on Praxis. I threw the sand above him and shouted, "revelabo sulitiam."

"No, Aiden, revelabo stultitiam," Vedi corrected me.

The sand bounced off something that let go of Praxis. I pulled my Empusa friend over to and into my car and closed him in. I jumped in the other side and backed out of there as quickly I could.

Vedi's voice prattled in my head. *"The spell would have worked if you just knew your Latin."*

We reached the barricade. I put the car in drive and merged into traffic. "Sometimes a car works better than a spell."

"Car's don't show you what's invisible."

"But cars keep your friends from being yanked off ramps to their death."

Praxis only heard my side of the conversation and I didn't want him to know about the other side of it so I smiled. "Sorry."

60

Chapter 59

Praxis squinted. "You said cars work better than spells but sometimes keep your friends from being yanked to their deaths? You want your friends yanked to their deaths?"

"Bad context for a 'but,'" I answered.

He sat back and gave an exaggerated nod. "Oh. Okay."

"Something invisible tried to kill you there. I'm guessing whoever it was wanted to blame it on me."

"That evil Oceanid and her hack boyfriend would be my guess."

"Is there an ideal place for me to drive you? I don't want to be accused of kidnapping."

"There's a parking garage in Oakland."

"I think I know the place."

"So, Thaumus let you use his portal to reach the caverns?" asked Praxis.

"Yes."

"Why?"

"He wanted me to stop the summoning by rescuing my brother-in-law."

"I guess, dragon, he had no idea the summoning would work without the sacrifice."

"That's how it seems."

"As well as that after failing to stop the summoning, you would defeat Scylla."

The conversation stopped. We rode a red river of tail-lights, the three of us, Praxis, me, and awkward silence. I broke it. "You know she started the fight?"

"Yes. We all knew that. We thought she wanted to make an example of you."

"I did what I had to."

"You convinced us we needed Thaumus to protect us from those who can bring dragons to Earth."

"My defeating Scylla did that?"

"Yes."

"You know I was set up and so was Scylla?"

"I do, dragon, but most of the Empusa don't think past the simple result. You defeated the ominous Scylla, so we must despair to share the world with you."

"Doesn't our truce mean anything in this thinking?"

"Our original matriarch was betrayed to death. That's what my people know. We honor our truce with you only because we cherish our honor. I alone, accept the simple truth that you are even more strongly bound to your honor than we are to ours. The rest believe you capable of treachery."

"And these Titan portals, do they have any idea who the third one belongs to?"

"We didn't even know there were two. The one we used was the only one we were aware of in the caverns."

"Well, that's interesting. That brings us to where we are right now."

"I'm afraid I don't drive enough to know where we are," said Praxis.

"Someone wanted you to die for the sake of their plans, and you didn't."

"Oh, you mean in that way."

"I think it's critical that I leave you with your own and not count on you making any lonely walks to get there."

He pulled out a phone. "I'll call ahead."

I grabbed his wrist. "Can you wait until we're just outside the parking garage?"

"You think whoever it is can listen in on my phone calls?"

"It's just that I really don't want framed for your death right now."

"Okay. I'll make the call just outside the place. We can't have you getting framed for my death. That would be awful for you."

He spoke those lines deadpan, but I caught the intended sarcasm. I thought it ironic, considering the frame would cause me more trouble than the grief involved. Decency still made me apologize.

"I'd miss you Praxis and I'd rather not in such a permanent way." Awkwardness and I are good friends.

"From you, dragon, I'll take that to be the kindest words I should expect."

One block from the parking garage, he made his call. "Yes. It's me. Something invisible tried to kill me and the dragon saved me by taking me into his car."

He paused to listen to the other end and continued. "He's driving me up to the gate and he won't leave me until some of you arrive to take me inside."

The sight of four men in dark suits appearing in a blur by the garage gate startled my cognition. Their size and demeanor intimidated but they arrived so instantly, like nothing I could easily conceive as real. Before my mind caught up, my passenger door swung open and Praxis left to join them. They left with him into the building before I could say anything.

"And with that, Vedi, Praxis is safe amongst his own again."

"I hope he's safe."

"He should be. They're an honor-bound collective."

"You like those things?"

"No, but I respect their honor."

"Of course, you would. Now, what have we learned?"

I resumed driving. "I've got nothing but speculation."

"I'm not going to run with it, like the people Epimetheus warned you about. So, please share."

"Whoever tried to get Praxis killed probably wanted to frame me for it, and that would cause all communication between me and the Empusa to stop."

"I don't see how that achieves much, considering how little they know."

"Riddles, my dear Vedi, riddles."

"So, you don't know much either."

"No. What I mean by riddles is that in solving riddles, like other logic problems, we should look for who has and who has not. They don't know much, but through Praxis, I just told them important things they didn't know."

"So, they can look into it for us?"

"Perhaps that could be useful, but more to my point, perhaps the one who wanted Praxis killed, wanted to keep the Empusa from finding out what I know."

"Good thinking. You surprise me at times, pretty boy. Maybe if you'd learn some Latin I could make a witch out of you."

I shivered. "Please no."

"Whatever the case, your reasoning is sound, sound enough that Nix wants to get us back to that portal in the caverns as soon as possible."

"I'm not sure Zeke can get me back into that vault."

"It's not going to be so difficult this time."

"And why is that?"

"Remember that ancient storehouse in the Himalayas?"

"I never wanted to see the inside of that place again."

"But if your life depends on it?"

"You realize half of me sees no value in that argument."

"Maybe Imhullu's still there."

"If it is, I could end myself there. You're using a desperate strategy, Vedi"

"It's your life I'm strategizing to save, a desperate fight I desperately want to win."

Until then, I thought her confidence exceeded mine. We both worried, but at least we worried in tandem.

Chapter 60

The airline staff at the SFO ticket counter played hot potato with my request for a flight to the Far East when my name wafted in the rafters. "Mr. Aiden Ferris to a courtesy phone." I wondered what shoe was about to drop.

Gabe's voice echoed over the phone. "You must be one important person to need all these flights at the drop of a hat."

"Are you holding me up?"

"No. I'm the Johnny on the spot who's being asked if the red flag you keep raising with Homeland Security needs to be disregarded again."

"I'm on the verge of getting to the bottom of a big lead."

"In Kathmandu?"

"I suspect Olympus will want to know what I'm about to find out."

"Do you care to tell me why, Aiden?"

"It wouldn't be wise until I know that myself."

"You almost sound like Athena when you say that. Only for her it's a matter of timing, not knowing."

"So, can you clear me?"

"Yes, of course. I just wanted to make sure you're properly moti-vated. While that's true, Athena's behind you."

The phone clicked, and I hung it up. A woman from the ticket counter met me half-way there. "So sorry for the delay, sir. God's speed on whatever you're doing."

Between Homeland Security and whatever Athena was up to, I just went from suspected terrorist to agent of the people. If only I could have figured out how I was Gabe's lesser evil and what the greater evil was.

On the subject of greater evils, my old instructor in dragonlore and all things magical, Harold the Dread, made this trip easy back when. We teleported a couple times. This time, I needed a couple long flights, a car to the edge of civilization, and some words in my driver's language from Vedi. His English seemed good enough, but Vedi's words sent him on his way like a horse running to the barn.

"What exactly did you have me say to him?"

"The truth, only in a way he'd best understand."

I didn't understand. I saw fear in him. "The truth doesn't scare me."

The dark of night and the lack of mortal eyes in the area allowed me to take flight. I used a handheld GPS to navigate the darkness. Oliver had kept the ancient warehouse empty of its arti-facts ever since the day I first came upon it. I can't say I found it. A strange acolyte with a goblin fetish gave me its location.

Thanks to me though, a new artifact was recently added, awaiting the moment when Oliver might be able to collect it, Imhullu. I wondered if he found the time yet to move it. My guess was that I'd know if I found a guard there.

A man who appeared native to the region sat in a thick woolen coat, warming his hands by a fire. The high valley around was barren. His pitched tent blocked the entrance to the cave I needed and appeared too coincidental to not be intentional, but he clearly was not an Olympian.

I landed far enough from the camp to not be seen, but he had exceptional hearing.

"Who is there?" he called into the darkness.

The truth, I've learned, can expedite many a mysterious encounter. "Aiden Ferris."

The man's response confirmed one suspicion but dispelled another. "Imhullu isn't here."

I entered the light of his fire. "Then why are you here?"

"Oliver told me not to bother lying to you."

"You're working for Oliver?"

"Yes."

"And why does he have you here?"

"To let him know if you come seeking Imhullu."

"Does he know about my curse?"

He read me somehow. "You mean, does he think a lust for power possesses you? No. He knows of your self-destructive-self. He wants to know if it has driven you here."

"You can tell him it hasn't, not exactly anyway. I'm here for a reason I'm pretty sure Athena knows about. He can ask her."

He turned to the fire and warmed his hands. "I will do that."

"I still need past your tent."

Without looking, he pointed at the tent. Its stakes jumped out of the ground, folded itself into a backpack and no longer blocked the entrance.

I walked through the cave. Its dimensions tempted flight, but I remembered passing this way before. The collisions with the walls make flying more painful but not so much faster in the end.

The ancient underground warehouse at the other end caused me to pause. A place once filled with magical flying machines stood empty. The sconces lining the walls remained, many broken, and all of them absent their torches. The destruction displayed a small bit of my legacy.

"Is the son of order here to destroy things?"

Vedi snarked. *"I do find that sexy."*

"But, seriously, how often have I destroyed things? Could it be I betrayed my nature long ago?"

"Now, Aiden, no. None of that. Destruction is the residue of making order out of chaos."

"Was that the meaning of your words that night about my

impact on your life being monstrous and you pleading with me not to stop?"

"That night outside of here? I remember that. You stopped at third base."

"As I did until marriage."

"I thought that was monstrous, but I guess I got what I asked for."

I sprouted wings. "So, where's the portal."

"According to Nix, it's right where you left it."

"Far end." I flew the five hundred yards down the length of the chamber and landed. An iron ring with a twenty-foot diameter sprawled across the floor from the wall where it once stood. It lay in two pieces. "It's broken, Vedi."

"Then fix it, oh Henry."

I never went to summer camp, but Vedi had. Based on what John told me of such things, she must have been a terror for the counselors. To her experience I owed the knowledge of silly songs like 'Oh Henry' and the 'Wheels On The Bus.'

Her reference called for me to ask how, but I wasn't in the mood. Instead, I placed my hands on the two pieces and watched them glow and become one. "Done. I suppose I now need to stand it back up?"

"Yes, and you're really no fun sometimes."

A question prodded its way out of me. "How did Nix know I could fix this? It wasn't something I could do until recently."

"It wasn't something she could know until recently."

"She doesn't want to answer my question, does she?"

The portal glowed blue.

"Shut up and fly through."

Chapter 61

I flew through the portal and into the cavern complex. Air pressure jumped. Dagger and sledgehammer force hit me from all directions. The pain clamped my skull. I screamed like a boiling tea kettle.

I landed on the edge of the lake of lava and rolled into a ball. Like a slow working aspirin, my body eked its way to equilibrium with the air, until I became capable of speaking sentences again. "Ouch! Vedi. What kind of transition was that?"

"Sorry, my love, but it would have taken over a week to do that properly, and unlike most, you can take it."

"Take it? If I knew I was flying into that, I don't think I'd be here right now."

"Why do you think I didn't warn you?"

The hammers and daggers stopped, but my head ached, and stiffness affected all my muscles. I dared not try to fly in that state. Instead, I trudged. My feet drug with each step.

"Good thing I had nothing to fight on this end."

"I am so sorry, Aiden."

The stiffness left soon enough to fly most of the way to where we left the portal of the yet unknown Titan. I landed short of the suction, secured the shard in the pouch, and leaped into the vortex. My last experience made me think about the likely ability of Oceanids to deal with sudden pressure changes. A silly thought, I concluded. Unlike me, they knew what to expect, or did they? In any event, Titan portals have tunnels between the terminals which allow for gradual pressure transitions.

This one's tunnel passed along invisible floors, between invisible walls, and under a ceiling indistinguishable from a cloudy sky. Puffy white clouds obscured below as well, wherever might be land or sea.

"I seem to be walking through the clouds in the sky," I said.

"When you reach the portal at the end of the path, be prepared to fly in turbulence."

"You know where I'm going?"

"Nix hopes not."

"What does that mean?"

The girls in the void offered silence. I began to feel more like the iron pawn than the son of the iron dragon. The other side of the second portal greeted me with calm.

"No turbulence so far."

"There's no good news for Nix here," said Vedi.

Long shadows stretched across clouds I walked on. Distant thunders growled. In the extent, a large silhouette drew in the horizon's light. I took wing and closed.

A sacred calm encompassed the air. I dared disturb it with a whisper. "I see a large figure ahead of me. Could it be a Titan?"

"Be careful, Aiden."

"Nix isn't telling me something."

"She needs to know as much as you do."

The form moved unnaturally, pulsing a chill down my arms, but then it didn't move. It hadn't moved. A shadow shifted and tricked my senses.

I closed enough to transform my perception. The form presented a man but of stone, not flesh.

"It seems to be a statue."

"Of what?"

"A man, a Titan-sized man."

"Astraeus! He's been turned to stone."

"Either that or he acquired a statue."

"Is it in a normal statue pose?"

"It's leaning over like someone about to pull something out of an oven."

"Not a normal pose. It must be him. Someone has turned him to stone."

Patterns in the sounds of breezes broke behind me, I had a presence in my company. Melina threatened. "I turned the Titan to stone. I can do the same to a dragon."

Truth rode her words but my eyes, self-destructive or otherwise, saw gold. "That's a potent force, transformation. How did an Oceanid ever get a hold of such a power?"

"I'm persuasive."

The object of Astraeus' bent-over reach remained in his stone grasp.

"Persuasive enough to get a wand like that?" I asked.

"Of course."

She lied. The pieces logically fell together. The gold stick in Astraeus' fingers was a wand of transformation. He must have tried to disarm Melina just as she used it on him. His effort left her unable to use it again as it remained stuck in his stone grasp.

With my back still turned, I launched at her. Surprise smiled on my efforts like justice had Astraeus'. I held her in my grasp as relentlessly as he held that wand. She clutched at something and vanished, but I still held her. She scolded. "Let go of me, lizard."

"You'll wish I was a lizard if you don't tell me what you're up to."

"Tundo."

She slipped out of my arms like water through a hose. I flailed at the air and grabbed nothing but. I faced the wand and listened to the air—nothing.

"She got away?" asked Vedi.

"Yeah. I hate that word."

"Me too. It's from a language more ancient than Latin and ancient Greek."

249

I whispered. "Nothing but air moves out there and hasn't since I lost her."

"Unless she can fly, she's got nowhere she can go from there."

My lessons from Harold offered an idea. "Check me, Vedi. Transformation curses protect their victims from destruction for the duration?"

"Yes, that's right."

"So noble Astraeus is indestructible right now?"

"What are you thinking?"

"Is there anything in Astraeus' home here that's vulnerable to sound?"

"Please, Aiden put the shard in its pouch first, and no, it's all magical force walls."

I did as she requested and then let loose my roar. I tried to modulate to not be fatal to an Oceanid, but lack of practice made that iffy. The trumpet-foghorn lasted five seconds but its echo returned twice. A thump followed the first sound of my roar. Groans followed the second, and the clatter of a small object rolling away followed the third.

Melina's body appeared dropped ten yards away, sprawled to a side in a mist. She lay motionless. Her chest neither rose nor fell. I rushed to her and placed my hands on her. A glow healed her. Bones snapped together, and I let go before the process finished.

She rolled onto her back and let out a scream. Her eyes rolled back into her head. I took the time to get the shard back out into my hand.

"Okay, Melina, time for you to give me some answers."

She gazed up and fainted. The same ability I have to tell the truth of words would have caught an attempt to feign uncon-sciousness.

"So, she lived through it?" asked Vedi.

"Yes."

A large raven fluttered off in the distance. I decided not to chase what I guessed to be Charly. I had more answers before me than he'd be likely to offer.

Vedi scowled. *"It's almost a pity she didn't."*

"Almost but catching her is only the beginning of the end."

"What do you know, Aiden that I don't."

"She didn't persuade her way into that wand. Whoever gave it to her is who we're really after."

Chapter 62

Vedi's voice carried urgency. *"Quickly before she comes to again, follow my instructions carefully."*

"I'm listening, shoot."

"Look at the chaos shard. Do you see the three crossed lines, like the chaos portal over the altar?"

"Yes. I hadn't noticed them before, but yes."

"Place your thumb on the triangle part so that only the lines sticking out remain."

I did as she asked, covering the triangle and nothing more. "Done."

"Now, holding your thumb there, touch the shard to her forehead and say, 'ventilabo.'"

I followed her directions. "Ventilabo."

Black lines like spider legs extended from where I touched her, spreading across her face and hair. "What did you have me just do?"

"It's okay, Aiden. You just confused her magic for an amount of time. She won't be getting any joy from her power word for the duration."

"For how long?"

"The lines will leave her when it ends. When you see that re-cast it on her."

I made sure my thumb remained obscuring the triangle. "What's the deal with covering the triangle?"

"The spell requires a glyph with just the outer lines. Normally it would be drawn onto an object or right on the targets forehead, but there's nothing to use for that near you. Ironically, I'm having you use an amazingly rare shard meant for a far greater purpose."

The hairs on the back of the hand I held the shard in raised. "I'm not comfortable channeling your wizardry, Vedi."

"What a pair we make, pretty boy. Now, how about you explain why you seem convinced our Oceanid here is working for someone else?"

"A wand capable of casting a transformation curse is like a nuclear-tipped ICBM. Rogue Oceanids and generals don't just use them. Someone more powerful than them pulls that trigger."

"Did Harold the Dread teach you that?"

"Being the former victim of such a curse, it's a subject he knows well."

Melina's eyelids twitched. The black lines still radiated from her forehead. I readied a question when she came to. Her head moved.

"Can you stand up?"

She pushed her upper body an inch off the ground and cried out. "No. What did you do to me?"

"Good. That serves my purposes. And, what I did is called in scholarly circles a sonic blast. Certain vibration frequencies do physical damage."

"You creep."

"I'll happily heal you completely, once you tell me what I want to know."

"You're going to torture me?"

"This isn't torturing."

"Haven't you cursed yourself enough? Of course, this is torture."

"I'm guessing you've got several broken bones. That must hurt, but that's just a consequence of what it took for me to catch you, not torture."

"Then heal me now."

"If I heal you completely you're likely to run away. Maybe you can tell me enough to make that less of a concern for me?"

She closed her eyes and stopped talking.

Vedi filled the vacuum after the silence. *"You're a far better inter-rogator than I'd expect you to be. A little bit scary, and lot sexy at the same time."*

I wanted to tell her to stop with the teasing banter, but I didn't want Melina to hear me.

"So, Melina, how much longer shall we wait before I heal you?"

Her eyes sprung open. "You may as well heal me now because no matter what I tell you, it won't lessen your concerns."

Her truth intimidated, but only for as long as it took me to remember my cursed state. "How so?" I asked.

"Did you let the raven fly away?"

"Yes."

"He got away with the wooden statue."

"Yes, I know, one of the magical toys you seduced him with."

"It's called Palladium."

Vedi's words jumped into my head. *"For the coven?"*

"Is he taking it to the coven?" I asked.

Melina sneered. "Soon the coven will be a real witch's coven."

The black lines vanished so I pressed the shard against the side of her head. "Ventilabo."

The lines returned, and her pupils dilated for a second. "What? You're casting spells? How?"

Her eyes rolled back into her head and shut. I shook my arm to remove a chill running along it. "I hate this stuff."

"Aiden. We'll need to get back to Milpitas soon. My brother could be in danger."

"Shouldn't we get what we can out of Melina first?"

"Yes. I hate to say it, but yes."

"So, what's the danger of your coven getting this Palladium?"

"Palladium is said in legend to have been the property of the cities of Rome and Troy. It will make whatever community possesses it invulnerable. Both cities only fell after it was removed from them."

"So, it's a collective thing?"

"Yes, and that's why Hunter could be in danger. Charly will have to get him out of the way to use it."

"Without the magic sword Epimetheus broke, that should be difficult. Nonetheless, I'll see about speeding things up here."

I nudged Melina's face. Her eyes opened. "Tell me, Melina, who you're working for in all this. Then I'll heal you completely."

She moaned and Vedi spoke. *"I'd have demanded more for that."*

Melina closed her eyes. I grabbed her and readied to shake her awake again, but she shot out a name. "Thaumus."

"Thaumus planned to trick me into bringing this curse on myself?"

She gritted her teeth and nodded. Her eyes begged for my mercy. I changed the nature of my grip to gentle and let the glow happen. Snaps and crunches jolted her body. Her face relaxed.

I pulled her onto her feet. "Now you're going to lead me to him."

She flinched around pulling at my grip. "Tundo."

The word achieved nothing. I smiled. "That's a fun word now."

The healing of her body brought only a short calm to her face before a new brokenness found it. I scolded myself for the pleasure I found there.

"Don't you want to know what he's up to before we get there?"

"Considering how we're going to need to travel, I expect you'll have time."

Chapter 63

I needed a way out of Astraeus' place fast enough to get me to Thaumus before he could provide Charly Chord with resources he'd need to overcome Hunter.

"How will we need to travel?" asked Melina.

"I'll need to think a few moments on that, but whatever way that is will require some time."

I squeezed the shard and hoped Vedi took the hint. My nudges encouraged Melina to start walking toward the Titan portal.

My patience vanished as we walked, but Vedi spoke up. *"It will take Nix the better part of a day to redirect Astraeus' portal to a place near Santa Cruz."*

"Where the San Andres meets the sea there?" I asked Vedi, but Melina assumed I said it to her."

"Do you think I can transport you to there?" responded Melina.

"No. I'm just talking to a voice in my head."

The voice in my head answered me. *"Yes."*

"And there isn't another portal already on the same beach?"

"No. Nix sees no portals there."

I wondered where Thaumus moved his portal's endpoint to.

Other than dragging her feet, Melina gave me no trouble in

walking where I wanted her to go. I had another question for Vedi, which fortunately would sound natural to the context perceived by Melina. "Would it take the better part of a day for me to fly to Santa Cruz from here?"

"Much longer," said Vedi.

Melina laughed. "I'd be days sitting on your back. Do you still intend to torture me?"

Vedi scoffed. *"Such a prissy bitch. Why not let her know you're talking to me? I could let her know a few things."*

I smiled at the thought of what Melina might think of hearing my answer to Vedi. "If she knows too much I might have to kill her."

Melina stuttered. "Is the voice in your head telling you things again?"

"Don't worry, Melina, I'm on the side in that discussion of keeping you alive."

She stumbled, recovered, and picked up the pace more to my liking. "My sister's the one who set you up to curse yourself."

"And while I was being set up, you were arranging for the coven to get this Palladium under the leadership of Charly Chord. Are you telling me Thaumus wanted that to happen?"

"Yes."

"You know I can tell if people are lying and Thaumus honestly likes Hunter Asta, not in the way he first suggested, but he does like him. So, why would he want Charly Chord to usurp him?"

She absorbed that question over a few seconds. "I don't know."

"What do you think? Could he be playing you and Hunter's allies against each other?"

She raised her voice. "I don't think so. He planned on you defeating Scylla because he wanted the Empusa to turn to him to be their patriarch. That would give him authority over all the remnants on land as well as at sea."

"But he had you get close to a hack like Charly Chord, just so you could get me involved in the first place."

"He's a clever Titan."

"He pretended to be my friend and committed treachery against me, why not you too?"

"He told me my highest priority was to get Charly in charge of the coven and to give them Palladium. I've done that. As for you, you're marked for death. I don't see any treachery toward me."

"Your one lie in that reassures me and bothers you. Charly isn't currently capable of taking over the coven. That means you haven't done what Thaumus told you was your most important task. So, tell me. Did you trap yourself here or did Thaumus send you here, into a trap?"

She stopped, and I nudged her. Her feet drug as she resumed making progress to the portal. Her chin met her chest and rested there until we reached it. Once there, I grabbed her shoulder.

"We need to wait most of a day here before going through. Until then you would only get blown right back."

She peered at me. "You're going to make Astraeus' portal go somewhere else?"

As much as I would have loved to say yes, I had to be honest. "We will wait, and it will change."

"Titan portals don't work that way."

"Have a seat Oceanid. We're going to be here a while."

"But you want me to lead you to Thaumus. How can I do that if you don't have a way for us to get out of here? We should fly out. You can carry me on your back."

"I don't lie, Oceanid, when I tell you we will be able to use this portal to get to Santa Cruz, I am saying that because I know we will. I don't guess and call my guesses the truth. Now have a seat so I don't need to break any bones."

She plopped to the magical floor. I sat as well. Her head turned like she couldn't find the notch to set it securely into her neck. "What sort of help do you have? You must have help to do this."

"You don't need to know and are better off not knowing."

The lines vanished; I lurched over and touched the shard to her forehead. "Ventilabo."

The same chill that climbed my arm the last time made it to the top of my head, which I shook and shivered. A paleness crossed Melina's face.

"You're possessed," she said.

"I'll let you think that because it's as close to the truth as you dare get. Any closer and you might know too much."

My shivers echoed. "Spell-casting bothers the heck out of me but I'll keep doing it as long as it takes to get us to Thaumus."

"What sort of being possesses you that can change the course of Titan portals?"

I made sure to glare. "The sort of being that couldn't trust you to live with the knowledge."

She shut up. We waited in a full day's silence. In her thoughts, I figured she questioned if she had the right employer. I figured that because I wondered if I hadn't become employed by Nix and thus had a similar crisis.

Chapter 64

When I struggled beside Harold the Dread, he hid his deceit. I didn't realize his treachery until he achieved his goal. This time I worked with Nix, again not knowing the endgame. Am I a fool? What's the difference between a teenager and an adult?

"Nix has changed the destination of Astraeus' portal to Santa Cruz."

I resisted the temptation to ask why Nix cared to help me. Besides, I probably knew the answer I'd get, something about me knowing when the time was right, but not before, lest I risk Vedi never returning.

I stood. "Okay, Oceanid, it's time for us to move."

She rubbed her legs and hobbled toward the portal. A proactive thought passed my lips. "Just keep in mind, I can outrun you even in the ocean, so don't test me."

I decided to trust Nix to have common cause with me. Unlike with Harold, I knew her ulterior motives existed. I just didn't know what they were. She also hated my presence in her void. Somehow, I could trust someone who disdained my presence more than someone who claimed to be my friend. Her disdain carried truth instead of deception. Maybe I'm not as foolish as I once was. I placed the shard in the pouch.

My prisoner and I stepped through the first portal and walked the invisible bridge to the second. She mumbled.

"What was that?"

Her voice rose and fell like a rollercoaster. "There's something wrong with this. Only Astraeus should be able to control his portal."

"Instead of panicking at things, let's just get to Santa Cruz."

She stopped short. "This magic is against the Earth."

I put my arm around her and pushed us through. On the beach in Santa Cruz, we were greeted by the sun as it escaped the mountains. I pulled the shard back out. Melina threw her hands at the sun. "No."

"I doubt you've cursed yourself, Melina. Now, where's Thaumus?"

"You really did it. I don't want to believe you really did it. This has to be a nightmare."

"I'd love to have you think that. Then you might more freely answer my questions, but nonetheless, I'm asking you how to get to Thaumus."

The lines needed to be renewed. "Ventilabo."

My right side shivered. My stomach chilled. Melina noticed my discomfort. "Your constitution doesn't agree with the demon."

"Demon!" cried Vedi.

I grabbed my head to dispel the pain. "Please, Oceanid, don't guess at things, or killing you may become my only path of relief."

Vedi's tone changed to concern. *"It hurts you to cast this spell?"*

I didn't care if Melina heard me answer. "More each time."

The dual meaning worked. Melina led me to the street. *"Then we need to be done with Melina's help soon."*

I touched Melina's back. "Lead me to Thaumus without giving me trouble and leave me to him. Do that and I promise to let you go unharmed."

Vedi grumbled. *"Where does your mercy come from, Aiden? You're the son of order, not the son of goodness and mercy."*

Goodness and mercy had nothing to do with it. To kill her at that point would be treachery. Reinforcements for Vedi's arguments, however, beat me to calling a cab. A familiar old car pulled up and its driver got out.

Zeke scanned Melina. "Son? No offense, but I worry about your choices in female companionship."

Melina reciprocated. "Old man."

"She's my prisoner."

"You pimp your prisoners on the street?"

"Zeke, you're a gentleman, right?"

"Apologies, son, but you're not the only one hating all of this."

"Okay, Zeke, how did you find me and why?"

"I'll explain when you allow me to drive you where you want to go."

I climbed into the back seat with my Oceanid prisoner. Zeke pointed to the seat-belts. "Where to?"

I nudged Melina's elbow.

"South end of the east hills," she said.

I could have guessed that much, but Zeke had us in motion and time to get more details from her would come.

"Zeke. Why are you here?"

"The Children of Galinthius are paws-off for this thing you're investigating, but thanks to you, we're very interested in how it's going."

"I told you I'd let you know when I had something solid, no speculations someone might be tempted to run with."

Melina inserted herself into our conversation. "That's very wise, dragon."

Zeke half chuckled. "Your prisoner agrees with you. Hmm. She's solid. This is one of the two wayward Oceanids Electra is looking for, right?"

"Yes, and I have her helping me."

Melina screamed. A loud thump caused a dent in the top of the cab. I alerted my detection abilities. Zeke bashed out his window with the barrel of his Desert Eagle and fired a shot into the sky. My thoughts had distracted me so I was the last of us to see the threat.

Three harpies buzzed us. I opened my door and Melina cried out. "He knows we're coming."

Zeke made the car swerve. Other cars honked their horns and left the road. He finished knocking out the glass from his door's window. "He? Who's he?"

"Thaumus," I said before climbing on the roof.

Zeke pulled his head and shoulder through his door. "Stupid Titan. If he wants to kill her, can't he wait until we're out of public view?"

A harpy swooped at him. He fired his gun. She waggled, scraped the road with her talons, but recovered back into the air. The other two circled.

Physics problems ran through my head. I knew the car loaned me its velocity, but air resistance would cause the loan to run out if I took flight, but how fast? I preferred not to risk losing my prisoner to Zeke's bosses and decided to cling to his roof.

Claws on my feet dug in while I tried to keep the claws on my hands minimal. I stood like a scene from a movie about a giant gorilla. Harpies buzzed about out of my reach. One tried to come in low on the passenger side, but with my feet firmly attached to the roof, I leaned down caught one of her wings. I gripped it tight and swung her onto the roof. She screeched. I flung her away.

She managed to gain control of her flight and keep going. The other two followed her.

Hot rounds from Zeke's gun and the futility of getting around me convinced them their efforts were pointless. We popped back in.

Zeke returned the car to its proper lane while yelling. "That's what we should expect from the Titan we're going to trust to administer all the remnants on land and sea?"

He didn't understand Thaumus was the schemer. I didn't plan to tell him before I knew why.

Chapter 65

I reached across the car and mended Zeke's window. "Do you know if he's got anything other than harpies to throw at us before we get to his mansion?"

"There's a truce between you and the Empusa and we're on land, so he's basically out of enforcers. He's just going to have to question her or do something else. Something more sensible than having his harpies attack a car in broad daylight."

I touched the bowl-sized dent in his roof and mended it. "Thanks for the ride, Zeke."

"It's the least I can do."

He laughed and added, "and the most too."

"Are the police going to come after us for all that commotion?"

He tugged the brim of his hat. "Nah, son, you're with Ezekiel Roe, special agent of the Children of Galinthius. We *are* the law."

"Then we're home free."

Melina and I exchanged glances. I hoped to read something in her to tell me what she thought of Zeke's ignorance and if she might be likely to let him know. Mischief danced in her eyes. "Mr. Roe, sir, do you know the dragon is possessed or something?"

"That's Field Marshall Roe to you, and if you mean the boy's penchant for order, that's what I'd call an obsession, not possession."

Her grin grew across to her dimples. "He has a voice in his head that he talks to."

"*Stop her,*" said Vedi.

"This thing, my self-destructive side is like another me."

I hoped by changing the subject in a way close to the original subject, I could cut her off.

"Well, yeah, that curse the boy has. It makes me sick to think of it. Are you bragging about causing it, fish-lady?"

"No. Whatever he talks to helps him cast spells."

She was determined to push the boundaries of the conditions by which I'd be bound to let her live.

"What's she smoking, Aiden?"

I hate figures of speech, especially when aimed at me as a question. Normally I'd ask for clarification, but that option seemed fraught with problems, like having to tell him about Vedi, Nix, and the chaos shard. The other option made my stomach hurt because it was ever so slightly less than completely honest.

"I wouldn't let her smoke in your car, Zeke."

My stomach disliked me. I wondered if Zeke might catch onto my evasion tactics. I didn't wonder for long.

"Well, son, there's some smoke being blown in my car for sure."

Melina leaned her head past Zeke's head-rest. "He casts spells."

"Fish-lady. Get your head out of my space. We're all suffering the consequences of your being a low filthy bitch. As for you, dragon, I'm done asking you questions this trip, so you can settle that gut of yours."

"Thank you, Zeke."

"No need to thank me. I've learned when you feel a need to keep something from me, it's probably in my best interest to let you."

Melina's chin found her chest and stayed there all the way into the east hills. I liked the silence, but once the car began the climb I had to ask her more.

"So, Thaumus is in his mansion?"

She turned her head without lifting it from her chest. Silence followed where I expected words.

"Well, is he?"

"Is he what?"

"Are you trying to get hurt?" I asked her.

"No. Is he what?"

"Is Thaumus in his mansion?"

"I want to live. Yes. As best I know, he's in his mansion."

"Do you have any idea how he's guarded, if at all?"

Zeke turned his head. "Why do you want to know that? What are you worried about?"

"Zeke. I need you to trust me to let you know when the time's right and not before."

"But you will tell me, son?"

"Yes. Now, Melina, about how he's being guarded."

She threw her head back and gasped. "He's been keeping Empusa around him lately, but his harpies are usually around somewhere."

I had to think this through to myself, no telling Zeke or Melina any more about what I was about to do. The Empusa were good news and bad news. On one hand, they wouldn't fight me, on the other I couldn't fight them. The harpies thus far were little more than harassment, but I imagined they would up their game once their master was on the line.

We pulled up to the mansion. Its grounds remained the same barren hillside lawn I saw a few days ago. That bothered me. He could have used magic to spruce the grounds up by now, and even if out of caution he wanted to go the natural route, where were the saplings or garden beds? It was almost as if the mansion's sole purpose was to give me a place to find him.

His guards presented a minor challenge, but the one challenge I couldn't predict was him. If he wanted me here, surely, he planned to deal with me. I gripped the shard. "Let us out at the gate and leave us here."

"Son. I don't know what you feel you must do in there, but try to minimize the mess."

"I can make you no promises."

"Shit."

He drove off.

I think I shared his sentiment. "Just so it gets said, voice in my head, I love you."

Chapter 66

Vedi kept silent. Melina stomped ahead. "I want to get this over with."

I followed her across the lawn.

Her aggressive steps percussed her voice. "You and that voice in your head. I want to be finished with you as soon as possible."

Two well-dressed, as usual, Empusa nodded as we passed through the front door. I could tell from their manners, they knew who both of us were. Once inside, two more greeted us. I recognized these two, Kern and Praxis.

Kern scowled. "Planning to save the wretched Oceanid, are you, dragon?"

Praxis nodded like the two outside. "Good work in catching her, son of order."

I thought to myself that sparing is not the same as saving, but I had to get my mind on more immediate things. "Where is Thaumus?"

Praxis gestured me to the back room with the view. Kern stuck to my side. "What, you feel a need to kill every Titan who dares be our patriarch?"

"I have nothing against you, Kern, and I wish killing Titans was as easy as me setting my mind to it."

"You're afraid, dragon?" asked Melina.

Kern cocked his head. "Yes. Yes, he is. I smell his fear."

I wondered what fear smells like, especially considering Kern's meaning was literal. In that back room, I found what fear most definitely didn't look like. Thaumus' human form reclined in a plush leather chair, facing the view. His red and purple Hawaiian shirt presented a festive clash with his dull expression.

Praxis rushed to his ear. The Titan listened with feigned surprise and smiled wide. The chair swiveled.

"My wife will be most pleased with your unsolicited help, Aiden."

I recognized his cleverness for the first time. "But are you pleased?"

"Yes, dragon of order, I am."

"You have me right where you want me, don't you?"

"I am pleased with your help indeed."

He slapped his knee. His show of glee failed to deter me. "You're a scheming Titan, even more than your sister."

He stood and gestured to the Empusa with an insincere pleasantness. "Leave us, gentlemen. We wish to speak as friends. I'll not need your protection."

Meaning evaded his talk of friends but confidence supported the part about him not needing protection. Kern left without hesitation, but Praxis slowed as he left. They shut the doors behind them and he spoke.

"You flatter me."

"Melina told me about your schemes."

He winked. "And you believe her?"

"I'd know when people lie to me and when they tell me the truth. It's part of what I am."

Melina returned his wink and smirked.

"And besides, it's what you wanted her to tell me and what is most likely the precise time you wanted her to."

He laughed, not maniacally, but as if told a good joke. "So, you see what's happening?"

"I've seen through much of it before Scylla's summoning. I just didn't know it was you."

He bent over, holding his middle. "The fly knows from so far away that he is flying into the spider's web, and he does nothing about it? He just announces that he knows what's about to happen to him and cries treachery. That's amusing, indeed."

Melina laughed. "What a fool to play you are, dragon."

I plunged the depths of my cleverness for something to answer them with but found nothing. Nothing, that is, besides my self-destructive side. "If I have entered your trap, you have better spring it."

He held a hand up. "I will, but first I have a reward for my able servant, Melina. Please come over here, clever Oceanid."

She walked over to where he could place a hand on her shoulder. "You are probably the cleverest of Oceanids indeed. Playing this dragon's nature against him was well beneath your talents, but I am grateful you lowered yourself to the task. Completing it was important to me."

"You're most welcome, my lord."

His gaze turned. "Hmph. You just stand there, waiting politely for what I have in store for you. Melina, face him so you can help me with one more task."

She turned with a grin. "My pleasure, my lord."

His hand glowed red. "You're probably wondering what it will take to kill him. It will take a special blade. A sword bathed in red flames appeared in his hand. He showed it to her.

Her grin grew wider. "You want me to use it on him?"

"I want you to hold it."

He pulled her back onto the blade. Its point burst out of her chest. Her eyelids lurched open. He studied her face. "So sorry, Melina, but you know too much. I can't let you live."

He pulled the burning blade out and her body hit the floor with a loud thump.

"Are you going to kill Kern and the rest of your Empusa guards as well?"

He glanced past me and waved. One of the doors to the entryway slammed behind me. I never heard it open since the two Empusa left.

"Only that one," whispered Thaumus.

Kern's voice filled the room. "Do you need help, Lord Thaumus?"

"Yes. Come over here."

"I think he means to kill you..."

Kern moved too quickly. Thaumus thrust his blade through Kern's heart before he could realize the danger. The magic ignited his body, countering his regeneration, and Thaumus kicked him over the balcony.

I shouted. "I'll not go down so easily."

He held a finger from his free hand over his mouth. "Not so loud, dragon. You don't want your friend Praxis to have to die too, do you?"

I didn't. I stepped toward the Titan. My wings spread.

He held the sword out to his side. "Of course, this blade isn't the one for dealing with you. This one is the one for loose ends."

My claws came out. The glow from eyes announced my readiness for battle.

He wagged his finger. "Nice try, being so non-verbal. Very intimidating, but that shout of yours has me worried. I think I need to kill all my guards just to be safe."

My legs pushed me across the room to him. I tackled him with enough force to send us rolling over the balcony and past the embers of Kern. I dug my claws into him. They found spaces beneath his shoulders where I could tear him apart.

"Tundo." He said.

That damned word, or at least it should be. He escaped my dug-in grip as if water and stumbled through a glowing circle. I put the shard in its pouch and jumped through after him, a proverbial fly after a spider.

Chapter 67

The portal carried me to the path between giant brail scribbles. Thaumus' agility belied his plump human form. He darted ahead. Drops of blood burned where they landed along the path, but he risked no excessive loss.

I pulled the shard out of its pouch. "He wants me to follow him. I'm playing into his plans, as I have from the beginning."

"Then why not turn around?"

"Because sooner or later I have to come after him and right now I have an ace he doesn't know about."

"What's that?"

"You. What's a good spell we can cast on him? Preferably one that doesn't require me to touch him?"

"We can only cast simple spells together, but there may be one we can surprise him with, ventilabo for sure, but we'll need something else."

"Something to counter fire?"

"Point and say 'extinctus,' and what you point at will stop burning."

"That's a start. Going through the other end. Talk to you on the other side."

The shard returned to the pouch and I stepped through the end portal. Thaumus' thrown room greeted me. He stood next to his thrown. It dwarfed his human form. I pulled out the shard and clutched it in my hand at the ready.

I whispered. "I'm here."

"I welcome you, dragon."

Of course, he did. Otherwise, I couldn't stay.

"Why do you welcome me?"

"Because you and I are fellow agents of order."

I lunged. Something smacked my face like a freight train, me. I had run headfirst into an invisible wall.

As the twisted bells stopped ringing in my head, I managed to make out Thaumus' words. "Do you like the magical wall? I borrowed it from my cousin. As you must know by now, he won't be needing it back for a while."

"You didn't go through all this trouble to get me here just so you can talk at me."

He gestured to an object on his throne, covered in a black drape. "We'll get to everything on the agenda soon enough."

"Why waste time? You know half of me wants you to kill me."

"Ah yes. That curse, and that's just the thing. You see, I'm sure we'd both agree that what this world needs is a champion of order. Chaos constantly threatens to consume civilization. Sometimes it more than threatens and at times like that, someone needs to step up to the challenge and beat it back."

"Then why kill me?"

He pointed at me. "And that is the question, isn't it?"

"Is all of this some sort of lesson you intend to teach me?"

"You could say that, and you could really say that, son of order."

"Then teach me, if you can, please."

"It's almost as if I need to hand you a mirror. You're supposed to be the champion of order, but you have a critical fault, an Achilles heel, dare I say, as large as the sky."

"Larger than your ego?"

"Your nature, that magical contract that makes you what you are, the son of order, it's like a leash and harness I can drag you around by. You went wherever and did whatever I wanted you to because of it. It makes you a most inadequate champion of order. I, on the other hand, have no such weakness. I can do whatever needs to be done for that cause, and I will."

"What does treachery have to do with order?"

"You and I are fortunate that I discovered your weakness first. Can you imagine what could have happened if someone truly chaotic and evil ever did?"

I couldn't deny his point, but I still doubted his merit. "How does giving Palladium to Charly's coven serve the cause of order?"

"The Olympians are as weak and flawed as you are. They conquered Earth only to abandon it. I need to re-ignite the spark of magic in the mortal humans, so they can help me guide them. Far better than letting them stumble around blindly like the Olympians have chosen to have them do."

"You think the Olympians will let you do this?"

"Even as we pulled your strings, dragon, we've been planting the seeds of suspicion against the absent goddess Nix. The Olympians will soon be very much distracted and by the time they realize there's nothing to fear from the void, the coven will have recruited promising acolytes from around the world. Their footprint on Earth will have grown too big for them to forcibly remove, and Olympus will have to negotiate with me."

"And you'll become the treacherous God of Earth?"

He sauntered away from his throne. "Not the treacherous God of Earth, dragon. You see it's not treachery if the ruler of all the Earth does it. If order is my ends, as opposed to chaos, all means are justified."

"What's the point of order if innocent people are made to suffer for it?"

He turned as if tripping over my words. "No, no, no, dragon. Order is its own point. That magical contract you made was a foolish one, a serpent that will eat itself if one can just show him his tail. Order cannot afford a champion so flawed, so for order's sake, you will do it one more service."

He snapped his fingers and the black cover fell from the throne. On the seat, a sword called to me. The same dark metal of the shard made up its blade, the one weapon capable of slicing through me with ease.

He took three quick steps further away from it. "You recall I hadn't lied when I spoke of using the correct blade to kill you? Well, there it is, and here's the beauty of my cleverness, you will be the one to use it. Kirkos."

"What?"

"Oh, that word, kirkos? A very ancient word. It's one of the controls on my cousin's wall. You'll now be able to reach my throne. I really do respect you, son of order. That's why I'm leaving you to your own thoughts before you fulfill that contract of yours. I'll be sure to give you a hero's funeral."

Vedi shouted. *"Percutiens, Aiden, squeeze the shard and say percutiens."*

The sword spoke to me louder than Vedi. My self-destructive side, after a long wait, had only a few steps and swift thrust to its goal.

Caught between them I squeezed the shard and took the steps to the throne.

"Aiden. No."

"It's right there, Vedi. I have to use it."

Chapter 68

Thaumus returned to find my body as he expected, slumped over his throne, the sword-hilt in my hands. Satisfaction on his face as he greeted me. His plan to rid the world of my weakness was almost complete. He only needed to get my body to a grave, but something confused his clever mind.

"I've always wondered what dragon's blood looks like. Is it this clear liquid I see?"

"Dragon's blood is the same as human blood, and so are our tears," I said.

I turned and tossed away the sword. Its blade had become a crude club with a faint remnant of a chaos rune in its surface. His face went gaunt. "What happened to the dark blade?"

"It's what happens when two pieces of the dark metal combine. They meld, becoming neither thing they were before."

"But how could you do that, not fulfilling your contract?"

I wiped a tear from my face. "I had to choose between multiple evils."

Blue lights swirled around his arms and legs. He cocked his head. "Tears? You cry at the thought of not fulfilling that contract of yours?"

"I'm not sure you'd understand. You only value people for what they can do for you."

The swirling lights covered all of him. "People? What does any of this have to do with people? Without order, there is nothing. Sacrifices have to be made for the greater good, even if it's you."

The air around him grew thick like a mist bordering on rain. I sprouted my wings, extended my claws, and stepped back. "I can satisfy my contract later, but I would give myself more to atone for if I didn't first deal with the greater evil."

"Your intellect and honor disappoint me, dragon. You think that I am somehow the greater evil? Not only are you too weak to be order's champion, but you are too foolish and lacking in character."

"Order serves the individual, not the other way around. You would not be order's champion, only a tyrant."

The swirling lights exploded and faded, leaving Thaumus' Titan form in their wake. One of his hands glowed red. Tongues of flame danced up his arm and shot out his fingers, swirling into cones, combining to form a fiery blade as long as my human form was tall. He pointed it.

His voice boomed. "I see your game, dragon if I should even call you such. You have become corrupt, trying to find a reason for your continued existence in the causes of people who put themselves ahead of the greater good."

"There is no such thing as a greater good, Thaumus, except as a myth used by tyrants."

"I am the champion of order and you are the champion of those who put their own fortunes ahead of the greater good, individuals indeed, a most unworthy bunch."

"I can't let you go on as you are, Titan. That is order's call on me."

"Such a shameful place you put yourself in. You won't remove yourself in honor, so I will do it for you."

I found my cause, my greater evil. Order is my nature. For Thaumus, order was an excuse for him to gain power and an excuse for him to kill. For me, dealing with the greater evil meant sacrificing my precious link to Vedi and risking my life to slay him. My tears were for Vedi and my blood was about to be spilled for the cause.

He started to speak, "kir…"

I launched my human-sized body at his throat and interrupted him. His non-burning hand batted me away as if I were a mosquito. I thought of the mass issue as I tumbled to the ground.

He coughed but managed, "tundo."

His sword's light grew an intense and almost white blue. I had taken on my first dragon form, about his size. A buzzing roar escorted his blade as he swung it. I dodged enough that it only grazed my belly, but it left a blazing trail on me.

I didn't want any more of those power words from him. My teeth came to bear at him, but only as a feint, which he fell for. He swung at it. Having planned on it, I dodged, but more importantly, my tail slapped his windpipe.

He grabbed his neck and struggled to speak. He only coughed.

My healing managed to smother the burning line across my belly. "That's a nasty blade you're wielding, Thaumus, but can it actually cut me?"

He continued to cover his neck with his free hand while pointing the blade. With a crackle, it doubled in length. I could no longer out-reach it with my tail.

I took flight and hovered. More feinting partial dives caused him to jab at me. I changed the angles of my approaches to read his ability to react. The results tempted me to try something, but considering how well he played me to this point, could I trust what his actions told me?

I made one more feint. This time moving so far that he could touch me with his blade, but only its point. A quick hard flap of both wings and a whip of my tail to turn me around, and I moved behind him. His blade scraped my already wounded belly, reigniting the old wound. A cross burned on me, but the important part was that I moved to his back faster than he could move his blade.

I took his head in one claw, his torso in the other and with my tail's help, snapped his neck. His own sword allowed me to finish him by piercing his heart. His body ignited. The flames consumed both his body and his sword.

I returned to my favored human form and picked up the piece of dark metal with a sword's hilt and useless remnants of runes.

I gathered my thoughts. I slew the greater evil. Only John's search through my hoard remained to delay my contract. I took the Titan portal back to where it took me from.

Chapter 69

Praxis stood over the burned remains of Kern's body. My arrival didn't stop him from staring at it, but he knew. "You found the source of the curse, didn't you?"

"How'd you know?"

He spoke slowly. "I saw you fight Scylla. Fire isn't your gift, but it's what we expected it to be. It's what Thaumus expected it to be."

A voice called from the balcony above. "Hey there, son, get up here fast."

Zeke peered over the railing. I sprouted wings and addressed Praxis. "So, you knew it was Thaumus?"

Praxis rubbed his temple. "I don't need to be Epimetheus to see things too late."

"Son. Get up here. The sooner you're with me, the sooner Thumper won't be interrogating you."

Zeke knew how to motivate. Of the two evils, being interrogated by Zeke or Thumper, Zeke seemed the lesser, and yes, someone from the Children of Galinthius had to interrogate me. I could finally tell him everything, as in everything except about Vedi and Nix.

He drove me to Milpitas while I told him my complete recollection of events from when I brought Melina to Thaumus to when I killed him. He didn't ask annoying questions until I finished.

"Good job, son. My boys are fetching that Palladium thing from Charly now, and good thing for him as he got himself hopelessly lost over the Rockies, but there's one question my bosses will insist I get an answer to. Why did you have a chaos shard on you?"

"It was Vedi's. Hunter gave it to me."

He squinted. "My boys are now having to catalog multiple magic items that hack had on him. That should keep them busy. So, back to the chaos shard, is that the answer you want me to go with?"

"You know it's an honest answer."

"Of course. It's your answer, so it couldn't be anything other than honest. Now, as for the truth, that's another question. There's something in what you're not telling me for me to know the truth."

"Zeke. Will you understand if I tell you Athena knows."

He hit his steering wheel. "Blast you, dragon, she keeps enough mysteries without including you in them."

"I'm just telling you Athena knows."

"And someday the time will be right, right?"

"I'm sorry, Zeke."

He pushed himself back. "I may hate it, but the answer you gave should at least be good enough for my bosses, but I'm telling you, I'm on to all that smoke you throw and it's beginning to get in my craw."

His words hurt. "I'm sorry, Zeke. I need to try harder to avoid these messes."

"I've got no clue how you manage to stumble around, get yourself into trouble, and keep winning, but if you want an old general's advice, do you know what I'd say?"

"I should take all the tips I can. What does the general have for me?"

"Whatever it is that makes you different than all the other agents of order, don't lose it."

Silence owned the rest of my ride to my house. I waited there until nightfall and called John in Slovenia. "John. How goes the search through my hoard?"

I expected him to sound dire or annoyed but instead, a lift carried in his voice. "Aiden. Do you know of a Titaness with rainbow colored wings?"

"No, why?"

"Because she visited me on the mountain."

"In broad daylight?"

"It was late night, about nine hours ago."

"What did she do?"

"She told me my empathy for you would bother me, and it did. I kept waking up in a cold sweat, but she told me to take courage because you'd triumph."

"Thaumus turned out to be the schemer behind all of this. We had it out."

"Woohoo! That's the dragon I know. She said you'd call me afterward right around this time."

"So, she's some sort of prophet?"

"Not that I can tell."

"Okay, John, what do you call someone who's good at predicting things?"

"Athena."

"What?"

"This Titaness' name is Iris and she was sent with messages from Athena. That's why and how she told me what she did."

"That was thoughtful of Athena and curious. Why should she care so much about your sleep?"

"Perhaps so I'd wake up for your phone call and pass on her message for you."

"She's got a message for me and she gave to you instead of me?"

"Yeah, yeah, I asked about that too. She said your phone call to me would be the best time and medium for it."

I could better understand Zeke pounding on his steering wheel. "She seems to be the master being cryptic. I hope her message isn't too much so. What is it?"

"I guess it's not too cryptic."

"John. What is it then?"

"She advises you to get your rest tonight because the morning will bring a very busy day."

"Okay, fine, now, besides Iris, how goes the search of my hoard?"

"You know it's huge, Aiden, but I think I'm halfway done."

"And nothing that can kill me?"

"There's a sword with runes on it suggesting it's a dragon-slayer, but it's broken. With great reluctance, I sent pictures of it to a sword-smith in England. He said it would be impossible to repair it with the engraving intact."

"And that's all you've found?"

"That's all, now follow Athena's advice and get some rest, boss."

I tried to follow her advice, but the loss of the shard kept waking me up as if I could still avoid it, as if the past could be reversed. Whatever the next day had for me, I begged it to come and distract me from it.

Chapter 70

In the morning I rose with the sun. If not for Athena's advice I would have risen sooner. A man in a tan three-piece suit stood in my driveway and studied my car. When he turned, I recognized Athena's psychoanalyst, Gabriel Schalken. I opened my front door. "Are you analyzing my car?"

He grinned. "I was, but now that you're available, you're much more interesting."

I gestured him past my front room. "Did Athena send you?"

"No, but I'm sure she's aware I came and approves."

"So, how much do you know about what I've done since Georgia?"

"You've killed a Titan and the curse remains."

I plopped onto my couch. "I lost the shard."

"You misplaced it?"

"I placed it onto a dark blade and they merged."

He gave my shoulder a squeeze and sat. "Did you know that would happen?"

"Yes. I had to do it."

He nodded. "You found a greater evil."

"Yes. Thaumus already intentionally caused the death of several

Empusa and an Oceanid, and he had more in his sights. His tyranny was only about to begin. I had to stop him."

"And you sacrificed the shard, your surest connection to Vedi, in order to do it."

"Was I foolish, Gabe?"

"No. You saved Olympus and Earth from Olympus' neglect. You're a noble man."

"Does nobility always hurt?"

He stood. "Do you have coffee? Can I get you some, Aiden?"

"Yes, thank you. The maker's on the counter next to the microwave."

He left my last question unanswered and returned in a few minutes with two cups of coffee. "You must have really impressed Epimetheus. It's because of him that I came to see you."

"He talks to you too?"

"Not until a couple days ago. He's secluded himself away from everyone for thousands of years, but after meeting you he contacted Olympus, asking for favors on your behalf. By the way, he still intends to write you."

"So, Olympus wants you to finish counseling me?"

"Olympus may be foolish and neglectful at times, but they're not stingy with help once they decide to give it. Oh no, Aiden, I'm here to take you to meet yet another Titan."

"I don't understand. How is me meeting another Titan supposed to be a big help to me?"

"Drive me to Thaumus' old mansion and you'll meet him and find out."

We moved to the car and I drove. I wanted Gabe to tell me more about this Titan, anything, but he kept the conversation about places he might want to see in the San Francisco Bay area.

The gates of the mansion were left open and I drove all the way to the front door. Empusa stood guard and Praxis met us as we got out. "Dragon. It is good that you've come to meet our new patriarch."

He opened the door for us.

"New patriarch? Already?" I asked.

Praxis opened the door to the back room. "Yes, dragon, Iapetus."

Gabe patted my back. "Go on in, Aiden. I'll wait out here."

"Anything I should know, Gabe?"

"He's a good guy. Athena personally talked him into volunteering."

Praxis whispered. "He hadn't been heard from for so long, we thought he was dead, but wherever he's been, he's become quite wise. He should be an excellent patriarch for us."

The room's furniture left it since my last visit. Melina's body did the same. A man stood over the spot where she fell. His posture could put almost anyone to shame and his frame could model statues. He bowed to me. "Dragon?"

Out of politeness, I bowed as well. "Iapetus?"

He stepped up and shook my hand. "You're the dragon who fells Titans. I am honored to meet you."

I looked into his eyes because I wasn't reading the sincerity of his words. I must have looked too long. He stepped back.

"I'm honored to meet you too, Lord Iapetus."

"Allow me, dragon, to update you on what's been decided since yesterday. Olympus acted quickly to fill the gaps left by Thaumus' death. His widow, Electra, will take over his old responsibilities over the remnants of the sea and I will administer the remnants of the land."

"Electra seems like a good choice as long as she doesn't have a grudge against me."

"I don't think she does, I really don't. Now, closer to home, my first task when I took this job was to select a new clan leader to replace the late Kern. I chose Praxis and I believe he has something to tell you."

He held out his hand and Praxis stepped up. "After explaining to the others what happened to Kern and why, we have come to an agreement that we should forgive you, and as their leader, I do so for all of us now."

My self-destructive side performed a melodramatic death scene in my head. 'Give my regards to Terra Del Fuego,' were its last words.

"Thank you, both of you."

Iapetus patted Praxis' shoulder. "Well done, clan leader. Now please leave us. The dragon and I need to speak in private."

He waited for Praxis to close the door. "I had to meet you once, Aiden Ferris, because we should never meet again."

"I don't understand."

"And that's it. What you don't sense about me is why we must not be in the same place again. But I just had to meet you once. I never had a worthy adversary when I probably should have had one, but you would have been."

"I can't tell if you're telling the truth or not."

He pointed at me. "Try not to think about that too much, Aiden, and you'll save both us and the world a lot of unnecessary trouble. We are both men who were cursed in terrible ways and found redemption. That's why I was so anxious to take care of yours."

"May I ask what your curse was?"

He walked to the door. "I won't answer."

I took the hint and left. I had a couple questions for Gabe once we got back in the car. "Why didn't you tell me?"

"You mean about Iapetus?"

"That my curse would be lifted."

"I suppose I could have, but I was more concerned about his immunity to you reading him. It's very important the ever-paranoid Empusa not know about that. I thought it best not to tell you anything than to have you wondering about me telling you partial truths."

"Fair enough. He and I both require special handling. Now, how long are you visiting?"

"How long do you want my services?"

"At least long enough for you to observe me talking to a clear night sky. I need the affirmation that I'm not crazy."

72

Chapter 71

In a tavern in Slovenia I hope to never go, drinks were on a certain American. John couldn't contain his joy at the news of the passing of my curse. He assured me the other tavern-goers only knew some American's best friend was no longer going to die, and he wanted everyone to share in his happiness.

I let him spend my money for that, but on the condition that he handle a real-estate transaction for me first. The backing of my hoard made it trivial, and he spent most of his last night before his morning flight, providing Slovenians with free drinks.

Meanwhile back in California, I showed Gabe the highlights of San Jose, statues of snake gods and all. I passed time until the sunset and drove out to a good spot for stargazing.

We left the car. The clicks of our doors reminded me of better times, times when Vedi and I would ride into the hills to watch fireworks over the bay.

"Tell me where you want me to be," asked Gabe.

I had to smile at the man who rode into the California wilderness in a three-piece suit. "Just far enough away that you can hear me and tell from my volume who I'm talking to."

For him, that turned out to be a surprising distance, maybe fifty yards. He turned away and seemed to orient himself by the stars. His finger moved like he could draw in the air.

Sadly, the stars ignored me. Giant balls of burning gas usually do, but a meaning assigned itself despite my knowledge of astronomy. A cold grip wracked my being as I wondered if Vedi would speak to me.

"Vedi?"

Something like her voice chimed, but I feared a bird teased me.

"Vedi?"

My breathing stopped, and I listened to the air.

"Aiden?"

"Yes, Vedi, I'm here."

"Aiden. What did you do with the shard?"

"It merged with the dark blade, so I could stop Thaumus."

The silence lasted too long. I panicked and sprouted wings as if I might fly into space. My rational mind slapped the silly thought down.

Her voice came. *"Nix is pleased that you stopped him from turning Olympus against her."*

"I only wish I didn't destroy the shard to do it."

"Oh, Aiden, I wish that too. We'll only be able to speak like this until Nix's plans are ready for me to return."

"When?"

"You know the answer I need to give you. Time is different here."

"Vedi. I'm virtually immortal, I can wait a long time, it may tear my heart apart, but I can wait a long time. You, my love, you're not immortal."

"Nix assures me I won't age while I'm with her."

Some feelings shouldn't mix but do. Relief attached itself to her not aging but the familiar lump in my throat had another station. "How long can I be expected to deal with you being gone?"

"You fought back your self-destructive side, born of that curse. You can handle this."

"Vedi, it's so hard. I want you back so bad."

"I know, Aiden. It's not fair. Time passes much faster for me here than it

does for you there, but you're my dragon, my champion. You can do it because you must like you always do because you must."

"At least, now I know where you are and that you're coming back someday."

"I love you, my pretty boy."

"I love you too."

My words may as well have been spoken to the cloud rolling overhead. She probably didn't hear them, but I knew she knew.

I walked back to talk to Gabe. "Well, did you hear me talking?"

"Yes."

"Am I crazy?"

"Are you grieving her loss?"

"No. She's alive, but I sure miss her like crazy."

"You and I know she's alive. You have rough emotions ahead of you, but you're functioning, making progress. You're no longer stuck in a stage of a grief you never should have been going through in the first place."

We got into the car. Gabe tapped his door window. "So, what do you plan to do with this land you've purchased?"

I put the car in gear. "Pitch a tent."

"You want to catch every moment of every clear night sky?"

"Yes."

"You'll find that to not be a practical option."

He broke his pattern. He jumped to a conclusion rather than leading me to it.

"You don't expect me to resist your counsel on that?" I asked.

"I expect you to stop before you run Iris off the road."

My headlights caught a rainbow in the night. A rainbow-winged Titaness stood on the road. I slammed my brakes.

Gabe removed his head from the dashboard. "She's the messenger of Olympus."

"Not Hermes?"

"You can quibble later, Aiden. For now, you should go see why she's got a scroll in her hand."

In my distraction, I hadn't noticed. She held it out to me but wouldn't approach. I put the car into park and came around. As I reached for the scroll she pulled it back.

"Are you Aiden Ferris?"

"Yes, and a good thing considering. Imagine if I was some ordinary mortal and you showed up like this."

"This scroll is from Athena and its seal can only be broken in the city of Milpitas during a summer snowstorm."

"Sounds like never to me."

She held the scroll up out of my reach. "The seal has the force of Olympian law behind it. I can only give it to you if you understand and respect the conditions under which it can be broken."

"I reside on Earth at Olympus' mercy. I won't open it unless its required conditions are met."

She allowed me to take it from her, and flew into the clouds. I returned to the car.

"Did you hear that, Gabe?"

"Yes, and I saw her coming well before you did, apparently. That's why I told you that you'll find catching every clear night won't be a practical option."

"What kind of nonsense is this? A Summer snowstorm in Milpitas?"

"I know Athena better than anyone and while I don't know what that scroll says, I can tell you its conditions for opening will be met, and when you open it, snow in a time and place where it doesn't belong will probably be the least of your worries."

"So, I guess I'll use the tent until then."

"You might pick up a warm jacket in town. It's summer, you know."

73

Bio

K. D. Menzies has a varied education ranging from Bachelors degrees in psychology from Asbury University to computer science from the University of Central Florida, with a lot of ancient writings and oral traditions in-between. He also has a Masters of Divinity from Asbury Theological Seminary.

For all of K.D. Menzies' books, as well as all those from JaCol Publishing, please visit www.jacolpublishing.com

Acknowledgments

I'd like to thank JaCol publishing for believing in my work, to Writers World Boot camp and the other members for keeping us on task. I'd like to thank Mark Payton and Karen Brosinsky for their work on my cover, and to my editor Randall Andrews.

www.ingramcontent.com/pod-product-compliance
Lightning Source LLC
Chambersburg PA
CBHW071859020726
47502CB00003B/819